Rainbow Tales

Rainbow Tales

Kathleen Murphey

jms books

JMS Books LLC
PO Box 234
Colonial Heights, VA 23834
www.jms-books.com

Printed in the United States of America

ISBN: 9798428109245

WE STAND AT the moment in history…when we are just beginning to explore the properties of human relationships. Imagine what a language could be like that had thirteen genders. Oh, yes, one says, masculine, feminine, and neuter—and what…are the other ten? We are laying the foundations of a way of life…and [human beings'] imaginations will be both sheltered and imprisoned within the limits of [what] we build.

—Margaret Mead, *Male and Female* (1949)

Contents

Beau and the Beast

ONCE UPON A time, in a small and far away kingdom, there was a young, spoilt prince; his name was Nathaniel. His parents doted on him, and though they were sweet and kind and regal, he was not. He was short-tempered with the staff, the servants, and his peers. He was blessed with good looks: pale skin, big blue eyes framed by dark lashes, thick, curly, auburn hair, full lips, a square jaw, height, and a muscular frame. He was swoon material, and he knew it. Young women were always interested in him, but he wasn't particularly interested in them. No young woman he met caught his interest, and he often rebuffed them in the cruelest manner. No one dared to complain to the king and queen about their son's behavior, so they were naïvely unaware.

Nathaniel slowly came to realize that he was attracted to other young men. He lingered at training sessions and fighting practices. The muscular arms, shoulders, backs, and chests of boys and men excited and humiliated him. Homosexuality was unheard of; males liked females, and females liked males. There was not a male-likes-male or female-likes-female option. He, on the other hand, would get hard-ons looking at and thinking about certain young men. He even dreamed about them. He masturbated thinking about young men—particularly about Luke—his regular sparring partner.

When Nathaniel was eighteen, he was particularly cruel to Isadora, the daughter of his parents' envoy to the neighboring kingdom to the south. She paid a lot of attention to him, and he made fun of her clothes, her looks, and her attempts to flirt with him. He had the audacity to call her a cow at a court party, and, mortified, she ran out of the party and sought the solace of the gardens. A sobbing young woman in the royal gardens caught the attention of Fairy Kate.

"Why do you cry, child?" Kate asked.

"Prince Nathaniel was beastly to me. He ridiculed me in front of everyone. He called me a cow," she sobbed.

Fairies, especially fairy queens, did not tolerate extreme vanity in humans, and Fairy Kate was a fairy queen. "Beastly?" Fairy Kate repeated, grinning with a sudden satisfaction. "I like it. Beastly he will become. I'll test him first, but I have heard about him before. A reckoning is in order." And with that, Fairy Kate left the young woman and waited.

On a stormy night, Fairy Kate sensed that activity in the castle was low. She sensed the young prince near the kitchens and knocked on the back door, transforming herself into the shape of a poor, old woman. A servant answered the door, and Kate asked to be let in from the storm and given a bite to eat. The servant led the old woman into the castle immediately and led her to the fire.

The prince, seeing the old woman, was aghast. "What are you doing?" he asked the servant.

"My prince, in this storm, we are obligated to give shelter and aid," she answered.

"To this Troll?" he answered. "She is odious. Get her out of here. I will not stand her presence."

The servant stared at him. "My prince, it is not done. You could hurt yourself. She could hurt you."

"That hag? How on earth could she hurt me? She is nothing, a beggar," he scoffed.

"Please my prince, the fairy folk test us. If you fail the test, I hate to think of what could happen," stammered the servant.

"The fairy folk—do you believe in such old wives' tales? Out! Get her out!" he screamed.

Mortified, the servant turned to Kate, "Oh, my lady, have mercy on me. I must obey my master."

"A blessing be upon you, my child. I am not dismayed by you. You tried to warn him," and she turned and looked at the prince and transformed into her most radiant fairy queen self.

Nathaniel was stunned, and he was suddenly afraid. He had revealed his most uncharitable nature to a fairy queen. He couldn't imagine the punishment. "My lady," he began.

"Silence, it is too late for apologies. You were beastly to Isadora and to me, and so a beast you will be and remain forever more unless you convince a mortal to love you," she smiled in sweet satisfaction as she spoke the words, because she couldn't imagine his arrogant personality ever swaying a mortal's heart beyond the monster she would make him appear to be.

She raised her hand toward him, and he felt it rip through him: pain and transformation. His body twisted and grew and sprouted. He grew huge: seven-foot, hair sprouted all over him, his jaw extended with his teeth turning to fangs, his hands and feet transformed into paws with claws. He howled in rage. Rage—human reason in this form was difficult to attain and almost impossible to verbalize—he howled again. The fairy disappeared, and he raged against himself in the castle. He ripped through rooms, destroying everything in his reach. He refused to look at himself in a mirror. Finally, he took himself outside and simply ran on four legs through the forest.

He had done this to himself. He couldn't believe he had been so stupid. His mother had told him story after story about the dangers of vanity and false pride. Zeus and Hermes, the Ancient Greek gods, were notorious for disguising themselves as beggars and visiting humans to see if the unsuspecting humans showed the proper deference to a guest. One old couple, he remembered from the stories, had given the disguised Zeus and Hermes the best of everything they had and had been rewarded with a never-emptying stew pot and a never-emptying wine jug. Hubris, arrogance, human pride, had brought him to this, to being a beast.

As he calmed down slightly, analyzing his situation, he

realized that he could sense the other animals in the forest. What surprised him was that the other predators were wary and scared of him. Was he so monstrous that he frightened even wolves, bears, and beasts of the forest? Yes, apparently so. When he was absolutely exhausted, he returned to the castle, found his bed, and passed out.

The light streaming through the windows woke him the next morning. Nathaniel lifted his head, and he saw himself in the mirror. He was like some kind of werewolf: huge, fury, fanged, clawed, hideous, an animal. He shattered the mirror. He wandered the castle and found that he was utterly alone. His life was horrid for a long time. He ran in the forest and through the grounds. He destroyed different parts of the castle, but he never touched his parents' apartments. Their spaces were the only places he found holy, touched with the unconditional love they had always shown him and, therefore, worthy of a reverence he had not shown other castle spaces in his rage and anger.

The castle provided for his wants and needs. A bath was provided for him at six in the evening, and the family dining room produced dinner for him at seven. Sometimes he ate there, but more often than not, his attempts at civilized eating infuriated him. He could not handle the cutlery with his paws and claws. Even handling the fine china plates and dishes reminded him of how different it had been when he was human. Thus, he often ate in the forest, taking down a deer, a beaver, or some other animal and eating it raw like the beast he was.

He longed for company, any company. He had never realized how devastating it was to be isolated and alone. Even the taunting fairy would be better than this abandonment. In fairness, he knew the fairy had not taunted him; she had corrected and punished him for his inappropriate behavior. But this knowledge did not end his loneliness. He started to seek out people—the odd wood gatherer or traveler—but whenever he revealed himself, they screamed and ran off in terror.

After several years of misery and isolation, he ran across an old woman who was preparing to camp in the woods for the night. Her grandson was out collecting firewood. She was sitting on log by the fire. She sensed him and called out to him.

"Hello, Stranger. Come and warm yourself by our fire. Can I offer you some tea?" she said kindly.

It had been so long that Nathaniel couldn't resist. "I don't want to frighten you or impose," he said hesitantly.

"Nonsense," she said laughing at the thought. "Where are you from?" she asked.

"Not far. There is a castle through the forest," he began. He wondered when she would start screaming as he drew close to the fire and to her, but she just sat there contentedly. When he sat down on the ground near her, she reached out with a tin mug of steaming tea for him. He was sure that she could see his face, though he kept up the hood of his cloak, and she could see also his clawed paws, and yet, she did not seem phased. By the light of the fire, he could see that she had light brown skin, dark hair streaked with grey which was braided in a single plait, and dark eyes. He took the mug from her awkwardly and thanked her for it.

"You're welcome," she answered. "A castle? There was the Brandenberg Castle, but there was a great tragedy there. I thought it was abandoned," she said slowly. "What is your name?"

"I am Nathaniel," he answered quietly. He couldn't look at her.

"Nathaniel Brandenberg?" she whispered.

He knew she knew then, by the way she whispered his name, and their chance encounter was about to be over. She would scream, and the grandson would come, and they would run away and never speak to him again. It was all too much. He started sobbing and choked out his response, "Yes...I am...he," and he forced himself to look at her. For the first time, he noticed that her brown eyes were rimmed with a whitish blue. Her face searching his, did not fill with terror but with a dawning sadness, and he realized that she was blind. "You can't see me, can you? What is your name?" he asked softly.

"No, I can't see you, Nathan." He gasped. His mother called him that. "I am Gwyneth, and I know you beyond your name. Do you know me?" she asked, a smile forming on her lips.

Gwyneth was the midwife who attended his mother through her miscarriages and then through his birth. There had been something she had said about his destiny after he was born. He had been told, but he couldn't remember. "Yes," he said hesitantly. "You were my mother's midwife. You birthed me," he said overwhelmed by the emotions that crashed over him—memories of his parents, his mother, their life as it had once been. He started sobbing again.

"I warned her," Gwyneth whispered. "The night you were born, the stars, the portents were…ominous. The deaths of the others…they would worship you too much, your parents. You could become the kingdom's undoing. And you have, haven't you, my child," she added solemnly.

He choked out the words, "It…is…everything…you…say. I was spoilt. I insulted a fairy queen. I…am…a…beast," he said.

She got up then. She was a tiny, little woman, but she sat down next to him and hugged him. He was so stunned at the gesture, at the contact, at the forwardness, that he didn't resist. He sobbed onto her shoulder, and he realized that she rocked him back and forth against her body. He sobbed harder; he was so lonely. This was the only contact with another human being he had had in so long.

"Grandmother?" a voice called, the voice tinged with surprise and alarm.

The old midwife released Nathaniel and turned her face to the voice, "Beau, do not be alarmed. We have a guest," she said firmly.

The firewood that had been in the young man's arms crashed to the ground. Nathaniel saw the young man's face change from alarmed surprise to full alarm and revulsion as he saw Nathaniel's face and paws clearly. "Gran, that is not a guest; it is a beast. Get away from it," and he drew a large knife from its sheath at his side.

"Beau, I know what you see, but the beast you see is not all he is. He is a young man underneath, and that is the part you can't see. Put the knife away and throw some new logs on the fire," she said commandingly. She waited, but the young man was frozen, gaping at her as if she had lost her mind. "Beau!"

Her shouting his name seemed to pull him back to himself. He hesitated, but then did as she asked, sheathing the knife and reaching for two of the logs he had dropped, throwing them on the fire. He kept his distance from Nathaniel and sat on the log near his grandmother. She patted his knee once he was seated. "Beau, this is Nathaniel Brandenberg. Nathan, this is my grandson, Beau."

The young man again was staring at his grandmother as if she had completely lost her mind. "That's not possible, Gran," he began, but she interrupted him.

"Nathan, tell Beau your story, all of it," she said demandingly.

That two people were still sitting with him, even though they knew what he was, was a miracle in and of itself. He dared not hope for anything further. He sensed that only complete honesty and humility with them would be tolerated. As a midwife, Gwyneth would have heard and seen it all (heard every lie and seen every deviant thing a human could do), and he had nothing more to lose. So, he told them of his spoilt childhood and the vanity and arrogance and distain he felt for others, except his parents. He told them how he hid his behavior from his parents who had always tried to teach him to be kind, generous, and empathetic. He told them about his indifference toward young women. He told them about his attraction to certain young men. He told them about what he said to Isadora and then to the Fairy Kate. He told them about his transformation and his years isolated and lonely in the castle. Lastly, he told them about his attempts to see others and about his encounter with them.

He had watched their faces intently as he told his story. Both the grandmother and Beau had suppressed their reactions at two points of his story: his indifference to young women and his attraction to young men. Were they shocked and revolted? Surely, the old woman had known of same sex relationships; she was a midwife. He couldn't be the only young man who got turned on by other young men, could he? The old woman had flashed a look at her grandson, and he had blushed and carefully avoided returning her look. Nathaniel knew that her eyes couldn't see, but her other senses must react in such a way as to give her an accurate enough impression of what was going on. It was as if she could see through her blind eyes. What did that mean? He gasped suddenly. What if Beau also was indifferent to young women and liked young men? He couldn't imagine the emotions flashing over his face, but he doubted that they could read them through the fur and beast's muzzle. He forced his face into the most neutral expression he could manage. The old lady was watching him intently with her blind eyes. A smile played at the edges of her mouth, and Nathaniel could have sworn that she made the tiniest nod of her head as if she had read his thoughts and was confirming their accuracy.

"How long?" Beau asked, a mix of emotions playing across his face, shock, sympathy, confusion, and curiosity.

Nathaniel looked at Beau before he answered. Beau had the same dark looks as his grandmother: he had light brown skin; dark, glossy, curly, short hair; sparkling, and strangely tender-looking, dark eyes; and though he was modestly dressed, his muscular frame was pronounced through his clothing. He was very different looking than the fair haired and blue-eyed Luke, but Beau was strikingly attractive, at least to Nathaniel. Nathaniel answered hesitantly, "I am not sure. It has been years, but when everything was misery, I stopped paying attention. I just don't know." Nathaniel's mind filled with the memories of the endless days of isolation and loneliness.

Gwyneth's voice interrupted his thoughts, "My prince, why don't you allow us to accompany you to the castle?"

That she could call him prince shocked him more than he

could have possibly imagined. His animal rage flared. "Don't call me that," he said harshly. "I am a beast; there is nothing noble left."

Though he spoke harshly, she was unintimidated by his words. He guessed that women in the throes of childbirth had said unimaginable things to her (curses, threats, promises of vengeance). "But you are not a true beast. You are a human in a beastly form. Find your better nature and redeem yourself," she said quietly.

Nathaniel stared at her. Redemption, could it be possible for him? He shook his head softly.

"We have brown bread and cheese, Nathan," Beau said quietly. Nathaniel was surprised at being called by the endearment, but the young man's grandmother had used the name, so he understood. Beau rummaged in a bag by the fire and doled out the bread and cheese. Gwyneth got them all more tea. Nathaniel pushed back the hood of his cloak. He looked at Gwyneth as he did so, but the woman's expression only showed warmth, and perhaps, slight appreciation at being trusted with such a revelation. Nathaniel next sought Beau's face, which seemed to hold curiosity more than anything.

Once they had eaten their small meal, Gwyneth insisted on bed. Beau produced blankets from another bag, and they gathered themselves around the fire to sleep. Nathaniel, before sleep overtook him, felt profound relief. He was connected to people again. There was an irony to the fact that an old woman was that vehicle since an old woman (at least so he thought) had been the vehicle to his isolation. He felt hope for the first time in a long time. Even if neither of them came to love him, he would not be alone, and then sleep claimed him.

When the old woman stirred in the early morning, Nathaniel's beastly senses woke him, and he offered to get fresh water. By the time he returned, she had rekindled the coals from the fire and had the tea leaves in a pot waiting for the water. Beau still slept, so they spoke quietly to each other.

"You do not have to come to the castle with me," Nathaniel said, knowing that it was true and yet wanting it more desperately than he had ever wanted anything.

"No, we don't. But I am a midwife, and my primary task is to relieve suffering. You are suffering, and so is my grandson, though he will not speak of it to me," she said quietly.

Nathaniel knew only too well his own suffering and pushed it from his mind. He knew also that when the old woman spoke of her grandson's suffering, she was speaking of Beau's attraction to young men. "You are not repulsed?" he asked, genuinely curious.

"Child, insecure and hypocritical men are repulsed or fake repulsion. Love and desire are what separate human beings from the animals. Animals reproduce by instinct, not love or desire. Sexual attraction and pleasure, not reproduction, drive human relationships. As a midwife, I know this. Just because reproduction happens between a male and a female doesn't mean that all males are sexually attracted to females or all females are sexually attracted to males. Neither does it mean that the sex between a male and a female is pleasurable. It should be, mind you. However, if pleasure is the defining characteristic of sexual relations, which I believe it should be, take pleasure where you will, female-male, male-female, male-male, female-female, and any other coupling you can think of among consenting human beings."

Nathaniel stared her open mouthed. "How can you say those things?" he asked.

She looked at him with all the compassion of her calling, "I bring life into the world, and I try to alleviate suffering. We are all God's creatures. I refuse to believe in a punitive model of God's relationship with human beings. A parent, a true parent, loves all his or her children, regardless of their idiosyncrasies and differences from their peers, their parents, or even their siblings. You are different for many reasons, Nathan. You are a prince, whether you acknowledge that or not. You are your parents' child—a position I hope you reclaim. And you like other young men—a situation you are not alone in—and you being open about that could change the world for all those young men (and others) who have, like yourself, hidden for too long. You all should come out and be who you want to be and love who you want to love."

He could only stare at her. He had hoped with wild desperation that she might understand, but that she could articulate his barely self-acknowledged longings was incomprehensible to him. "Gwyneth...I am...just a beast," he said.

"No, Nathan, no beast of the forest could talk to me of such things. Be the human being that you can be." She stood up, and for a tiny, old woman, her presence was powerful. Perhaps it was all the lives that she had brought into the world or saved from worms or whatever illness or broken bone. He quavered under her penetrating blind gaze.

"I am...unworthy," he choked out.

"So, make yourself worthy," she spat back at him in a challenge.

Worthy? If he were worthy, he could be loved. "I will try," he answered.

"There are some who would answer that to try is not enough, but I will accept you trying," she answered.

Beau stirred, and Nathaniel and Gwyneth stopped talking and got a small breakfast together. With Beau up and about, they ate quietly and then packed up their things. The walk to the castle started well, but after a short time, the old woman was clearly struggling.

Just as Nathaniel felt a tinge of annoyance at having to slow his pace, he realized that the logical thing to do was to carry the old woman. Beau could do it, but Nathaniel was much bigger and stronger. He stopped and turned to face them.

"Nathan?" the old woman asked.

He smiled, or tried to; he wasn't sure he pulled it off too well. "Let me carry you," he said softly, and he took off his cloak and knelt so that she could climb on his back.

"No, my prince, it would be unfitting," she said backing away from him, but he reached out and took her hand in his paw.

"There is no kingdom, so there is no prince. You honor me with your company. The journey is hard for you, but it is nothing to me. Allow me to ease your passage." He saw her face change from resistant to something softer and more accepting. He let go of her hand, and he turned to Beau who watched them both in surprise, "When she is in place, can you tie the cloak around us, to hold her better?"

Beau took the cloak and nodded. The old woman climbed on Nathaniel's back hesitantly. She was so tiny that her arms around his neck were almost uncomfortably tight, and her little legs barely reached around his waist. Beau wrapped the cloak around the two of them, his fingers fumbling awkwardly and his face flushing slightly as he tied the edges of the cloak across Nathaniel's chest. Once the cloak was secured, the old woman was able to loosen her hold, and Nathaniel laughed. It was strange sounding to him. A kind of bark with a laugh in it. He realized that he had never laughed in his beastly form. The thought was like a kind of grief—for all that he had lost.

"What is so funny?" she asked, a tinge of irritation in her voice.

Her question and her tone jolted him back to himself. He shook his head, clearing his thoughts. "You're just so light and tiny, like a child," he answered. More quietly, he added, "It has been so long," and he could hear the ache in his voice. He hadn't been touched since he had been transformed, except when she had hugged him the night before.

She seemed to read his thoughts. "Like a child, am I? Perhaps, then, it is fitting. It seems like yesterday when I held you, cleaned you up, and handed you back to your mother." He couldn't see her face, but her voice was gentle, and he felt her tiny hands patting his neck. He was touched more than he could say.

"Thank you," he whispered.

"Don't dwell on what you can't change," she said softly, and there was a sadness in her voice.

Nathaniel wondered what was the cause of that sadness. "Why did you leave the castle?" he asked.

"A blind midwife isn't very useful," she answered stiffly. "I chose to leave, to return to my family and life in the villages," her voice was warmer. "Beau is studying with me; it is unusual for a male to train as a healer, but then Beau is an unusual young man," her voice filled with pride.

Beau's head turned toward them at the mention of his name. "What are you two talking about?" he asked.

"I was just talking about your training," she answered raising her voice so that he could hear her clearly. "Tell us a story," she commanded.

Beau obeyed and launched into the story of "The Happy Prince."

Nathaniel listened, fascinated and charmed by the story. The prince and the male swallow clearly loved each other. It was a sad and sweet story. He wished it had a happy ending instead of the tragic one. The story had an author unlike traditional fairy tales, Oscar Wilde. Clearly, this man lived in a kingdom that did not condone male-male relationships—that had to be the cause of the tragic ending. They could love each other, but the people would reject them. Despite the intolerance of the people, God and the angel knew the love and sacrifices of the prince and the swallow were the worthiest things in the town. There was hope in that, Nathaniel thought.

They passed the rest of the journey amicably. The castle came into view, and he heard Beau gasp. He smiled. He hadn't felt pride at the sight of his home in a long time. Then he thought of the damage he had done, and he was filled with shame. His body stiffened with tension.

"What is it?" the old woman asked.

"After I was transformed, I was very, very angry," he said quietly. "Much of the castle…" but he couldn't finish.

"You raged through the castle. I can imagine. It will give Beau and me something to do," she said softly, patting his neck again for reassurance, and they both felt the tension leave his body.

On the grounds, Nathaniel knelt, and Beau untied the cloak and helped his grandmother down from Nathaniel's back. They entered the castle through the kitchens. Beau whistled at the destruction. "Is it like this everywhere?" he asked, more with curiosity than condescension.

Nathaniel shifted uncomfortably. "Not my parents' apartments. I will show you to those rooms. You must be tired."

"My prince, we could not," the old woman said firmly.

"You must stop calling me that," he said more loudly than he intended.

"Alright," she said, "but then you must call me Gwyn."

Nathaniel reigned in his emotions, "Okay, Gwyn," he said in a more measured tone. "My parents' apartments are the only rooms in which it would not humiliate me to put you."

"Nathan, Beau and I will find a room or rooms that we can tidy up and be happy with. We are servants," she began.

"No!" he said so loudly than she and Beau both jumped. "You are my guests, and I am a beast," he said lowering his voice in response to their reactions.

Recognizing the pain in his voice, she smiled, a warm, grandmotherly smile, full of understanding and compassion, "Show us the way."

She was humoring him, Nathaniel knew. He led them through the halls and up the stairs. Beau took special care to lead his grandmother so that she wouldn't trip. They passed room after room; most bore witness to previous violence.

"Which ones are yours?" Beau asked, but he was amused.

"They are coming up, Beau," he said dryly.

Turning a corner, Nathaniel waved toward a door on the right, "These are my apartments," he said solemnly.

Beau ducked his head in and saw the overturned bookcase in the study and saw past that to the bedroom with the smashed mirror. He whistled again. "You must have been really angry."

"You have no idea," Nathaniel answered bitterly. "Being a beast didn't help either. I lost it for days. When I couldn't take it any longer, I would run through the grounds or through the forest. Anything to burn off the anger and rage."

"Well, you are not alone now," Gwyn said gently.

Nathaniel turned and looked at her, "No. Thank you for being here," he said sincerely.

"Whose rooms are these?" Beau asked. "They don't look disturbed."

Nathaniel followed Beau into the rooms across from his rooms, taking a turn at leading Gwyn. Once inside the rooms, he stared around him wildly. He remembered slashing through these rooms almost as viciously as his own rooms, but they were in perfect order now. The bookcase, the chairs, the tables, the bed. There was a note on the bed.

"What is it, Nathan?" Gwyn asked. She couldn't see the rooms, but she could read the distress and tension in his body.

"I destroyed these rooms," Nathaniel answered.

Beau had walked to the bed and picked up the note. "Um, these are apparently my rooms," he said, holding out the note, with a surprised look on his face.

"The castle is enchanted," Nathaniel said hesitantly. "Perhaps…"

"Perhaps it knew we were coming?" Gwyn finished for him. She sounded excited. "Do I have rooms?" She tugged at his paw, and he laughed his strange barky laugh.

"Let's find out," he said, caught up with her excitement. "The castle has never fixed itself before," he mused.

"Perhaps it is not the only one changed," and she squeezed his paw.

He felt the tears prick in his eyes, "Perhaps," he said in a strangled voice, and he felt her squeeze his paw again. Gently, he squeezed back.

They crossed the hall again, and the rooms were again in order though he remembered trashing them. More interesting to him was that they were decorated in a more feminine manner than his or Beau's. Different than his mother's rooms but distinctly feminine. Additionally, there was a hand rail that ran at waist-level around the walls of the rooms. Nathaniel led Gwyn to the rail and put her hand on it. The rail was at her precise waist-level. Holding the railing, Gwyn navigated the first room. She was approaching a set of chairs and a table that obstructed her way, and Nathaniel was about to cry out, but she stopped suddenly, and successfully felt her way around the obstructions.

"How did you do that?" he asked.

"The rail told me the chairs and table were there," she said in wonder. Then after a moment, she said, "Describe the rooms to me?"

"The walls are painted a marigold yellow," Nathaniel answered.

"I so love yellows," she said absently.

"There are solid, golden-colored, velvet curtains at the windows," he continued. "The bedding looks to be of the same golden velvet. There are flowers, roses, in vases, throughout the apartment. Your study has books and a desk." He fell silent as he watched her cross into the other room to the bed and feel the coverlet. Though she was an old woman, her excitement made her seem like a small girl.

"I feel like a princess," she said, giddy with enthusiasm, making her giggle and laugh at herself. "Our rooms here are bigger than our cottage, Beau." She flopped herself onto the bed. "It is so soft. It is like lying on feathers."

Nathaniel was both pleased and ashamed by Gwyn's pleasure in her apartments. She had been a trusted member of the royal household, but only as a servant. These rooms were grand compared to the servant quarters but nothing like the grandeur of his parents' apartments. What he took for granted was made splendid and special through Gwyn's vision of it.

"They will always be your rooms, Gwyn, for as long as you live, whether you visit often or only rarely," he said with conviction.

Gwyn sat up and looked at him, "Nathan, you can't do that."

Yes, he could. Whether she understood it or not, she and Beau were his family now, his only tie to his humanity. They had not run from him screaming in the forest, and they had agreed to stay with him. He would owe them more than they could possibly imagine. Before he could get emotional on that point, he shifted his thoughts. "Dinner is at seven, usually, in the family dining room. The castle usually provides me with a bath at six, just in case it does it for you as well. We have a couple of hours until then, but you may like to rest and get to know your rooms, so I will take my leave and look forward to seeing you at dinner," Nathaniel bowed to them and left.

Nathaniel entered his own rooms a little bewildered. The castle had cleaned up Gwyn's and Beau's rooms but not his. Why? Perhaps it was not ready to accept that his rages were over. Could he really blame it? The first ones had lasted for days. A day of civilized behavior on his part was nothing compared to before. Instead of retiring to his room, he wandered the castle, following his paths of devastation and regretting them. Eventually, he retired to his rooms. He took the bath with more pleasure than he had ever remembered. Despite his fur and his claws and fangs, the water made him feel clean for the first time in a long time. After his bath, he found dress clothes in his closet, and dressed with anticipation.

Dinner was lovely. Though Nathaniel had smashed dishes and thrown cutlery in the family dining room, it had escaped relatively unscathed, and whatever damage he had inflicted, the castle seemed to have mended, so that the room was as elegant and welcoming as it had been before Nathaniel's transformation. Beau looked unbelievable cleaned up, in a smart suit, smiling from ear to ear. Gwyn was bursting with happiness; her dress of golden silk flattered her frame in all the right places. The table was set when they entered, the fire was comforting, and then the food just appeared on their plates—their favorite dishes. Beau helped his grandmother into her seat, and then he and Nathaniel seated themselves. Nathaniel was at the head of the table, with Gwyn at his right side and with Beau at his left. Nathaniel's meal was fingerling potatoes, cut glazed carrots, and beef steak which had been cut into strips. Though he was relieved that the steak had been cut, he flushed with embarrassment, as he considered what a fool he would have made of himself trying to use the silverware. Gwyn, perhaps sensing his tension, turned her face toward him. He clenched his jaw and concentrated on trying to pick up his fork. It fell from his clumsy paw, and he resisted the urge to slam his fisted paw onto the table. Fury coursed through him, but Gwyn's voice intruded on his dark thoughts.

"I have always thought that the excesses of table manners were ridiculous," she said softly, "and since the castle has gone to such trouble to give us all relatively bite sized portions and I can't see where the food on my plate is, I hope you won't mind if I use my fingers." She then moved her hand over her plate and found a piece of roasted potato and popped it into her mouth.

Nathaniel stared at her, his fury melted away, and he felt only gratitude and compassion. Gwyn could hold the cutlery in her human hands, but she was right. Without her vision, she would not be able to spear the food on her plate with her fork without hacking at it. His paws were still clumsy, but he could spear his food with his claws and eat it effectively.

Beau, perhaps also sensing the tension in the room, breathed an audible sigh of relief, grabbed a piece of roasted duck with his fingers, and said, "Sounds great to me, Gran. I never know which damn fork you are supposed to use with what anyway." Then he put the duck in his mouth and ate it.

After that, they ate their meal contentedly and talked comfortably about what they might do the following day. It was decided that they would work at cleaning up the castle in the morning, and then in the afternoon, Nathaniel and Beau would go through the grounds and perhaps some of the forest to collect herbs and items that Gwyn always liked to have on hand as a midwife, and that Beau should have experience preparing. Then, if they had time, Nathaniel had promised to train Beau in fighting skills, his beastly form permitted.

After dinner, Nathaniel led them across the hall to a small chamber he had not entered in years. Comfortable chairs and sofas were grouped together. There was a piano forte and several other kinds of musical instruments along the back wall. After Gwyn was seated in a comfortable chair, Beau picked up a fiddle and played folk songs, and so they spent a pleasant evening before retiring to their rooms for the night.

When the sun streamed through his windows, Nathaniel woke. He lay quietly for a while, feeling content and almost happy. He was not alone anymore, and he felt comfortable in the company of Gwyn and Beau, even though he was a beast. He looked forward to the day, and he couldn't remember the last time he had felt like that. Sitting up, he gasped in surprise. His mirror was intact, completely mended, as were the other things he had broken in his rage. Tears pricked in his eyes; perhaps Gwyn was right, and the castle noticed that he was changed. He dashed the thoughts from his mind. It was dangerous to hope for too much. He rose and washed and dressed himself. He knocked lightly on Gwyn's door, and she opened it almost immediately. They exchanged pleasantries, and he escorted her to the family dining room where a light breakfast was set out for them. Though the table was set for three, Beau was apparently sleeping in, as could be expected from a young man—who wasn't a beast.

While waiting Beau's arrival, Gwyn suggested that Nathaniel read to her. He agreed, and he left her seated by the fire on a padded bench while he retrieved a book from the library. He braced himself at the door. The second day after his transformation, he had tried to read a book to distract himself, but he couldn't turn the pages and had wrecked the place. To his amazement, the library was perfectly in order when he opened the door. All the books were in place and nothing was broken. "Thank you," he whispered. "Thank you *so much*." A book lay on the nearest table, John Milton's *Paradise Lost*. It seemed fitting somehow, so he took the book and returned to Gwyn. He sat next to her on the bench and held out the book to her. She took it, opened it, and turned the pages until he told her where to stop. They read together like that: he reading the words and telling her when he finished a page, and she turning the pages for him and listening to the story. They hadn't gotten very far when Beau joined them. He begged them not to stop, got himself a cup of tea and a slice of toast, and joined them near the fire to listen to the story.

After Beau had eaten, they made their way to the kitchens to start cleaning at least one of them. To their surprise, one of the kitchens was already completely in order. Nathaniel quickly explained about his room and the library. Nathaniel led Gwyn to a table and chair, and he and Beau brought her jumbles of things that she could sort by shape and feel, like silverware and napkins and such. Nathaniel got out a broom and dustpan and set about sweeping up broken china and pottery. Beau picked up scattered pots and pans, washed them, dried them, and then put them away. After about an hour between the three of them, that kitchen was in order, so they moved on to the larger kitchen. This one took them two hours, but when it was done, Nathaniel felt so much pride and satisfaction that it surprised him. In his previous life, he had never really had to clean things. The servants had done all that, but completing the task from start to finish, seeing the transformation of the room from chaos to order, fixing a mess that he had made—all of these things gave him pleasure—and best of all, the work was much more pleasant in the company of others. Sometimes they talked, but other times they just worked in a companionable silence.

When they were done, they returned to the family dining room and found lunch waiting for them. After they had eaten, both Nathaniel and Beau expressed concern about leaving Gwyn all alone for the afternoon, but she scoffed at them. She had found a knitting basket in her apartments and had started on a shawl for herself. She knit so well that she didn't need to see what she did; she could feel what she did and needed to do. She had them escort her back to her rooms, showed them her newly started project, and sent them on their way. Beau brought his knife, a basket and a sack from the kitchens in which they could store their finds. The castle's kitchen gardens were not in as bad a shape as Beau had assumed. They were full of weeds, of course, but a lot of the herbs were still alive, fighting for their space among the weeds. Beau cut swatches of lavender, rosemary, chamomile, tansy, peppermint, spearmint, and sage. He found rosehips in the formal gardens and collected those along with a range of different medicinal flowers like roses, foxgloves, dandelions, and pansies. Next, they set out for the forest. Beau was remarkably good at finding certain kinds of mushrooms, and he even found some truffles. Nathaniel watched Beau work with fascination. Some tasks Nathaniel could help with, but though he couldn't help with the majority, it was still interesting and educational to watch Beau foraging. Beau tried to explain what each item was and how it could be used in various remedies, poultices and other healing means. He was kind and patient and very much like his grandmother, Nathaniel realized.

When they returned after several hours, Nathaniel went to get Gwyn. Beau set out the different things on a big kitchen table in the smallest kitchen and got bowls for some things and string and scissors for tying up herbs to dry. Then the boys left Gwyn to work in the kitchen while they experimented in the training yard. By trial and error, they found that Nathaniel could wield a staff, while Beau tried to come at him with a sword. Nathaniel was over a foot taller than Beau and much stronger and faster. They were in fact quite evenly matched, despite Nathaniel's extensive former training, which gave him an advantage. It was thrilling to do something more physical than just run. They spent several hours going after each other until they were both dripping with sweat, thoroughly sore, and nursing various bruises and abrasions. They walked back to the castle together to see to Gwyn. She was waiting for them. Bunches of herbs had been tied together, and she had lengths of string ready for them. She put them to work, hanging the herb bunches to ceiling beams where they would dry. After the herbs, came the flowers. The rosehips would dry in a colander, and she had placed the mushrooms and truffles near the stove in case the magical beings who created the castle's enchantments, wanted to use them for the food.

They retired to their rooms, badly in need of their waiting baths. Dinner was again delightful. They ate contentedly and shared the events of their separate activities. After dinner, instead of music, Beau read to them from *Paradise Lost* until it was time for bed.

After retiring to his room, Nathaniel spent a lot of time thinking about his day, especially his time alone with Beau. He had not allowed himself to do so before, because he did not want any awkwardness between them, but now it was all he could think about. He thought about Beau's quiet gentleness and grace, his kindness and patience, his beauty. He was beautiful, a dark Adonis, and they had touched while training. Nathaniel tried to empty his mind, but he couldn't. He kept thinking about Beau, wanting to touch him more, and wanting Beau to touch him in return.

The days fell into a happy rhythm, cleaning in the morning with Gwyn and then Nathaniel and Beau foraging or training until it was time for dinner. On the odd rainy day, they played games or read in the afternoon. Nathaniel and Gwyn usually paired off against Beau in games. He became her eyes, and she became his hands. As the days turned into weeks and months, they grew incredibly close. Nathaniel wasn't sure exactly when it had first started, but Gwyn's good morning and good night kisses seemed so natural to him that it was hard to imagine life without them. The one pattern that did change was that one morning, there wasn't a room in the castle that needed cleaning. They had either cleaned those that were damaged or the castle had mended them. In the absence of that chore, they read or played games in the mornings until the young men went out on their own.

A couple of other things changed as well. Nathaniel's feelings for Beau only strengthened in intensity, and Beau began reciprocating those feelings. They held hands occasionally. In addition to training with the staff and the sword, they competed without weapons, which almost always disintegrated into a wrestling match. During one such bout, Nathaniel had Beau pinned beneath him, his weight and height making it easy for him to do. Beau had been struggling against him, but then suddenly stopped, and when Nathaniel looked down at him, Beau was staring at him, his lips parted, his breathing heavy, and a hunger in his eyes that made Nathaniel gasp. Nathaniel pulled away slightly.

"Nathan?" he heard Beau ask him.

"You can't want me. I am a beast," he said bitterly.

"You're not a beast. I do want you. Gran and I both love you; surely, you know that, don't you?" Beau asked.

"Love me?" the words were strangled. They were everything Nathaniel had ever hoped for, and yet he didn't feel worthy of them.

"Let me touch you," Beau pleaded, and he reached out his hand to touch Nathaniel's face.

Nathaniel felt as if he was melting, his fur, his size, his shape. The next thing he knew, he could feel Beau's hand on his bare skin. Beau looked just as surprised as he felt.

"Nathan, you're human again," Beau whispered.

Nathaniel couldn't believe it. He wept, and Beau wrapped his arms around him and let him cry. When the tears stopped, Beau kissed him. Nathaniel had wanted to do this for so long that he nearly started weeping again. The kisses slowly deepened, and they touched each other. In between touching and stroking, they made each other come, both feeling happy and content. Then they shrugged into their clothes to go and find Gwyn. Nathaniel struggled with his overly large clothes, but he didn't mind.

To their surprise, Gwyn was not alone in the kitchens. Fairy Kate was with her. Both women were seated and beaming at them.

"Prince Nathaniel, I have never been so happy to have been wrong," the fairy queen said with a radiant smile.

Nathaniel knew not only that the curse was broken, but that he was forgiven, and he felt profoundly humbled. He inclined his head to the fairy queen, "I am not a prince, My Lady, but I am truly grateful to be human again. It was a tough lesson, but I am happier now than ever in my previous life," he said quietly.

"Your kingdom will be returned to you in a short while, and you will be a worthy prince. You and Beau may want to get cleaned up, so that you can greet your parents in proper style," said the fairy.

"My parents...what...do I tell them?" Nathaniel looked awkwardly at Gwyn and the fairy, but they understood that he was thinking about his love for Beau.

Gwyn spoke first. "They love you, Nathan, as I love you. They will want your happiness more than anything else. Being different and bringing change is hard, but it is important."

"Plus, I have a gift for each of you," and Fairy Kate moved forward and gave each young man and Gwyn a kiss on the forehead. "You are all marked with my kiss. It will protect you and bring you luck."

Gwyn gasped suddenly, jumped to her feet, and knelt at the feet of the fairy. "My Lady, how can I thank you?" she began.

Fairy Kate held out her hand and pulled Gwyn to her feet. "You are skilled, my dear Gwyneth, and you have much more life to live. To make the most of your skill and aid your people, it is my pleasure to return to you your sight," she said softly. "It is time for me to leave. Live well, all of you, and love each other," and she disappeared in a flash of sparkling dust.

Nathaniel, Beau and Gwyn hugged each other. They were all so happy and grateful for so many things. They talked excitedly until they retreated to their rooms to get ready. After his bath, Nathaniel stared at his reflection in the mirror for a few minutes, turning and checking to see that no patch of fur lingered on him. He felt amused when he opened his closet and found a completely new wardrobe, designed to fit his human form. Nathaniel, Beau, and Gwyn walked hand-in-hand through the castle to the grand ballroom, and were not surprised to find the castle in a flurry of activity, with servants rushing about and guests milling around. Nathaniel led his friends into the ballroom and froze when he saw his parents. They looked the same as always, utterly unchanged and unharmed.

"It's okay, Nathan; you are the one who has changed, not they," Gwyn said to him quietly.

Nathaniel hugged his parents passionately, and they seemed bemused by his enthusiasm. He presented Gwyn as his permanent guest at the castle, and Beau as his boyfriend. The king and queen welcomed Gwyn and Beau warmly, and with a light and happy heart, Nathaniel and Beau left Gwyn to catch up with the queen while they went to dance the night away.

Snow White and the Huntsgirl

ONCE UPON A time, there was a king and a queen who loved each other very much and wanted a child more than anything. Queen Theresa and King Michael were good and just rulers, and because of that, when the queen asked the fairy queen for her help in granting them a child, a girl with hair as dark as ebony, skin as white as snow, and lips as red as blood, the child was conceived and then born. They named her Snow White, and she was a sweet, kind, and loving child. She was also very beautiful.

When Snow White was eleven, her mother grew ill, and despite the doctor's efforts and the constant tending of King Michael and Snow White, the queen's condition worsened, and she died. The king and Snow White were bereft, and they withdrew from society. The royal court allowed them their grief for a while, but then they demanded their re-entry. It was easier for Snow White; she was a child after all. She made appearances and then disappeared to the kitchens and was coddled by the cooks. From the kitchens it was easy enough to escape to the kitchen yard with the other children. Shirking off her royal status was often a blessing, so she often felt like a regular child and not a princess.

Her father drifted. Sometimes incredibly attentive, and sometimes incredibly absent—lost completely in his grief. A half-brother drew him abroad. Months dragged by. Snow White was so lonely, and then suddenly they were back, and her father, her half-uncle, and their entourage; a woman accompanied them. Lady Lauren was stunning, one of the most beautiful women Snow White had ever seen. Where her mother had been fair, Lady Lauren was dark with golden-brown skin, thick, tightly-curled, dark brown hair, and cat-like golden-brown eyes.

Her father and Lady Lauren were married shortly after the royal party returned, and they were happy. Queen Lauren loved King Michael, and she was kind and loving to Snow White. And then a sickness fell upon the land, and King Michael was struck with it. Queen Lauren and Snow White cared for him in shifts, but to their horror, they watched him deteriorate. He was dying, slipping away from them, and there was nothing they could do, so they loved him as much as they could for the time they had left. When he died, they knew that each of them had done everything that she could have done and that they had loved him with their complete souls and hearts.

Snow White withdrew into herself, and the queen let her as much as she could. Queen Lauren dealt with matters of state as best she could, and she was amazingly good at it, considering that she was a foreigner. Snow White heard the compliments that were made about her step-mother and was pleased. The queen oversaw Snow White's education, placing her in the capable hands of Lady Jessica, a distinguished tutor. The queen made time each day to lunch alone with Snow White so that they could talk intimately. Snow White grew to love the queen, not as a replacement of her mother but as a kind of second mother, and the queen loved Snow White and never tired of noting what looks the princess had inherited from her father or what mannerism of his that she used quite unconsciously. It made Snow White feel closer to him somehow. So, the months passed in a contented rhythm, and soon it was years, and Snow White found herself facing her fourteenth birthday.

Though Snow White had not found the idea of turning fourteen any different than turning thirteen, she was mistaken. When she had finished her morning lessons with Lady Jessica, she led Snow White to the queen's private council chambers. There Snow White found herself being formally introduced to the queen's advisors. She had known them for years of course.

What excited and frightened her now was that she was being introduced to them not as a child but as a peer and equal. The queen now expected Snow White to learn to rule, and to do so she would need to work with these ladies and lords. She glanced nervously at Lady Jessica, but she had withdrawn. She next glanced at the queen, who smiled at her reassuringly and nodded to confirm that Snow White had guessed quite correctly. After the introductions had been made, the queen led Snow White to barracks of the Queen's Guard where she was likewise introduced. Captain Davidson winked at her and introduced his men with authority and respect. The queen then took Snow White to meet the chief cooks and housekeepers and healing women and doctors. It struck Snow White that the queen knew all these people by name and details about their lives and their families. Finally, they ended up in queen's private dining room where a small lunch was laid out for them. As they took their seats, the queen handed Snow White a round flat package. It contained a delicate diadem which the queen took from Snow White's hands and placed carefully on the girl's head.

"You have been a young woman for some time, Snow White," she said tenderly, "but now you are a queen in the making. It is time for you to wear a symbol of what you are," she said sweetly, and bent to kiss Snow White on the forehead.

"Thank you, my queen," Snow White said shyly.

"Don't be silly, my child. Nothing significant has changed between us. You must use my given name when we are alone," she said with a smile. "Eat," she commanded, and so they ate, and the queen explained that Snow White's days would change now. She would have morning lessons with Lady Jessica as usual, but on days when there was court business to attend, Snow White would attend the queen and watch and learn. On days when there was no court, there were other things the queen wanted to show Snow White.

Learning the business of becoming a queen was often incredibly dull, but other times it was full of unexpected surprises. In formal court session, about a month after Snow White's birthday, she was shocked to hear King Arthur of the neighboring kingdom ask for Snow White's hand in marriage for his son, Prince Kenneth. Snow White thought that she might burst into flames at her embarrassment, until she caught the mocking gaze of Captain Davidson watching her with such suppressed mirth that she felt a rush of anger. He saw her change of expression and amended his face to a more deferential attitude of apology that was somewhat convincing. She later learned that princes had been asking for her hand for years, with both the king and the queen putting them off on account of her youth.

Another surprise was the deference with which the queen held the household staff (the cooks, the housekeepers, the healers/doctors, the teachers and tutors of the children). "Never dismiss the servants, Snow White. They run the castle; they know things. You need them as your allies, and they need to know that you respect them and value them. Have the servants as your enemies, and you fail because you fight on all fronts. But it isn't just politics, Snow White. They are good people; you have selected them as such—acknowledging them as such, it is just what is due. Life has granted us privilege, Snow White, but never forget that you could be one of them and lucky at your good fortune." Snow White bowed her head in acknowledgment. She knew this was true from her time in the kitchens with the cooks and their children.

One afternoon, the queen invited Snow White to her private apartments. The queen led her into the large changing room. Snow White followed, increasingly puzzled. The queen opened a large armoire at the far end of the room. Snow White came to stand by the queen's side, peering curiously at the inside of the armoire.

"Come, Snow White, this is my greatest secret," the queen said very softly, and Snow White felt the queen take her elbow and help her inside the armoire, shutting the doors behind them and casting them into darkness. Snow White felt a rush of fear, but then the queen waved her arm, pushing aside a dark curtain that Snow White had mistaken for the back of the armoire, and there was a little hidden room before them. It was small and sparsely furnished. Two small couches sat by a large low table. In the center of the room, a brazier burned unnatural blue, steady flames gently lighting the little room. Opposite the couches stood a great, magnificent mirror, gilded with both silver and gold. Runes made a winding, twisting silver band around the edges of the great mirror while pictures of animals real and imaginary made another in gold.

Snow White stared at the great mirror and then at the queen. "What is this place?" she asked in a whisper.

The queen steered them to the closest couch and sat down. Snow White sat next to her. "Your father let me store the Magic Mirror here. We used it together while he lived, and I have used it since to rule the kingdom," she said simply.

"Magic Mirror?" Snow White repeated numbly. "What does it do?"

"It grants wishes, Snow White," the queen answered.

"Wishes?" she found herself repeating again. "Any wishes?" and Snow White found herself both excited and alarmed at the prospect.

The queen straightened herself and looked at Snow White carefully. She felt the scrutiny of the queen's gaze, probing her, trying to decide if she had been mistaken in trusting this secret to the girl. "The Magic Mirror is a powerful object, Snow White. It can be used for great good or great evil. I am only human, but I have tried to use the mirror for good—to enhance the lives of our people. In my own land, my cousin learned of the mirror and wanted it. He was a cruel man, and I knew he would use the mirror poorly, so when I met your father and he seemed like such a good man, I asked the mirror about him, and it showed me that he was good and that we could have a good life together. So, I confided to him the secret of the mirror, and he helped me hide it and then get it here safely. Not even your half-uncle knows about the mirror. Now you are the only other person who knows about the mirror."

Snow White shook her head, trying to process this information and trying to order the questions that were screaming in her mind. "How does it work?" she asked speculatively, looking from the queen to the mirror, glistening in the odd blue flames.

"Snow White," the queen said sharply. "It is not a toy. It is a great responsibility to have access to such an object. You must be very respectful with how you use it."

"How do you use it?" Snow White asked sincerely.

The queen relaxed a little. "I use it to see things in the kingdom that I would not otherwise see. I try to alleviate suffering where I can, but I also try not to pry too far into the lives of our people," she answered.

Snow White still clearly did not understand. The queen sighed and turned toward the mirror, "Mirror, Mirror, on the wall, show us those who suffer in our land so that we might lend a hand."

The queen reached quickly for a large notebook that had lain on the table and a quill which she adroitly dipped in an inkpot. Snow White had failed to notice these objects on her first scan of the little room. She could not imagine what the queen wanted with them, until suddenly the mirror flashed to life. A baker's store front came into view, and inside in the living quarters an angry man was lashing his son savagely. Angry red marks cut into the boy's bare buttocks, and both Snow White and the queen flinched as they watched the beating. The queen scribbled notes in the notebook, and the image changed. A woodcutter's cottage deep in the forest, and a woman's face gaunt with hunger divvying out a meager stew to her four skinny young children. Another entry in the notes. The image changed again—a tavern, two men sat conspiring, one was being paid to set fire to the other man's neighbor's barn. More notes. The image changed again, a girl was being coerced into a marriage that she didn't want and was too young for. The images flickered, and the queen wrote about it all in the notebook. When the mirror went clear again, the queen picked up a different, smaller notebook and made a copy of the notes in the larger book. Snow White sat quietly watching, and as the queen finished this second set of notes, she asked, "What will you do?"

"Captain Davidson will see the baker and send his men to see about the farm dispute and some of the other situations. Sometimes a male intervention is better than a female one, but there are others that are suited to me and, now, me and you. The woodcutter died a little while ago; I should have realized, but I had forgotten. With children so young, she should be moved out of the forest. We will pay her a visit and help her get relocated. Some nanny goats and chickens would help her support her family," the queen answered.

So, Snow White began to be schooled in the power of the Magic Mirror. Beauty, the queen counselled, was as much in the soul and heart as in the face and the body, and the beauty of one's heart and soul could be seen in the actions one performed for others. The danger of the mirror was that one could see too much. Seeing too much could strip people of their powers of free choice and their agency over their own lives. Help where needed was the goal, not control over others. The prayer was for the sight to help, and Snow White felt a profound satisfaction traveling with the queen and giving aid to her people. Most were unabashedly gratefully. The queen's gifts were answers to their most secret prayers. The woodcutter's wife had fallen to their feet crying and sobbing a strangled thank you. A few prideful to the point of idiocy tried to refuse the queen's gifts, but she skillfully turned the gifts into loans which they were to repay with interest.

That spring it seemed like the countryside bloomed in invitations, dances, balls, festivals, and/or ceremonies. Snow

White could not remember a season with so much activity. The queen had a dressmaker come specifically to update Snow White's gowns and to make quite a few new ones. Her new gowns were different; they were more fitted and sophisticated. They were not the gowns of a child, but the gowns of a young woman, and Snow White realized that the flurry of invitations was in acknowledgment of her being of marriageable age, and she felt a sense of dread at the thought.

At lunch with the queen, Snow White asked about it, "Do I have to marry?"

The queen looked at her, the startled expression on her face softened as she read the anxiety on Snow White's face. "No, my child. You don't have to marry, but you might like to, some day," she added gently.

"Some day?" Snow White toyed with the words. Relief that imminent betrothal was not her fate washed the tension from her body.

"You are very young, Snow White, but it is time for you to be presented to the neighboring royalty. Perhaps in a few years, you may get to know someone you like. Our lands are relatively peaceful; we have allies already, and I do not see the need for marriage alliance, but if one should present itself that wouldn't be undesirable either." The queen paused. She saw that her words did not comfort Snow White. "Your desires are also important, Snow White. I would not see you married against your will."

The queen and Snow White went to every event. Snow White was introduced to scores of young men. She danced and talked with them, but Snow White had always been a solitary child. She liked being with Mother and Father, with Lady Jessica and some of the other tutors, with the cooks, with her father and Queen Lauren, and then with the queen. She had acquaintances among the ladies-in-waiting, but no close friends. Her closest friend was Tanya, the Huntsman's daughter, who often accompanied Snow White when she rode. Tanya had taught Snow White how to hunt with a bow and arrows, and they had an easy friendship. The spring had been so busy with Snow White's turning fourteen, assuming more adult responsibilities, and being presented to royal households that Snow White had scarcely seen her friend.

One evening, Snow White was dancing with a young man with straight black hair and dark russet skin; he smelled vaguely of the outdoors and horse, and Snow White wished she were dancing with Tanya. They would be laughing easily at all the fuss over dresses and costumes and all the intrigue over who might marry who. Some of the young men she met were handsome; some appeared to be very nice; some even appeared to be handsome and nice, but none of them grabbed her attention, and none of them were as fun to be around as Tanya.

The next evening, they were at her half-uncle's castle. Lord John and Lady Rebecca had introduced Queen Lauren and Princess Snow White to the ladies and lords present, and Snow White was dancing with her half-cousin, Lord Peter, when a party of guests arrived late and was introduced. Lord Thomas and his sons were presented, and suddenly, the queen was at Snow White's side.

"Lord Peter," she interrupted, "please get Snow White out of here as discretely as possible and then go and fetch your father," she whispered. Both Snow White and Lord Peter were alarmed at the strain on Queen Lauren's face and the deathly pale of her skin. Before they could say anything, the queen disappeared into the crowd. Her half-cousin followed the queen's example and disappeared with Snow White into the crowd and out of the back of the hall.

Lord Peter took Snow White to his father's private counsel chamber and left her there with the queen while he went to get his father. Lord Peter returned with Lord John and the head of the Lord's Guard, Captain Richards. Queen Lauren explained that Lord Thomas was her cousin, the man she had fled when she agreed to come away with King Michael. Lord John understood enough to know that the queen and Snow White were in danger, and he ordered his son and Captain Richards to take half his guards and return the queen and the princess to their castle and remain with them. Lord John would see what could be done to get rid of the unwanted company and feign ignorance about the queen and princess.

They traveled as swiftly as they could in the darkness; it was dawn before they reached the castle. Grooms saw to the horses, and cooks and housekeepers saw to feeding and housing of Lord Peter and his father's men. The queen sent Davidson to fetch Tanya and her father, and she had clothes brought to her private rooms. The clothes, Snow White realized, were boys' clothes. The queen laid out several changes of clothes and had Snow White change into one of them. She packed three other changes of clothes. Davidson ushered a bewildered Huntsman and his daughter into the queen's rooms and stood waiting. He was rigid with tension.

"My cousin has found me," she explained. "He showed up at Lord John's. I don't think he saw me, but even with Lord John's denials, he will find out that I was there, and about Snow White. He will try to force a marriage alliance one way or another with me or with one of his sons and Snow White. He wants something from me, but I will destroy it to keep it out of his hands if I have to," her eyes looking meaningfully at Snow White. She nodded in acknowledgment. If the queen should fail to destroy the mirror to keep it from Lord Thomas, Snow White was to do it herself.

"Snow White must go into hiding. Tanya, will you take her? Disappear into the forest. Go far away. Keep her hidden," the queen implored.

"I will go with them, my queen," said the Huntsman.

"No, my friend; I can't let you go. It would be too obvious if you disappeared. Tanya we can make excuses for, and knowing my cousin's contempt for women, he will not think much of Tanya's skill and resourcefulness."

"What about me, my queen?" Davidson asked.

"You must remain with me also, my captain, but is there one among your guard that you would trust with such important task?" the queen asked.

"Yes, my queen, Nathan Daniels is a good soldier and a good man. I will go and make the arrangements," and he bowed and took his leave, pausing to wink at Snow White and wish her well.

The Huntsman embraced his daughter and wished both her and the princess well. Davidson returned with Daniels, and he led the three through the castle to the stables where he saw them mounted, armed, provisioned, and off. They were to ride for a few hours so that they were well clear of the castle and then find a secluded place to rest.

The three of them were so stunned by the recent events that they didn't talk much. The distractions of the spring countryside kept them entertained. They rode through any stream or creek bed they could find; they forded one river and then another. By about noon, they were well up in the mountains, and when they found a shaded clearing, they made camp. Snow White fell asleep at once after her sleepless night, and Tanya and Nathan took turns to watch the sleeping princess and hunt. They woke the princess at about five. They ate a happy little meal of roasted rabbit and wild yams, bread from the castle, and fresh raspberries. Snow White tried to explain what she knew about Lord Thomas to Tanya and Nathan (excluding the information about the Magic Mirror). Nathan had tried to use formal address with the princess and Tanya, but Snow White demanded that they use their given names under their distressed circumstances. They told each other stories after that and then bunked down for the night.

They rose at dawn and continued traveling. They stayed away from villages and settlements. They hunted, fished, and gathered food as their meager castle provisions were consumed. The days fell into a quiet rhythm. They were all anxious: Snow White about the queen, Tanya about her father, and Nathan about his brothers-in-arms and the queen. By unspoken compact, they didn't discuss their worries. After about a week of hard travel, they slowed their pace. It had rained twice since they had left—between not knowing the direction they had traveled, the rain, the measures they had taken to disguise their paths, and the significant delay Lord Thomas and his sons would have faced in beginning looking for them, they were pretty sure that they were beyond his grasp. Tanya and Snow White spent significant portions of their days together. They bathed together, and then they hunted and gathered together. Sometimes Nathan joined them to hunt and gather, but he seemed to enjoy his time alone too.

Weeks passed, and Snow White worried that if everything was resolved peacefully that no one from the castle would know how or where to find them to bring them back, but Nathan assured them both the Queen's Guard and the Huntsman would know. Spring turned into summer, and Snow White and Tanya bathed daily, and something began to change between them. They had always been friends, but Snow White realized one day sitting on the river bank watching Tanya combing her fingers through her hair that Tanya was the most beautiful person she had ever seen. With her dark hair and skin and her golden-yellow eyes, Snow White was reminded of a dark jungle cat from the stories she had heard. Desire flared in the bottom of Snow White's stomach, and she blushed at the direction of her thoughts. She remembered that night at a dance when she had pictured herself dancing not with the young man who held her but with Tanya. As if divining Snow White's thoughts, Tanya looked up suddenly and saw Snow White looking at her and blushing. Tanya smiled ruefully at her friend and came to join her on the river bank. Snow White didn't know what to say. Apparently, she had been attracted to Tanya for some time but had not articulated the idea to herself. How was she supposed to explain it to Tanya? What was more, how did or would Tanya feel about the matter?

Tanya didn't speak but simply took Snow White's hand in

her own and squeezed it. Snow White turned to look at Tanya who was looking at her with the same desire that Snow White felt, and all the awkwardness of situation seemed to fall away, and they kissed. It was gentle at first and exploratory, and then the intensity of it increased, and they were kissing passionately and running their hands across each other's body.

At first, they hid their relationship from Nathan, but he surprised them by telling them he not only knew but didn't care. Same sex relationships were not apparently as uncommon as Snow White thought. Nathan's paramour was the head stable groom, Harry Fraser. Nathan gave them his blessing—noting that now he wouldn't be responsible for the princess "technically" losing her virtue or getting pregnant—concerns that had apparently troubled the guardsman with their living rough in the wilderness.

Since Nathan knew, Snow White and Tanya curled up together at night, held hands when they wanted, and exchanged fairly innocent kisses. They continued their intimate moments when they were bathing or in the woods, and Nathan gave them a wide-birth for their exploits.

As summer drifted into fall, tensions ran high. All three of them were anxious for news from the castle, and though Snow White and Tanya could distract themselves with each other, Nathan missed Harry and could be snappish and irritable.

One morning, they woke to frost and the sound of hoof beats. They took strategic positions in the trees, arrows notched, and waited. The Huntsman, Captain Davidson, and Harry Fraser came in range and were hailed. It was a joyous reunion. Lord Thomas had tracked Queen Lauren back to the castle. His sons went after Snow White but couldn't find a trail. The queen claimed that she had left the mirror in her homeland and that it must have been destroyed if Lord Thomas had not found it. She allowed Lord Thomas' men to search the castle, and they tore apart every room they searched, but they failed to find the secret room behind the armoire, so they eventually left with Lord John's and Captain Davidson's threats that they should never enter the kingdom or threaten the kingdom, Queen Lauren, or Snow White again.

They rode hard to return, but opportunity was given for Nathan and Harry to spend time together. The Huntsman and Davidson got themselves used to the idea of Snow White and Tanya and were even happy for their obvious joy. Though they were not sure how the queen would take the news, they could and would attest to the happiness of the couples.

Queen Lauren was only happy and grateful. They were free from her cousin, the mirror was safe, and it could continue to be used to help their people, Snow White had come home, Tanya was returned to her father, Snow White had found a caring and attentive partner, Nathan was returned to the Queen's Guard and reunited with his lover, and Queen Lauren was re-bonded with Lord John's family. Snow White found it both bizarre and comforting to think of her life as queen with Tanya at her side, but she had many years to get used to the idea, learning and growing into the role under Queen Lauren's patient tutelage.

The Frog and the Transgender Prince

ONCE UPON A time in a small kingdom, there lived a princess. She was the apple of her parents' eyes. They showered her with affection and love, but she was not a happy child. Stephanie never felt quite right in a way that she couldn't explain to herself. Her father was dark-skinned, a deep dark brown that was nearly black. His hair was kinky and wiry. He wore it in tight thin braids and usually tied it back in a pony tail of sorts. His eyes were dark, nearly black. Her mother was fair skinned with wavy light brown hair and crystal blue eyes. Stephanie was somewhere in between. Not quite the image of her father and not quite the image of her mother. Her skin was a lighter brown than her father's, but much darker than her mother's. Her hair was raven black but had the texture of her mother's fine hair except that it was crazy curly—in tight corkscrew curls that were impossible to tame. Her eyes were a light brown flecked with green, but it wasn't just her skin, hair, and eyes. She never felt graceful like the other girls at court or in the castle. They seemed to glide through their actions, and Stephanie always felt like she plodded along. Once she hit puberty, she felt even more miserable. Other girls were naturally shapely in a feminine way, and she just wasn't. She didn't have hips; her waist was thick rather than slender, and she had broad shoulders. There were other things. She loved history and philosophy; she hated needle work and was not a good musician or singer. Her dancing drew a frown of the dance master, who often compromised by having her dance the less complicated male leads of the dances.

Feeling so out of sorts, she had few close friends. When she could, she went riding to be alone. She enjoyed hunting, and though women rarely accompanied hunts, her father allowed her to come with them because so few things seemed to give her pleasure. She watched the boys and men of the palace train with interest. The physicality of what they did looked like fun and engaging, but watching was all she was permitted to do.

For her eighteenth birthday, the princess had been given a golden ball. A traveling sorceress had given the ball to the king and queen, assuring them that the ball would transform the princess' life and lead her to true happiness. Stephanie had thought the whole thing was ridiculous, but knowing how her parents grieved over her discomfort, she had accepted the ball.

Shortly after her birthday, she had ridden deep into the forest. She had dismounted and was leading her horse through a stand of trees when the trees thinned suddenly to reveal a beautiful small pond. Her horse drank eagerly from the water. Stephanie sated her own thirst and then walked absently around the charming pond, admiring the wild flowers that grew around it. After her initial exploration, she sat down at the edge of the pond and ate her small packed snack of bread and cheese and dried fruit. She fed an apple to her horse and found herself drowsy, so she spread out her cloak and fell asleep to the peaceful sounds of the pond and the forest.

She woke with a start and had the uncomfortable feeling that she was being watched. She got up and gathered her things warily, but her horse was completely peaceful and contented, so she convinced herself that it had only been her imagination. To distract herself, she took out the golden ball and started playing with it. She threw it up in the air and caught it. Such a small and insignificant thing, she thought; how was a ball supposed to change one's life? Still it was made of gold, a precious metal. Perhaps that was the price of change—something precious. Frustrated by the seemingly futile train of her thoughts she threw the ball up higher than she had intended, and she realized that she couldn't catch it on its way down. She watched helplessly as the golden ball dropped into the pond and disappeared.

She was shocked by the depth of emotion that accompanied the disappearance of the ball. She had not truly believed that the ball could do anything for her, and yet with its loss, the potential for her true happiness was lost too. She sat down on the edge of the pond and wept. She had been so consumed with grief that she did not notice that something was trying to talk to her. Finally, she realized that a voice was speaking to her, and she looked up in shock.

"Miss, please, miss, why do you cry?" the voice said. It was coming from a frog who seemed to have come out of the pond. The princess stared at the frog. I have finally lost my mind, she thought, and looked around frantically to see what her horse was doing. If a frog could talk, perhaps Star Blaze had grown wings and could fly as a Pegasus. But, no, Star Blaze stood grazing happily, four legs and a tail and no wings. Stephanie looked back at the frog who seemed to be eyeing her with amusement. There didn't seem to be any choice, so as foolish has the princess felt, she spoke to the frog.

"Are...are...you speaking to me?" she asked, the incredulity clear in her voice.

"Well, yes," the frog said softly. "You seem so upset. What is wrong?" it asked again.

Stephanie felt ridiculous, but she tried to explain. "My parents gave me a golden ball for my birthday, and I have lost it in the pond," she answered.

The frog looked from Stephanie to the pond and back again. "I could get it for you," the frog said slowly, "but you would need to do me a favor in return."

Without considering the consequences of such a promise, Stephanie answered immediately. "Of course, anything you want, so long as you fetch my ball for me."

"Anything I want," the frog repeated, looking at Stephanie carefully.

Stephanie felt a tinge of panic—what was she promising this creature obviously touched by magic? It is just a frog, some voice in Stephanie's head answered, dismissing the fears that suddenly presented themselves to her.

As if reading Stephanie's mind, the frog looked into Stephanie's eyes and asked, "Who are you and where do you live?"

With the vanity of nobility, Stephanie announced herself, "I am Princess Stephanie, the heir of King Marcus and Queen Rose." Realizing too late that she was giving the frog more information than she intended to. She didn't intend to keep her promise; she lied about where she lived, waving vaguely in the opposite direction from her father's palace.

The frog nodded. "I will hold you to your promise, princess," and then it turned and hopped into the pond and disappeared.

Stephanie stood and found herself worrying her hands together in anticipation. Just when she was concluding that she had imagined the whole thing, the frog hopped out of the pond and hopped to her feet, spitting out the golden ball from its mouth.

Stephanie stooped down and snatched up the ball. "Thank you," she said, and she meant that part. "Now it is time for me to return home," and she snatched up her cloak and started for Star Blaze.

"But, your promise, princess," the frog protested.

Stephanie ignored the frog, mounted her horse, and was gone without giving her broken promise a second thought.

The following day, Stephanie had convinced herself that her encounter with the frog had been a dream. So that evening at dinner, when the page announced the frog as "a guest of Princess Stephanie, heir to King Marcus and Queen Rose," Stephanie was just as surprised as her parents. The frog slowly hopped its way through the royal family dining room and stood before the king and queen.

"What is the meaning of this, Stephanie?" the queen asked.

Stephanie told the king and queen the story of her encounter with the frog at the pond. Both her parents looked stricken when she explained that she had promised the frog anything it wished—and she began to realize that promising anything was a very dangerous thing to do.

"What is it that you wish of our daughter?" the king asked cautiously.

"For now," the frog said politely, "I only wish to be the princess' primary companion. To eat with her and to be with her through the days and nights."

The king and queen relaxed slightly hearing these words. The king turned to his daughter, "You have heard the request, my child. Make the frog feel welcome in our home." Stephanie looked at her father, trying to recover from her shock. He was dead serious. He wasn't even faintly dismissive of a frog requesting to be her new best friend. She started to say something in protest, but her father shook his head slightly. There was no argument to this request; it was an order. Whether she wanted to or not, she had to befriend the frog. The frog hopped up on the table and helped itself to small scraps of her stewed meat. When they were all finished dinner, the princess retired to her room to save herself the humiliation of entertaining the frog in front of the court. Alone in her apartments, the princess ignored the frog. The frog didn't seem to mind and contented itself with looking through her books and possessions.

Stephanie was miserable. Previously unhappy and out of place, she now felt herself the butt of every joke, the subject of all the gossip in the palace, the object of every stare. She tried to ignore the frog as best she could, but her parents grilled her every day about how well she was being companionable to her guest. Worse, the frog talked to her. It told her all its favorite stories. It talked to her about its favorite periods of history and favorite philosophers. Stephanie found herself listening to the frog despite herself. They spent long hours alone in Stephanie's apartments. The frog would page through the princess' books. Sometimes the frog would read to Stephanie. The frog began to be fascinated by poetry and would read out its favorite poems. Once the frog had gone through all the volumes of poetry in the princess' apartments, Stephanie took it to the formal library and let the frog choose volumes of poetry to take back to their rooms.

Slowly, Stephanie began to talk to the frog. She talked to it about all the ways she didn't feel comfortable with herself and her life in the palace. She told the frog things that she had never told anyone. She wondered why she could tell it such things. Perhaps, she mused, because no one would believe a talking frog or perhaps because, as a frog in the palace, it was as out of place as she felt.

One day, they had been reading a story about seal-man whose pelt had been stolen by a human woman, so that he had no choice but to marry her and live with her in his man form, but she had grown to love him in that selfless way that is the way of true love, and she had given him back his pelt so that he could return to his home and his people. She had truly expected him to leave her then, but he had grown to love her as well, so he stayed with her until she died and only then returned to his home. The transformation part of the story fascinated and excited Stephanie. If she could only transform, perhaps then she would feel like she belonged. But transform into what?

"If I could transform into anything, what do you think I would be best be suited to turn into?" Stephanie found herself asking the frog.

The frog stared at her for a long time. Stephanie thought there was a desperate longing in the eyes of the frog, but it shook its head and turned away from her.

"What is it?" Stephanie asked. "Tell me," she demanded.

"Nay, princess," it said softly, "I cannot tell you. It is a selfish desire of my own, and I love you too well to speak it." The last few words were spoken so softly that the princess could barely hear them.

Stephanie stared at the frog. The whole crazy situation seemed to make perfect sense now. How could she not have seen it? How could she not have guessed? How could a frog talk? How could a frog read or know history or philosophy? How could a frog know the obligations of court and royalty? Only if the frog had in fact been a human and been transformed him or herself. "Who are you?" Stephanie demanded.

"No one of consequence, princess," the frog answered, but Stephanie did not believe it.

"Yes, you are! You are of consequence to me. Who are you and why were you transformed?" Stephanie demanded again.

The frog looked at her again with the sad longing present in its eyes. "Once I was a child every bit as spoilt as you, but I had the misfortune to be rude to a fairy queen who transformed me into a frog."

Excitement coursed through Stephanie's veins, "But then I can free you, can't I? If I love you and tell you so and kiss you, I can free you?" she said in a rush. And she felt like she had never wanted anything more. This was it; it was all true. The golden ball was transforming her life. It had brought her the frog, and the frog was a prince, her prince, and she would be happy. "I love you," Stephanie said breathlessly, and she bent and kissed the frog on the head. She stepped back to see the transformation clearly, but nothing happened.

"Nay, princess, I am a princess myself, and though I love you dearly as a friend, I need the love of a prince to save me," the frog explained slowly.

Stephanie stared at the frog. She felt as though the world had shifted under her feet. Of course, that was it. She sat down and looked out the window. She had never been comfortable as a girl, but it had never occurred to her to be a boy. The rightness of it took her breath away. Would her parents care? No, she thought firmly—they had only wanted her happiness. The frog could ask for anything—even her life. The frog could have demanded that Stephanie become her prince, but the frog loved her well enough to remain a frog forever, and she loved the frog well enough to make the change into a prince as much for her own sake as for the frog's.

Her name was even suited for it; she would change from Princess Stephanie to Prince Stephen. She laughed at the thought. "What is your name?" the princess asked.

"Julia," the frog answered softly.

"Julia, my sweet, Julia, I will be your prince, and you will be my princess, and we will be happy forever," Stephen answered.

"I cannot ask it of you, princess," the frog said carefully.

"But I give it freely. Nothing would make me happier—and you know this better than anyone could," Stephen answered firmly. "I love you, Julia; take me as I will take you," and Stephen kissed the head of the frog. There was a blinding light. Stephen felt a deep glowing flowing throughout zir body. Ze could not see. Ze could only feel the glowing coursing through zir body. Slowly the glowing stopped and the bright light faded, and he sat on edge of his bed naked, now Prince Stephen. Next to him sat a beautiful young woman with russet skin and long straight black hair with dark brown/black eyes.

"Julia?" he asked softly.

"Stephen?" she asked at the same time.

They nodded at each other and laughed. Shyly they reached out their hands and explored each other. Touching progressed to kissing, nibbling, sucking, and licking. Julia seemed to discover her own body as Stephen explored it, and perhaps she did, having been a frog for he didn't know how long. Stephen certainly found that he discovered his own body through Julia's exploration of it. His proportions all seemed much more natural in male form, and he felt a deep genuine contentment and self-satisfaction that he had never experienced with himself as a female. He made her climax using his fingers—his former self-pleasuring in female form—aiding this particular sexual skill. The sexual intercourse part was harder. They both knew that his penis needed to go into her vagina but beyond that both were novices. He was gentle. He entered her carefully and slowly. As they both got used to that, he proceeded slowly. Gradually, he could move in her easily, and when he climaxed, it was wonderful—filled with the same transcending sensational experience as it had been before—but different—the semen exploding out of him in pulsing spurts. They lay in each other's arms, kissing and talking softly. Mostly, they were so grateful to each other and so happy and fully together after having been alone for so long.

Finally, Stephen wrapped himself in a blanket, went to the outer room, and called for a maid. The young woman nearly fainted at the sight of him. He was recognizably Stephanie, only a young man now, not the young woman she had been an hour before. Stephen demanded the maid go to the dressmaker for a suit of men's clothes that would fit him. Next, he looked through his former clothes and helped Julia dress in the most beautiful clothes he had. Once the maid returned, Stephen dressed himself as best as could, the novelty of male clothing being new to him. Assured by Julia that he was thoroughly presentable, Stephen led Julia through the palace to find his parents and present themselves.

The king and queen were in their royal apartments. The queen was doing needle work, and the king was writing a letter. They looked up as Stephen entered. Their eyes went wide with both shock and recognition. Stephen smiled hugely at them and motioned Julia to his side—grasping at her hand and linking his fingers through hers.

"Mother, father, I have the most wonderful news. Julia is my frog, and I am her prince, and we are happy, really truly happy," he said in a rush.

The king and queen made the two tell the story again from the beginning. Having either Julia or Stephen go over bits they found particularly confusing again and again, until at last they understood. They also understood the joy and love that flowed through and around the young couple, and they gave them their blessing. They were married in the following weeks, and the kingdom rejoiced that the princess had found her true self as a young man and that their new prince had found joy with a princess who loved him.

Hansel and Gregory

ONCE UPON A time at the edge of a great forest, there lived a lonely woodcutter and his son, Hansel. The woodcutter's wife had died in childbirth some years before; the child, a baby girl, had also died. The woodcutter had so loved his wife that he withdrew from all society, except his son. There was a village nearby, but the woodcutter always sent Hansel to sell their wood to the villagers. Their life had a pleasant rhythm. They woke at dawn and fixed a modest breakfast—usually of porridge and goat's milk. Hansel would then feed the chickens and gather eggs while his father fed and milked the goats— separating the milk for drinking and cooking with the milk to set for cheeses. Then they worked in their small garden, weeding and picking ripe vegetables, fruit, and herbs. Done these husbandry tasks, they packed lunches of cheese, bread, and fruit and made their way into the forest with their axes, knives, bows, bundles, and Donny, the mule. Two dogs, Ben and Bertha, they left behind to guard the chickens and goats, but Sampson, the great boarhound, accompanied them. They set snares for rabbits and other small game as they made their way into the forest, knowing the sounds of their labors would send terrorized animals fleeing toward the waiting traps. Once set to cutting felled limbs, the work was hard but rewarding. After four hours or so, they had usually filled their bundles and secured a sizable load of wood in packs on Donny. Sometimes they managed to collect and cut an excess, which they would stack neatly to be retrieved the next day in a double run. Other times they would hunt or fish before returning with their loads and the contents of their snares to their homestead, the cottage, the garden, the smoke shed, the well, and the barn with the great lean-to that sheltered their wood and their wagon.

The evening before market day, they would eat a hasty supper and load the wagon with bundled wood. On market day, Hansel would hitch up the wagon to Donny and make his way to the village, leaving his father alone. Occasionally, Hansel would spend the night in the village with a friend. It was lonely, after all, for the young man with just his father and the animals, but he returned home in the morning with a few coins and the goods they needed like salt and oats, fabric, and the odd tool or book. It was a quiet but contented existence, and then everything changed.

One afternoon a storm came with particular intensity. It drove the woodcutter and his son home. They baked bread and read by the hearth. They mended clothing and made arrows. As evening drew close, the dogs started barking, and Hansel went outside to find the dogs ringed around a horse and two frightened figures on the horse. Hansel quickly called the dogs off; they retreated but sat watching the newcomers warily. With the dogs calmed, a young man about Hansel's age swung down from the horse and introduced himself.

"Good evening. Pardon our intrusion. We lost our way. I am Gregory Griffin, and this is my mother, Elena Griffin," he said politely, gesturing to his mother.

Hansel looked from the young man to his mother; they were strangers. He had never seen them before. They weren't from the village; villagers knew to keep their distance. Hansel flushed. He knew his father would be uncomfortable with guests, but there clearly was little alternative. Gregory and his mother would need shelter, and there was no one else around for miles. They would just have to make the best of it.

Hansel grinned at Gregory. "I am Hansel Hansen," he said. "Please, you must come into the cottage and warm yourselves."

Gregory was already helping his mother off the horse. Hansel took the woman's arm and turned to lead them to the cottage. He paused a moment when he saw the cottage door open and his father's strained face eyeing the guests and making a grim appraisal of the situation.

"Father, we have company," Hansel called, watching his father carefully. He sighed with relief as he saw his father carefully set his features and nod stoically. Reassured that his father would manage the situation, Hansel waved the griffins toward the cottage and then led their horse to the barn where she could keep Donny company. As quickly as he could, Hansel took the mare's saddle and bridle off and got her a portion of oats. Bubbling with excitement, he ran from the barn to the cottage.

He found the griffins divested of their sodden traveling outwear and holding mugs of steaming tea on a bench by the blazing hearth. His father looked embarrassed, but was busying himself at the far end of the hearth over the smaller flames with basting the roasted goose that was to be their supper. Hansel got himself a mug of tea and joined the griffins on the bench by the main fire.

Up close and out of the rain, Hansel looked over their guests. Elena was a pretty woman with thick chestnut colored hair, tamed in a plait, but the humidity had changed the small wispy hairs around her face into a mass of corkscrew curls that was most becoming. Her eyes were a strange golden color like a cat's. Gregory's hair was a mass of short, wavy sandy brown with a few of his mother's corkscrew curls at his temples and the same golden-colored eyes. They had been trying to get to the village, but the storm had spooked the horse, and they had lost their way. She was a seamstress and knew her trade well, Hansel thought. Her bodice and gown were fitted and flattered her frame quite well. The soft browns and mahogany piping matched her eyes and found an echo in the color of her hair. It turned out that Elena's husband had died in a fire five years ago. Her trade had kept them fed. Gregory worked when and where he could and made decent contributions to their maintenance, especially in the last few years. Elena's brother was the local smith, Tom Bradley.

They sought his protection. In their home village, on the other side of the ridge, the local brewer and pub owner, Jack Stephens, had been increasingly threatening in his desire for Elena's hand in marriage. So, they had left, leaving before dawn and having the ill luck to be traveling on the day of such a storm.

Fortunately, given the current circumstances, Hansel and his father had expanded the cottage. Originally, it had consisted of his parents' bedroom, his bedroom, and the main room with the great hearth. But they had added on two rooms on the far side of the main room. Hansel had taken the larger of the two for his bedroom. After drinking his tea, he retired to his room to retrieve some of his essential belongings, so that Elena could have his room for the night.

After depositing his things in the small bedroom next to his father's, he helped with the dinner preparations, getting bread and cheese and placing them on the table. Though a stranger, Elena knew her way around a kitchen and set out the dishes, cutlery, napkins, cups, and a pitcher of hard cider. Hansel's father took the goose off the spit and placed it on a platter on the table. Hansel found it easy to talk to Gregory and his mother. The three of them chatted companionably. Elena seemed intuitively aware that his father was unaccustomed to company and was content to leave him to his silence. Gregory followed his mother's lead and did not try to engage Hansel's father in conversation.

When the table was set and ready, Hansel's father surprised him by stepping forward and holding out a chair for Elena. "Madame, permit me," he said in a soft voice. Hansel's mouth dropped open, and he caught the look of surprise on Gregory's face as the young man looked to him for guidance.

Elena blushed but took the proffered seat gracefully. "Thank you," she said in an equally soft voice. "Please, call me Elena," and she smiled at him.

Hansel's father nodded awkwardly, "I am Hansel also." He paused thoughtfully. "Big Hansel long ago, but I suppose Old

Hansel now," and he smiled at his son. He drew out his own chair and sat down motioning the young men to sit as well. Once they were seated, Hansel's father said Grace and wished the griffins safety and success. They ate, and Hansel continued talking with the griffins. The earlier tension surrounding Hansel's father's awkwardness was lessened somehow with the exchange of first names and the breaking of bread and the sharing of drink. Hansel watched his father surreptitiously and realized that his father was watching Elena just as covertly as Hansel was watching him. His mother had been dead for ten years. He had been six when she and the baby died. His father had withdrawn from others in his grief, but Hansel wondered now, looking between his father and Elena, whether his continued isolation was more habit now than unrelenting loss. He gazed at his father—surprised to see him as a middle-aged man, solidly and muscularly built with russet skin, short black hair, brown-nearly-black eyes, and broad handsome face. He was stunned to realize that his father was attractive. The fact had not occurred to him before. He glanced at Elena who blushed slightly as she caught him looking from his father to her. He glanced at Gregory who seemed to be making the same assessment that Hansel was; he too looked slightly embarrassed and amused at the same time.

Elena seemed suddenly flustered and self-conscious. "Hans, thank you…for your…for your…h-hospitality," she said awkwardly, flushing.

"It is nothing, Elena," his father answered quietly, and he reached out his hand to pat hers, which rested lightly on the table next to him. She blushed even further, and suddenly, the atmosphere at the table seemed charged. Hansel felt like he was intruding on something private and powerful. Gregory went pale next to Hansel. Elena pushed back from the table, rose, collected her plate and cup, and took them to the washstand. Hansel and Gregory rose also with their things. Elena insisted on doing the washing. She seemed desperate to have something legitimate to do, so Hansel let her, collected his father's things and one pot from the hearth that needed cleaning.

Hansel's father sat down in an armchair near the hearth. With the distraction of routine food storage and washing, the awkwardness receded. Hansel, Gregory, and Elena resumed lighthearted conversation seated around the fire. Hansel's father didn't speak, but he looked at each of them, his eyes lingering on Elena when he thought no one was looking. When it was time, Hansel made sure that Elena and Gregory had fresh water in a pitcher and a basin in each of their rooms and a chamber pot. Wishes for pleasant dreams were exchanged, and each retired to a bedroom.

Hansel was too confused to try to talk to his father that evening. He retired to the little bedroom feeling relieved to be alone. He stripped out of his clothes. He tried to process the evening. He has heard of sudden attraction, the thunder bolt, some people called it. He had seen goofy infatuations between the village teenagers, but they usually ended, sometimes as fast as they had started. This was different—the charge was like a heat pulsing between his father and Elena. She seemed affected by it too. It embarrassed her. If they acted on it, they would have sexual relations. It was strange to think of his father as sexual. Of course, he must be. Humans were sexual from birth to death despite the best efforts of the church fathers to pretend otherwise. Thinking about sex aroused him. He touched himself with increasing vigor until he climaxed on a soiled towel and allowed himself to relax into sleep.

Hansel woke at dawn and was surprised to smell bacon being cooked—an extravagance usually reserved for holidays and special occasions. He hurried with his morning ministrations, relieving himself, washing, and dressing. He found his father looking simultaneously embarrassed and unrepentant. He wore one of the finer shirts he owned and was sitting on a stool frying bacon over a small fire, the pan suspended by chains above the flames.

"Pappa, what on earth is going on?" Hansel demanded.

His father blushed but looked into his son's face. "I don't know," he said honestly, "but I hope to find out." His father smiled sheepishly and continued minding the bacon. "Get some eggs and fresh milk and then see about the bread. Elena wrapped it in a damp towel, so it should be fine this morning."

As if divining the mention of her name, Elena emerged from her bedroom. She nodded at them. "Good morning, Hans and Hansel," she said quietly. She moved into the main room. Hansel's father watched her move across the room transfixed. By the time she reached the table, the two of them were blushing furiously. Hansel shook his head, grabbed a pitcher and a basket, and left the cottage. Any trace of the storm was gone, and the sun coming up shone brilliantly. He fed the chickens first and collected six eggs. Then he got feed for the goats and milked them. He used the pitcher that he'd brought and a bucket in the barn. He would see about setting the extra milk for cheeses later.

As he was getting food for the griffins' mare and for Donny, Gregory came into the barn looking exasperated.

"Good morning," Gregory said politely, but the effort it took him to say the words casually gave him away.

"I have never seen anything like it in my life," Hansel said sympathetically.

Gregory's handsome features spread into a mischievous grin, and he laughed ruefully, "At this rate, we could be brothers in a week." He shook his head, "I have never seen my mother act this way."

Hansel laughed as well, "Nor I my father. Quite frankly, my father has avoided people since my mother died. I can't remember the last time he talked to someone besides me," he said gravely.

Gregory looked at him thoughtfully for few minutes. "Perhaps, we should be happy for them," he said a little tentatively.

"Perhaps," Hansel admitted, "but I wish they could tone it

down a bit. It makes me uncomfortable to be in the same room with them."

Gregory laughed again, "Why do you think I am here? Thank God it is a nice day. I can't imagine being stuck in the cottage with them all day." He was smiling, and Hansel found himself smiling back. The prospect of spending the day with a person his own age was exciting. He did interact with the kids in the village on market day, but his primary activities were selling the bundles of wood and getting the supplies they needed. And it might not be just a day if this crazy thing between his father and Elena was as serious and powerful as it seemed. Could he have a brother and a mother? Could they be a family? Gregory went over and patted the mare; Patsy. Hansel picked up the pitcher of milk, and Gregory grabbed the basket of eggs. They walked to the cottage and found themselves hesitating awkwardly by the door. Gregory coughed loudly, and Hansel fumbled with the door handle for a solid minute before opening the door.

Hansel's father was scooping two fried eggs onto a plate that Elena held. The table was set with three other plates of eggs. Bread, cups, napkins, and cutlery were on the table. Hansel put the pitcher of milk on the table, and Gregory put the basket on the counter near the larder. Hansel's father stood up and followed Elena to the table, holding out her chair for her and seating himself next to her. Hansel and Gregory took their chairs. The time alone seemed to have benefitted Hansel's father and Elena. Hansel could still feel the charge between them, but there also seemed to be an understanding between them about just what to do about it and that helped. Hansel glanced at Gregory, who winked at him; he felt it too. They talked and ate amicably. As they finished the meal, Hansel's father suggested that the young men gather wood in the forest and do some hunting. He didn't suggest what he and Elena would be doing in their absence. Hansel and Gregory flushed slightly, but they were only too glad to go into the forest.

Hansel's father got them lunches while Elena started cleaning up at the washstand.

Hansel led Gregory to the barn, and they equipped themselves with axes, knives, bows, bundles, Donny, and Sampson. Hansel showed Gregory how to set snares as they walked through the forest. They talked. Gregory told Hansel about life in their village, Littletown. His father had been a carpenter. Life had been good in the village when both his parents had been alive. They had plenty to eat and nice clothes and possessions. It was harder after his father died. At first, he was slightly too young to get steady work, but it had been easier since he turned fifteen and looked more like a young man than a child. Hansel, in turn, told him about life in the woods and about the village. Hansel knew Tom Bradley. He admired the smith and told Gregory about him. Having met Elena and Gregory, Hansel could see the family resemblance. Tom had green eyes, but his sister's curly auburn hair. As a smith, he was well built and muscular like his father—something that Hansel had always admired about the smith. Looking at Gregory, Hansel could imagine him filling-out like the smith and found himself blushing at the thought. Hansel tried to do most of the axe work to spare Gregory's hands, but Gregory wasn't put off, working up quite a set of blisters by the time they stopped and tried a little hunting. Though unsuccessful at hunting, they had more luck with the snares and brought home three rabbits along with the wood. Hansel had Gregory drop his bundle and take the rabbits in to the cottage while he started unloading the bundles. Gregory returned quickly, shaking his head and snorting.

"I don't know whether it is better or worse," he said trying to make light of the situation. "But they are definitely *together*."

Hansel looked Gregory over carefully. "What do you mean?" Hansel asked.

Gregory smiled a little bitterly and said, "That charge thing is back. They are being careful, but you can feel it is an effort not to be touching each other. I have heard about love like that—love at first sight. But it is quite something to actually watch it happen—and to *my mother*. I don't know whether to be scandalized or glad to know that love is something one can enjoy past one's youth." He shook his head in a gesture that so completely expressed his bafflement that Hansel found himself snickering in agreement.

Finished with the wood, the young men returned to the cottage. The leftover goose had been made into a hearty stew with carrots, potatoes, onions, herbs and goat's milk. Hansel's father set the stew pot on a metal trivet on the table, and Elena dished out bowls of stew on to cubes of stale bread. Each poured cider for him or herself. After Grace, they talked about their days, eating in between descriptions. Hansel's father and Elena admitted to walking around the property, working in the garden, and taking a walk in the woods where they gathered mushrooms and wild strawberries. Gregory showed his mother his blisters, and Hansel's father glowered at Hansel for not doing most of the axe work, but Gregory silenced both of them by saying that given the circumstances it looked like he needed to build up the calluses. After a brief silence where both of the adults turned a satisfying shade of pink, Hansel had them address the immediate future.

"So, what happens now?" he asked. "You're crazy about each other; we get that," darting a glance at Gregory who nodded in approval and support. "Don't you think that you are rushing just a bit recklessly? I mean flash fires, flame suddenly, but they burn out. Have you thought this out or is it all impulse?" Hansel struggled through the last couple questions blushing furiously, but they all felt his genuine concern.

When Hansel couldn't continue, Gregory asked, "What are we doing, Mother, are we going to the village or are we staying here? Is there any plan?" Gregory glanced at Hansel who smiled at him gratefully for intervening.

Hansel's father reached out and took Elena's hand, twining his fingers through hers. Looking at Gregory, he said, "I would like you and your mother to stay...for a bit." Then he turned and looked at his son pointedly.

"Yes, of course, we would like you to stay," Hansel answered his father's demand automatically, but he felt another wave of pure excitement washing over him. Gregory would stay; Elena would stay. He was happy and then another batch of questions struck him. Where would they stay, he thought with horror—and all the implications of that thought. The last place he wanted to be was in the room by his father's bed—if she came to him in the night or if he brought her to his room—his room—not his parents' room. As these last few thoughts flashed through his mind, he caught a glimpse of Gregory's face draining of color—as if the same thoughts in reverse were occurring to him.

Hansel looked at his father who was blushing furiously, but who also seemed to understand the discomfort of the two young men. He nodded curtly. Hansel understood that to mean that Elena and he would change rooms. All of them blushed at that point, and Elena started nervously reaching for bowls to excuse herself from the table. Gregory grabbed cups, and Hansel cleared off the cutlery and the empty stew pot.

Hansel darted into the small bedroom and again removed his essential belongings. Gregory, in full sympathy with his distress, opened the door of his room, so Hansel could stow his things there until Elena had moved her things. After the delicate dance of musical rooms, they sat by the fire and Gregory and Hansel took turns reading. Elena sat in an arm chair next to which was a basket of assorted yarns and needles. One project, apparently started in the absence of the young people, was a scarf, Hansel judged from the short width of it. His mother's things, he thought, but pleased to see them put to use.

The next few days fell into an easy rhythm. They ate breakfast together and avoided discussing sleeping arrangements. The young men packed lunches and left the happy couple to the domestic and husbandry tasks of the homestead and to getting to know each other in every way possible (their histories and their dreams as well as their bodies and bodily pleasures). The young men grew close too, talking about everything from their pasts, to their parents, to their lack of success in relationships of their own.

Market day approached, and Hansel's father made the remarkable announcement at supper that they would all go. Hansel just stared at his father dumbstruck. Elena took his father's hand and squeezed it. "We need to see my brother," she said softly, "and arrange a wedding." They all went slightly pink at the statement, but the dinner of roast rabbits in mushroom sauce with fresh bread distracted them.

On market day, they loaded the wagon. Elena rode on the wagon with Hansel's father, and the young men rode together on Patsy. Hansel rode behind Gregory and was startled to find that about an hour into the ride that he was aroused. Gregory's tight, firm buttocks rubbing against him couldn't be ignored. He flushed with embarrassment and thought again of Gregory's uncle and how Gregory might fill out so muscularly. Gregory's back stiffened in response. Hansel felt a surge of shame. Was he repulsing Gregory? Were his feelings unnatural? Surely, his father and Gregory's mother would think so. Attraction for them was between a man and a woman. His attraction to Tom Bradley's muscular form and his lack of interest in the village young women suddenly seemed to make sense. He liked males, not females. But Gregory was close to being his brother. How would that complicate things for his father and Elena and Gregory and himself? Startling him, was Gregory relaxing against him, feeling his erection but not moving away from it. Gregory, it seemed, liked males too, like him. Hansel flushed with pleasure and excitement.

As they neared the village, the people that they passed stared at them. Old Hansel Hansen's return to society was taken due notice of. By the time they reached the smithy, Tom Bradley was waiting outside. He stood erect—tense trying to read the face of his sister and the faces of her three companions.

"Elena, are you well?" he asked, anxiety clear in his voice.

"I am well, brother," she said clearly and firmly. "We got lost in the storm, and the Hansens have been very kind to us." She smiled at him, and he smiled back, but eyed Old Hansel and Young Hansel.

Tom helped his sister dismount the wagon and led them all into the smithy. The accumulated crowd was left to stare after them as they disappeared indoors. Inside, Hansel's father asked consent to marry the smith's sister. Tom stared at them both, shocked at the proposition, but then Hansel and Gregory chimed in—explaining the circumstances and the attraction, and Tom looked at the bond that was so clearly between Hans and Elena. The marriage was arranged. Elena and Gregory would spend a few days with Tom and his family, and on Saturday they would be married, and then could permanently retire to the Hansen homestead.

They shared a spectacular lunch, and then it was time for the Hansens to leave and go back to the homestead. Tom looked curiously at the pained expressions of both his sister and his nephew as they saw Hans and Hansel off. Happy to be reunited with family as they obviously were, there was a melancholy about them too. Tom thought he understood, if Elena could meet and be committed to marriage in a matter of days, the separation would be hard. His nephew's grief, however, puzzled him. Did he miss his future father so much? That seemed unlikely. Did he miss his future brother? And if so, how? He shook his head. The impossible was happening. Hans Hansen had left his solitude—had left his solitude for his sister. Jack Stephens had been moving to compel his sister to marriage, and this thwarted his efforts and protected her in a way Tom would have been willing to do himself, but this was better—Hans, Hansel, and Gregory—but they were so isolated where they were. Could he get them to move closer to the village or even to the village? That would be best, he thought.

He let it drift from his mind as he integrated his sister and nephew into the fabric of his family, his wife and two daughters and two sons.

Tom watched as he saw his sister and nephew interact with genuine pleasure with his family, and yet feel a grief at their separation from the Hansens. It made him wonder exactly just what had passed at the Hansen homestead. He felt a vague sense of jealousy and confusion as the two primary warring emotions. What exactly had happened there? Jack Stephens and his men had arrived three days ago demanding Elena. Tom had been shocked, scared for his sister, and glad that she was not there. Now, now what? Elena loved Hans, and Hans loved Elena—that was plain. But what was it with his nephew? Why was he pining as much as she was at the separation? Was he in love too? That would be disastrous.

The days passed in a bustle of activity; it would be a small wedding in the Bradley home. Elena was to be dressed in a new gown of pale browns with copper colored lace highlights. Gregory was provided with new clothes that similarly brought out his eyes and hair color. Tom had had the dressmaker size up Hans and Hansel before they left town, and she had made matching garments for both of them. As soon as the Hansens entered town, they were ushered to the Bradleys to change for the quiet ceremony.

Tom watched with a mingled satisfaction and confusion at the joy of this reunited family—his sister, Hans, his nephew, and Hansel. Some of the dynamics he understood, between his sister and Hans, but between Gregory, Hansel, and Elena, he did not understand. But it was loving, he knew that much. And wasn't that all that really mattered? Yes, the voice in his head answered.

Formally married, Hans and Elena retired to the Hansen homestead, taking Hansel and Gregory with them. As the honeymoon wore off, Hans started to join the young men in the afternoons to harvest wood and haul it. That still left Hansel and Gregory the mornings (and presumably their parents) to be alone and intimate. And they were; Hansel touched Gregory, and Gregory touched Hansel.

The young men had gone fishing and had stripped completely to avoid soaking their clothes. They had caught a dozen trout between spearing them and using a net. Hansel was placing the last of the fish on the bank of the small lake when he turned to find Gregory staring at him with blatant desire and longing. They had embraced before and kissed, but something held them back—some sense that others wouldn't understand—even their parents. The church fathers were very clear on the matter of who were the appropriate partners of romantic love—and two males weren't an option. Plus, with their parents married, it was like incest even though they weren't real blood brothers. But there alone, naked in the shallow water, it didn't seem to matter. They were in each other's arms suddenly and all the suppressed passion and emotion of the last couple of weeks flamed. Kiss followed kiss. Hands roamed touching face, neck, breast, nipple, shoulder, back, buttock, balls, and penis. They made each other come and lay on the bank in each other's arms. When the languidness of post-orgasm faded and brought them back to more rational thought, they were engulfed in a sense of panic.

Gregory touched Hansel's face, "What do we do now?" he asked, his voice tense with anxiety.

Hansel looked into the golden eyes and shook his head. "I don't know. I…I…don't think we can go…go…back," he choked out. The thought of abandoning his father was devastating. But it was equally devastating to think of abandoning Gregory or attempting to live with him and not be with him as they were now, lovers. The bleakest thing was thinking of the disapproval his father would express at the subject of Hansel's love. He couldn't face that. He looked back at Gregory whose face was flooded by similar dark thoughts.

"I think you're right," Gregory said slowly, the regret and sadness clear in his voice.

They dressed slowly. They didn't need all the fish for just to the two of them, so they took four and went in search of a sheltered spot in which to spend the night. They found a cave, made a fire, ate, and snuggled into the comfort and the pleasures of each other's arms for the night. The next day they wandered in the forest. They brought down two ducks and found shelter beneath an overhang of rocky ledge. The following day they continued deeper into the great forest. They had not found shelter, and it was nearing twilight when they smelled wood smoke.

Following their noses, they came across the most curious cottage they had ever seen. At first glance it seemed to be made of food—of every delicacy imaginable—of candies and pastries, of tender slices of meat, of carefully cooked and seasoned vegetables, of wonderfully ripe fruit, of generously buttered breads, of flavorful cheeses. Gregory stretched out his hand to touch the wall closest to them, and the images changed. Suddenly, the two of them were staring at naked bodies, male and female all in the act of self-pleasuring. The two young men gasped and blushed furiously. They stared at the images before them, too shocked to speak. Hansel looked at Gregory. Yes, Gregory was seeing what he was. The pictures showed people of all ages and colors and sizes in blissful sexual ecstasy. It was both horrifying and exciting. If sex was natural, why not?

Hansel reached for Gregory's hand, and the two of them silently walked around the cottage to the next wall. They gasped again. The images were just as explicit except that they were of males and females in a wide variety of acts of sexual pleasuring, fellatio, cunnilingus, and intercourse. Again, the people came in all colors and shapes, but the ages of the actors did not include prepubescent children. They stood staring for some time working up the courage to see what was on the next wall of the cottage.

The next wall was full of images of female couples engaged in sexual play—cunnilingus but also pleasuring with hands and fingers and dildos. The females came in all colors and shapes again and again excluded prepubescent children.

With anticipation they rounded the final corner and gasped again. The wall was full of images of male couples engaged in sexual play—fellatio but also hand-jobs and anal sex. The male participants were youthful and old, black and white and yellow and russet. Some were lean and muscular, but others were flaccid and plump. All were post puberty judging from their pubic hair. Gregory and Hansel glanced from the images to each other. Perhaps, if the cottage could display all this variety in human sexuality, they weren't so abnormal after all—their faces said more clearly than either one of them felt capable of articulating. Gregory grinned and touched Hansel's face, which was breaking into an answering grin.

"Good evening," said a voice, jolting Gregory and Hansel back to their surroundings. Hansel let go of Gregory's hand, and they turned to see the person standing in a doorway they had not noticed. There was something odd about the person. Hansel couldn't tell if it was a man or a woman; he glanced at Gregory who looked similarly confused.

"Good evening," the young men answered cautiously. They moved toward the person—whoever this person was—he or she had answers for the questions they had about themselves and others. Closer, they froze and gasped—trying to process the aberration before them. He/she/it was half male and half female—a hermaphrodite—ze seemed the better pronoun under the circumstances—a combination, not a single gendered identity. That accounted for the oddness. Ze's hair was shoulder-length and a sandy blond color, but one side of the face and body had softer female features and parts (a big blue colored eye and long lashes, full lips, soft, hairless cheek, a feminine shoulder, a developed female breast, a slender waist, a full hip, the mounded pubic area of a female, a long shapely leg, a delicate ankle, and a small foot) the other side of the face and body had harder male features and parts (a heavier brow, a smaller blue colored eye, narrower lips, check and chin sprouting day old stubble, a broad, muscular neck, shoulder, chest, and arm, all sprinkled with coarser masculine hair, a tapering waist, a narrow hip, pubic hair that nested a ball and a penis, a hard muscular leg also coated with coarser masculine hair, and a larger foot). Ze wore a sheer robe, so the young men saw everything.

"Children, I am Herim. How can I help you?" Herim bowed theatrically to them.

"What is this place?" Hansel asked.

"It is my palace," Herim answered. "In the time before history, all knew my palace and found pleasure there, but patriarchal culture drove me into the depths of the forest or secret places. It made any sexual activity beyond sexual intercourse between the active male and the passive female forbidden or wrong. As if anyone should be passive or dominant in sexual activity; it's just the wrong metaphor. Mutually empowered, mutually pleasuring, and by mutual consent—that is the better dynamic. You pleasure each other, do you not? You love each other. You would not cause each other pain or force the other to do something that he did not wish to do, correct? I rant a little, excuse me. Being persecuted tends to distort your perspective—or at least, it distorts mine. Sexual pleasure is as natural as the need for food and drink, sleep, love—parental, platonic, and romantic—it is a part of both platonic love and romantic love."

Hansel and Gregory both exchanged glances of incredulity at these last words; Herim noticed and continued.

"Sex is just sex. Jettison it from the morality that you were taught. Restructure your world around pleasure for all and security for all. Love is the answer. Love is always the answer. Love is the better way—be the better angels of your natures. How could it be anything but better? Acceptance not exclusion. Enough. Enter my palace children, and see the ways of love." Herim ushered them inside.

Herim wasn't kidding. Stepping across the threshold, the modest cottage changed into a vast, sprawling palace filled with guests. People milled around in happy conversations; the atmosphere was festive. Herim encouraged the young men to explore the palace, but before Herim excused zirself to attend other guests, ze warned them.

"There is one absolute law for finding pleasure here; there is no coercion, no force. There are sheets of paper and pens in every room or alcove. In any sexual encounter, each participant must write down what he or she or ze wishes to do and wishes to have done to he/she/ze, even if that only consists of watching. Each contract is subject to verbal amendment. A request to stop must be honored by any and/or all participants. Violation of the contract (written or verbally amended) will result in public humiliation and punishment, including if necessary, banishment. Do you understand?" Herim asked severely.

Hansel and Gregory flushed at the explicitness of Herim's statements and their implications but nodded in agreement. The young men found all sorts of people flirting and dancing in the grand ballroom. In small private rooms, every kind of coupling seemed to be taking place including group sex—threes and even more.

Hansel and Gregory passed an empty room, and Gregory took Hansel's hand, and they walked into it together.

"What do we do now?" Hansel asked breathlessly.

"Anything we want," Gregory answered, moving toward the waist-high table in front of them with a blank contract laid out. They entered their names and the date. They blushed writing down what they wanted to do to each other and laughed together. It seemed strange and yet liberating to be so explicit about what they wanted. Both noted the "subject to verbal amendment" clause at the bottom of the page. They embraced and started kissing. They found themselves on the bed. They stripped each other of their clothing. The touching escalated, and they brought each other to climax—kissing, licking, gently nibbling/biting, sucking, blowing, stroking, and touching. After their lovemaking, they wandered around the palace. A man dressed as a woman offered them bits of roasted meat on small bits of toasted bread. A young woman about their age offered them glasses of cider. They continued to wander. In one corridor, they heard a smacking sound that they both recognized as flesh striking flesh. They looked at each other in alarm, not knowing what to do. A pair of women were nuzzling each other against one wall, but one of them noticed the young men's distress.

"It's is okay," she assured them. "They do it all the time. It's part of their contract. He likes to be spanked. The slight pain excites him and helps him climax. Different strokes for different folks, right?" she smiled suggestively, and then laughed at their embarrassment. "There is lots to learn here," she continued. "Find couples who don't mind being watched, and you'll see that there is much more variety than you might have thought." She laughed again at their deepening blushes, but then stopped as her partner tugged on her hand and suggested that they find a room of their own. The women disappeared down the corridor.

Hansel and Gregory found their way back to the grand ball room and contented themselves with dancing and watching the other dancers. As it got late, Herim found them and probed them about their future plans. They tried to explain why they had left. How they were sure that their relationship would not be approved of and might even be punished.

"Are you sure?" Herim had asked them. "Do you really think that Hans Hansen and Elena Griffin could stop loving his/her child because of who the child is attracted to when attraction refuses to obey laws of reason?"

Gregory and Hansel stared at each other and then back at Herim, "You know our parents?" they both exclaimed wide-eyed.

Herim laughed. "Yes, I know your parents. You'd be surprised at the people I know, though much fewer admit to knowing me," he said with a sly smile that held a mingled mirth and regret. "Let's see what tomorrow brings, shall we?" ze said and showed them to a bedroom that they could call their own for the duration of their stay.

Alone in their room, the young men felt overwhelmed by the revelations of Herim's palace. By unspoken consent, they did not entertain the implications that their parents knew Herim, had been to the palace, and knew its secrets. Both silently wondered in what capacity their parents had come there, but they forced such thoughts from their minds. They took off their clothes, climbed into the inviting bed, and found comfort and sleep in each other's arms.

The sun was up when they woke the next morning. They used the chamber pot, but they didn't dress. Hansel grabbed a contract and wrote out his desires while Gregory read them over his lover's shoulder, smiling and waiting to write out his own. Once the contract was written, they commenced to fulfill its particulars with great enthusiasm. Sometime later, they cleaned themselves off and got dressed. They found a small dining room and had just finished a light breakfast, when a boy appeared and said that Herim wanted to see them. The boy led them to an elegant library. Herim was seated at a grand desk. Two travel-worn, cloaked figures stood in front of zir.

Herim cleared zirs throat at the sight of the young men, and the figures turned revealing themselves as Elena Griffin and Hans Hansen—both of whom wore twin expressions of anxiety and worry. Those expressions faded at the sight of the young men to be replaced with expressions of relief and hurt.

Hansel felt a wave of guilt, and glanced nervously at Gregory who was also looking mortified.

"Hansel!" "Gregory!" Elena and Hans exclaimed at the same time.

Herim stood up. "I told you they were fine," ze said to them softly. Then Herim turned to the young men, "Let's all take a couple of deep breaths and sit down," waving to the four chairs clustered around the desk.

Herim had Hansel and Gregory sit directly in front of zir with their parents on either side of his and her son. With everyone seated, Herim spoke, "Elena and Hans, the young men ran away because they are gay and thought you would disapprove."

Hansel and Gregory flushed and looked at each other sheepishly, and then shot tentative looks at their parents. Hansel saw his father's face change from a forced calm to a one of contrition and self-remonstration. Hansel's father glanced past his son and nodded at his wife. His father took a deep breath, and then addressed himself to both young men.

"Hansel and Gregory, do you really think that we didn't know?" he asked softly.

Hansel stiffened. Know, how could his father know? Hansel hadn't even known himself. He felt Gregory go rigid next to him, apparently having a similar reaction. Hansel didn't remember talking to his father about his interactions with the kids of the village on market days—or at least not much. He certainly hadn't talked about romantic attractions because there hadn't been any. He gave up trying to tease it out when his father started speaking again.

"Do you think we care more for whom you are attracted to than for you?" his father continued.

Before Hansel or Gregory could respond, Elena cut in, "Do you disapprove of your father and me?" she asked.

Disapprove—Hansel thought with shock—they were adults, and they were heterosexual. It was sudden, yes. It was embarrassing to think of his father as sexual, yes, but he didn't feel he was entitled to disapprove. "What is there to disapprove of?" he asked in exasperation. "And even if we did, it wouldn't be our place to say anything; it is between the two of you."

"Exactly," both Elena and Hans said together. "What happens between romantic partners is their business. The church fathers have poisoned people's ideas about sex and sexuality," Hansel's father said quietly.

"Surely, even your short time here helps you see past the narrow teachings of the church fathers?" Elena added.

Gregory glanced at Hansel, and the two of them smiled with relief. Herim smiled broadly and cleared zirs throat, rising to zirs feet. "Ah, my dears," ze said to the young men, "I told you." Then sweeping his look to the whole group, Herim said, "You are all welcome here as you see fit," and then narrowed his gaze on Hansel and Gregory, "You can return and stay with your parents' permission." Herim bowed then and left them to attend to other matters.

It was decided that the young men would return with their parents to the Griffin-Hansen homestead where the young men would share the larger bedroom in the new addition of the cottage, but they would be free to return to Herim's palace in the future.

They took their leave of Herim and thanked zir for zirs hospitality. The young men rode together on Patsy, and Elena rode Donny with Hans leading the mule. And with occasional visits to Herim's palace, they settled into a happy routine of work and pleasure and lived happily ever after.

P Pan and Beyondland

KRYSTAL AND KYLE Barry were very close; they were twins after all. They played with each other always. They fought some, of course. A girl and a boy; she played princess and so did he. He played knight and so did she.

They could tell that their parents found them odd. It bothered their mother and father that the children could switch from female to male and male to female. They never said it explicitly, but Krystal and Kyle could tell. Their parents tried and tried to separate the children, but they snuck into each other's beds at night—to give each other comfort and support.

At school, the expectations were clear—there were boys and girls but nothing in between. They acted their parts. Krystal was a girl, and Kyle was a boy. It was so confining. Girls were supposed to be feminine—sugar and spice and everything nice—affectionate, cheerful, compassionate, gentle, loyal, shy, soft-spoken, sympathetic, understanding, warm, tender, yielding. In contrast, boys were supposed to be masculine—snips and snails and puppy dog tails—aggressive, ambitious, analytical, assertive, competitive, dominant, independent, individualistic, self-reliant, self-sufficient, stoic. Krystal and Kyle were so much more when they could move in between—when they could be both and more and anything in between. Wasn't that the point of being a full human being (being sympathetic and assertive, tender and self-reliant)—and didn't that mean being a blend of masculine and feminine? All they knew is that they didn't fit in.

One night they threw open a bedroom window and cried to the stars the heartbreak they felt. To their surprise, in the middle of the night, a figure loomed above their bed.

"What do you want and who are you?" Krystal asked timidly.

"I am P Pan from Beyondland, but please call me P. With what you said to the stars, I think you might like to come to Beyondland."

Krystal and Kyle listened to the words and then looked at each other. They looked back at this P and decided that they couldn't tell what he/she/ze was—ze was the better term they realized without being told. P was someone like they wanted to be, something in between or multiple instead of binary—male/female. Ze was about fifteen maybe, with light stubble on zirs face but eyeliner and lipstick, shoulder-length hair, the front pieces braided off to keep out of ze's face, tight-fitted clothes that only favored ze's ambiguous form.

"What are you?" Krystal and Kyle blurted out the same time.

"I am a human being," P answered, "the same as either of you; it's just that, in Beyondland, I can express any aspect of myself that I desire. That's why some choose to leave their homes and come and live with us."

"But are you a boy or a girl?" blurted out Kyle.

P cocked zirs head. "I am neither or both. I am non-binary. In Beyondland, gender is a spectrum—like a spectrum of colors from whites to yellows to greens to reds to blues and to blacks or like a big multifaceted rainbow. There isn't just white and black or male and female—there is a whole range of ways to see one's self." P paused, studying them. "From the things you said, I thought you were looking for somewhere where being more than 'girl' or 'boy' was appealing, but perhaps I am mistaken."

Krystal had taken Kyle's hand under the sheets and squeezed it. "Yes, P, we are, but we didn't even know a place like Beyondland existed. All we know is how it is here," Krystal struggled to explain.

The children weren't sure what to do. They loved their parents, but they also knew they didn't belong. They played at being a boy and a girl, but the roles were wrong—they weren't true to the core people Krystal and Kyle knew themselves to be. All these thoughts flitted over the children's faces.

P looked between them and smiled a sad smile, "It's a lot to take in and a lot to give up. You know how to reach me. Call me again if you're ready for Beyondland." With that, ze bowed and walked to the window—which the children suddenly realized had been open the whole time.

"P!" shouted the children as they watched ze leap out the window. The children, in horror, leapt from their bed and ran to the window to find P floating just outside the window and chuckling with mirth.

"Didn't I tell you or didn't you guess? There's magic in Beyondland. How else could I hear you to answer your pleas? Good night, sweet children, and call if you need me." P then raised zir arms and flew away.

The children, too astonished to speak, stared after zir until they couldn't see zir anymore. They got into bed and whispered to each other their imaginings of what Beyondland might be like—what the children did there, what they could do there, and how they lived. The next morning, they half convinced themselves that P's visit had been a dream—but they had never before dreamed the exact same dream. Then as they were washing up in the bathroom, getting ready for school, the bathroom mirror steamed up, and the two children froze as the words, "Beyondland is real," formed on the glass. Krystal wiped the words away, and afterwards, Kyle squeezed her hand—it was a secret between them—that was the pact.

School was tedious—the burden of the roles they played at school and for their parents—made Krystal and Kyle feel as if their true selves were being lost—consumed by the gendered performances that put others at ease. Then something frightening happened. Harry and Jamie, two young, sweet, kind boys, were found in the choir loft kissing. The two boys were dragged outside by a gang of older boys, yelling insults like "fagots," "Nancy boys," and "fairies." Krystal and Kyle were horrified.

The boys circled Harry and Jamie, jeering at them and punching them. Some girls stood by looking uncomfortable while other girls took up the chants of "fagots," "Nancy boys," and "fairies." A few female teachers appeared and moved to break things up, but male teachers appeared out of nowhere and blocked their way. Harry and Jamie were beaten bloody before it was through. Krystal and Kyle couldn't bear to watch, so they slunk away. The guilt they felt at not being able to help the two defenseless boys from the savage attack overwhelmed them. They had feared being exposed as different as well, and they had feared being beaten too. So, they hadn't intervened and had left. They found themselves vomiting alone in their separate gender-assigned bathrooms—rinsing the sick out of their mouths and the tears off their faces, and trying to compose themselves, so they wouldn't become targets themselves. Mercifully, the school day ended shortly after the disgusting spectacle without any explanation from the teachers or headmaster—making it clear that same sex attractions were punished by the cruelest of means and that boys better act like boys and girls better act like girls—nothing in between would be tolerated.

Krystal and Kyle fled home. Nanna made them snacks and talked to them. Nanna was always so kind and supportive. They let their guard down in front of Nanna. That particular day, Nanna seemed to know there was something very wrong with the children. She probed them, and finally Krystal blurted it out.

"Two boys were caught kissing at school, and the teachers let some of the older boys beat them up and call them names," she choked out, tears running down her checks. Kyle was crying too.

Nanna opened up her arms, and the children went to her and let Nanna comfort them. "There, there now, my sweets. There are always people who are different—that doesn't mean they're bad. Other people, unfortunately, feel threatened by people who are different, so they dehumanize them and persecute them, bully them, punish them. The good Lord gave us the golden rule: 'Love your neighbor as yourself.' He didn't qualify neighbors as people just like you. Neighbors are people from different households, from different families—people who are different—so the golden rule really is to love people who are different than you. But people in power are threatened by the idea of too much love and togetherness especially among common people. No, they find it more effective to seed conflict, to pit groups of people against other groups of people. People who like people of their same sex are generally gentle and peaceful, people who just want the freedom to live in peace and as they choose. What was done to your friends is horrible, and you should be upset. That more people aren't upset says a lot about the intolerance and division that our culture spreads. I am sorry, for you and for them."

Krystal and Kyle felt comforted by Nanna's words. They knew what was done to Harry and Jamie was wrong, but they couldn't articulate why it was wrong, and Nanna had explained that. She had also explained why people encouraged conflict and hate. They knew it was probably a lot more complicated than that, but Nanna had explained it to them in a way that they could understand. But more than anything, Nanna understood about people who were different, whether attracted to people of the same sex or people like them, and they knew that Nanna knew about them, and she still loved them. "Oh, Nanna," they murmured.

"Hush, my darlings. The world can be a cruel place, but you are loved at home. You know that, don't you?"

"Yes, and no," Krystal whispered.

"What do you mean, my sweet?" Nanna asked.

Kyle squeezed Krystal's hand, "We don't think Mum and Dad…well…we don't think they understand about us…about people who are different," he struggled to say.

"Oh, my darlings, your parents are good people, and they love you. I am sure they'll stand by you," Nanna answered a little too hastily. "Now off with you; you have studying to do." And with that, she sent them away.

They went over their lessons in Kyle's room, and when they were called down to dinner, they ate with their mother and father and talked superficially about pleasant things. After dinner, they all sat in the parlor where the children took turns at playing the piano. While Krystal was playing, Nanna announced there was a call for Mr. Barry. Their father stepped into the hall to take the call. It didn't take long—perhaps five minutes. And then, their father was back.

"Is there something you children want to share about your day today?" he demanded, something strange and tense in his voice.

Krystal and Kyle looked at each other alarmed. "Why?" they stammered together.

"That was Master Laurence on the phone. Two fagot boys were caught kissing at your school today. The Master called to say that they had been punished and expelled from the school."

"What?" Krystal and Kyle cried together.

Their father looked at them in alarm. He bristled and shook his head. "Quite right, children. We can't have this sort of thing. Boys should be boys, and girls should be girls. Boys should like girls, and girls should like boys. That is the natural way."

"It's true, children; it is just what is done," Mother Barry added after a pause.

Krystal and Kyle nodded mutely as the color drained from their faces. They excused themselves as soon as they could, and kissed their parents good night and good bye. They retreated to their separate bedrooms and got ready for bed. Once the house was quiet, Kyle slipped into Krystal's bedroom where they threw open the great window and called out to P.

"P, P Pan, we are ready; we want to go to Beyondland. Please hear us and come to take us away!" they called to the stars. Then, they gathered a few of their favorite books, fairy tales mostly, and a few books of poetry, a couple of changes of clothes, their brushes, combs, and toothbrushes, and things like that, and stuffed them into Krystal's pillowcase. They wrote out a note which they left on the bare pillow:

Dear Mother and Father,

We love you so much, but we are different. You've always known this, and it has always made you uncomfortable. Those boys you condemned from our school are more like us than we are like you or how you want us to be. Because you seem to hate them so, you must also hate us the way we truly are. So, we have gone somewhere where they don't care. We wish we didn't have to go, but we don't want to be beaten and expelled.

With love,

Krystal and Kyle

Then they laid down together in Krystal's bed and waited. Not much later, a familiar figure flew through their window.

"P!" the children cried.

"I told you I'd come," and then P stopped, and ze looked over the children more carefully. "What has happened? You're traumatized. Tell me," ze demanded.

And Krystal and Kyle poured out the whole horrific story—the brutalization of Harry and Jamie, their guilt and shame at not helping, and then, worst of all, the words of their parents. "P, could you help Harry and Jamie too," they ended.

"We leave here to get Jamie, but Harry isn't ready to go," P said gravely.

"Why?" the children asked.

"He loves his parents and sisters, and his parents know and sympathize. They are going to move and try again. Maybe it will work. I hope so. It gets a bit easier when one is a young man or a young woman. If one is discrete, there are communities of people who are different and who give each other the love and support they need. There are risks, of course. But some people never choose to leave. I don't judge, or try not to. I offer shelter in Beyondland for those who seek it; that's the duty of a Pan— to offer aid to other human beings," P explained.

"A Pan? What is a Pan?" Krystal asked.

P smiled and shook zirs head. "I forget that you probably don't know our stories. I really should be better at this by now," P said to zirself. "I am a Polly Pandora—one of the many descendants of Pandora who was sent by Gaia, the Great Mother Goddess, to counter the harshness of the world of the Titians' and then the Olympians' making."

The children looked at each other in puzzlement. This was not the version of Greek mythology that they were familiar with. "But Pandora was a trick that Zeus and the gods sent to mankind in punishment for Prometheus giving men fire and then showing them how to keep the better cuts of meat rather than offering them in sacrifice to the gods," Kyle said in a rush. The children had always enjoyed Greek mythology and were quite proud of their knowledge of it.

P chuckled and shook zir head again. "Not a bad answer, but you have, in your answer, the source of your misinformation."

"Misinformation?" Krystal repeated slowly, pondering what P had said. Krystal looked from P to her brother and then back again at P. She laughed. "Mankind," she said softly, "a world of men—that part always bothered me. It seemed ridiculous."

"What do you mean? Ridiculous?" Kyle asked, just a tad defensively.

"I mean the idea of a world of just men is ridiculous. They can't reproduce. In the story, all the other animals are there— male and female (I mean the animals for the sacrifice aren't all male or they'd go extinct)—and humans are just supposed to be a single sex race of specie. Common on, Kyle, it is ridiculous. The Greeks hated women or saw them as subhuman—so of course they are trivialized in all kinds of ways. A race of all men with a woman as a punishment and the source of all evil and sadness in the world. God, it's just another version of Adam and Eve. Men are the story tellers, so women get the bum-rap. That's right, P, isn't it? So, what is the real story?" Krystal said in a rush.

P was chortling with mirth, but ze mastered zirs features and answered, "Very good, Krystal. Pandora was a daughter of Gaia and one of the old gods. It was her task to offer aid and shelter where there was violence and conflict and hurt; she was hope and sanctuary. By following the Titians and the Olympians, human kind followed paths of violence and cruelty, hence rape and slavery and all the other misery that accompanies the pursuit of power over the pursuit of love. When Prometheus was punished for his aid to humans, Pandora healed him and set him free. Zeus was furious and took away her immortality. But as an old god, Pandora had power that Zeus didn't realize, and so Pandora's magic passes down her line from one Pandora to the next and the next—the Polly Pandoras or the many Pandoras, and I am one of the many, P Pandora," P said, bowing with a flourish.

"But why P?" asked Kyle.

P cocked zirs head, looking at Kyle. "Not really sure; it just seems true to who I am at my core. I don't really see myself as either a complete boy (whatever that is supposed to be) or a complete girl (again whatever that is supposed to be). Other Pans have; there have been Peter Pans and Polly Pans, Paul Pans, and Pamela Pans, but there have also been Paul Pans who have switched to Paulette Pans and Phoebe Pans who have switched to Patrick Pans. And Pat Pans have been somewhere in the middle. P Pan just seemed to suit me when I was called to serve as a Pan."

"Called to serve? What does that mean?" Krystal asked.

"Well, we age, but not like regular humans do. Beyondland is special; it's magical and beyond the scope of earthly time, but still we age. Pans intervene for children, so a serving Pan should be a child, someone from ten to seventeen, or at least look like a child of about that age range."

"Why that age range?" the children asked together.

"Because in many places, children are most vulnerable at puberty, while trying to figure out their gender identities and sexual orientations. In rigid cultures where only the binary of male/female is accepted, that is in most cultures, children need a Beyondland option, like you two and Jamie."

"Jamie," Krystal repeated. "We didn't help Jamie...we..." but she couldn't finish her thought.

"It's okay. Make it up to him. You will all meet lots of new and supportive people in Beyondland, but it will also be nice for the three of you to have each other. Shall we go? Do you have a few things to bring with you?" P asked.

Kyle took Krystal's hand with one hand and grabbed the stuffed pillow case with his other. "Yes, I think we are ready," he said, his voice full of nerves.

"It's okay. I won't let you fall. Each of you need to take my hand."

Krystal let go of her brother's hand reluctantly and moved to P's other side. Hand-in-hand they moved to the great window. "Don't look down," P commanded. "It might be better too to shut your eyes—at least for the initial leap."

Krystal whimpered softly, but pushed her chin up and shut her eyes tightly. Kyle didn't make a sound, but he shut his eyes too.

P pulled the children close to his sides and said, "Now when I say, 'Jump,' we all go together, okay?"

"Okay," the children repeated softly.

"Jump!" P shouted.

The shout so surprised the children that they jumped without thinking. Suddenly, they could feel the night air on their faces and blowing against them. Krystal opened her eyes and stared in wonder. She was flying, holding P's hand and flying. London seemed so different from the air, she thought. She looked around P to see her brother grinning back at her, flying on P's other side. Krystal had almost forgotten Jamie when she realized that P had stopped flying and had them floating down in front of a smart Brownstone house. One of the windows was thrown open, and P gently pushed the children, one by one, through the window before flying in zirself.

A surprised voice called out, "Krystal? Kyle? Is that you?"

Jamie stood before them, with a pillowcase in hand and the most surprised look on his battered face.

Krystal burst in to tears at the sight of him. "Jamie, my God, your face. I am so sorry. We're so sorry. We should have done something," she stammered as she gave him a hug.

Kyle was there too, laying a hand on Jamie's shoulder, "I am sorry as well."

Jamie pulled back from Krystal's embrace, his eyes watering with tears; he shook his head and looked at P. "P, I don't understand?"

"They're like you, Jamie, in a way. They don't belong here and want to come live in Beyondland," P said simply.

Jamie looked from P to Krystal and Kyle. The brother and sister smiled a little awkwardly and shrugged. Jamie laughed, part in relief and part from nerves, and the others joined in.

P, then, got their attention. "Right, that bit sorted, let's be on our way. Jamie, you have what you need?"

"Yes, P, I am ready," Jamie answered.

P opened a small pouch at zirs waist. "We fly a much greater distance this time," ze said addressing the twins. "You'll each need to fly on your own, though feel free to hold hands as you will. And for that, you'll need fairy powder." And before any of the children could ask, each were covered in a light dusting of glittering, simmering powder. It tickled and prickled the skin. Krystal was about to object, when she felt P pick her up by the waist and launch her out the window. She was about to scream, but then she realized she wasn't falling but flying, and the tickling and prickling feeling had disappeared. She was quickly joined by Kyle and Jamie, whose faces flashed what must have been the confusion of her sensations just moments before. Each of the boys held a stuffed pillowcase, but that didn't impede their flying ability one bit. P joined them then—more gracefully, Krystal noted, P's magic creating a more natural flight. P led the way, and Krystal watched as London fell away beneath her, the mass of twinkling lights receding. She felt sad in a way, but excited too for her new life.

P let the children enjoy the novelty of flying before ze started explaining things in Beyondland. There were chores to be done each day, some domestic chores and some gardening and husbandry chores. There were various gardens, the herb and medicinal garden, a three-sisters garden (maize, beans, and squash), a green beans and potato garden, a carrot and garlic garden, a broccoli and cucumber garden, an eggplant and spinach garden, and all sorts of other companion vegetable gardens, lined with marigolds and nasturtiums to keep the pests away. There were beds of strawberries, blackberries, raspberries, elderberries, and blueberries. There were small orchards with apples, pears, peaches, almonds, walnuts, chestnuts, figs, cherries, and apricots. The children raised chickens and goats and sheep, so there were egg collecting, milking, and cheese making tasks. The children made things from clothing from woven flax and sheep's wool to pottery and crockery, baskets, tools, cider (both regular and hard), and cabin making and maintenance. Children were assigned bunks at first and then moved in with a group of friends usually. Cabins usually housed four to six children. There were lessons on basics subjects for all. Quarterly, there was a week-long arts festival with competitions on anything one could think of from paintings to knitted or crocheted items of clothing to song writing and singing to play scripts and performances to the best apple treat. The absolute rules about Beyondland were that, one, all were welcome and supported. Two, that no one could coerce another person to do any activity, and sexual coercion was especially forbidden. Third, that no sexually mature person could have a relationship with a prepubescent child. Beyondland was an inclusive rainbowland of people from different races, religions, ethnicities, gender identifications, and sexual orientations. They were to become each other's family members now, and they needed to act like it. That didn't mean there weren't tensions and fights, but children were encouraged to work out those disagreements or tensions constructively through contests or writing about them or expressing them creatively in some other way. Someone who abandoned the principles of tolerance, acceptance, respect, and peaceful conflict resolution was subject to banishment. That had never happened, but that didn't mean that it couldn't. P had explained all this before, but ze did it again to reinforce the importance of the commitments they had made in coming to Beyondland.

Krystal had been contentedly holding Jamie's hand, so the two could share stories about all that they had hidden from their parents and their schoolmates before, when she realized that they were descending. The beautiful night sky, so lit up with more stars than she had ever imagined, was beginning to fade. Jamie squeezed her hand, and she followed his gaze to see a cluster of islands beneath them, and at the horizon, the threat of the sunrise was just beginning to light up the sky.

"Beyondland," P announced loudly. "The Main Camp is on the big island. That's where we're going."

"What's on the other islands, P?" Kyle asked.

"Crescent Island, that first one, has Crocodile Cove in the pocket of the crescent, and the merpeople generally school around the outer crescent."

"Crocodiles?" said Krystal in alarm.

"Merpeople?" said Jamie.

"We're a pretty peaceful lot," P began, "but we've been attacked before by pirates. Our bask of crocodiles is led by Ali Oop; he's a sly old devil. He caught the pirate captain unawares—ate the whole bastard himself—hat, watch, boots, and all. Not really sure what kind of magic watch that captain had, but it is still ticking. Ali still has his stealth, but that tick-ticking often gives him away now. The merpeople are fierce fighters. After defeating the pirates, we all agreed to move Crescent Island to the front of the Beyondland island formation for defensive purposes."

"Move an island? But that's…impossible?" exclaimed Kyle.

"I told you there is magic here," P said solemnly. "The Pans have magic, the crocs and the merpeople have magic. The fairies have magic, and the children begin to absorb it too. It's kind of hard to explain, but the way we live here creates a magic—between the land and creatures and us—the more we have, the more we give, the more it seems to grow."

"Fairies?" repeated Jamie.

"Not an insult, Jamie, real fairies, little people with wings and magic. You don't want to mess with fairies; there a long-lived people who can make a lot of trouble if you get on their bad sides," P responded.

Fifty or so cabins ringed a great series of common areas. They landed near what appeared to be a communal dining and eating area with tables and benches. It was still largely dark, but the glow of the impending sunrise was stronger than ever. The children were startled when two figures moved out of the shadows. One was an old woman, and the other a middle-aged man.

"P, we are glad you are back," said the woman, smiling warmly at P and the children.

"Who have you got with you?" asked the man, also smiling a greeting.

"Wendy and Peter, this is Krystal and Kyle and Jamie," P answered.

"Children, this is Mother Wendy, our chief midwife and healer, and Peter is a former Pan."

The children said their hellos, and then Wendy showed them to an empty cabin, showed them the outhouses, and bade them to get a little sleep or rest before being introduced to the whole crowd. Krystal wasn't sure she could sleep, but snuggled against her brother in a soft bed with clean sheets, she was asleep before she realized it.

Krystal woke with a jolt when she realized a bell was ringing in their cabin. "Children, have you had a good rest? It is about noon, and we are breaking for lunch, so I thought this might be a good time to introduce you to our band of Beyondlanders," Mother Wendy called. Krystal heard Jamie open his door and stumble out.

"Mother Wendy, I'll try," Jamie mumbled, clearly still groggy.

"My, my, what did they do to your beautiful face, my lad," she said softly. "Come see me after you're groomed and fed, and I'll see if I can put something on that to ease the swelling and bruising."

Kyle and Krystal came out of their room a little unsure of their reception, but Mother Wendy didn't bat an eye. She smiled, instead, and chuckled, "You two look as groggy as Jamie. Groom yourselves as quick as you can; there's food to eat and people to meet." Then she left them.

The three of them stood there a little awkwardly. Finally, Jamie broke the silence.

"Are you together, then? I thought P said you were more like me? I don't understand," Jamie said.

Krystal and Kyle blushed a deep red; he squeezed her hand, and she answered, "It's not like that between us. It's completely platonic. I am not sure I can explain it exactly. We are twins. We've been together since the womb—we're just attached. I don't know what that means when we become attached to others, but I guess we'll deal with that when it happens," Krystal paused. "Do you have siblings? Do you know that special love and devotion that many siblings feel for each other—or that they should feel for each other?"

Jamie was struggling to keep up, but he understood the part about loving one's siblings. "Yes, I love my brothers and sisters. They know about me, even though my parents don't understand."

Krystal laughed, "Children always know—that's why Pan must be a child," she said both to herself and to her brother and Jamie. "I think we are more like P than like you. I am thinking of changing my name to Kay—I feel gender fluid—not one or the other. I think Kyle feels much the same way, but he'll have to make that decision himself. I told you about how uncomfortable we felt growing up. We didn't need a beating to know they'd hurt us for being different. After what happened to you, and then what our parents said, we knew we needed to leave."

"Children," called Mother Wendy from outside the door.

They walked out the door to join her, where they found P and Peter too. Each took someone's hand, Mother Wendy took

Jamie's, P took Kyle's, and Peter took Krystal's. Peter introduced them all, and then let the children wander. Krystal and Kyle came to know that children were there for all kinds of reasons from physical abuse like beating and lashings and genital cutting to sexual abuse from uncles or step-fathers or teachers (in extremes forced marriages, rape, and sexual slavery).

Jamie, Kyle, and Krystal discovered that some children were straight and identified as boys and girls, but others were different and identified as everything from gay and lesbian, homosexual, to bisexual, transgender, queer, questioning, and asexual. People dressed in whatever they wanted. Some girls wore dresses and so did some boys. Most wore form fitting clothes. Many adorned their outfits with an accessory or two of a bright color. Nearly everyone wore make-up of some kind, and many sported elaborate braids. Clearly, grooming for the day was a communal event.

After they'd had something to eat, the children were surrounded by other children. They were together but in the center of a swirling group of children who asked them questions and studied them.

Krystal heard Kyle and Jamie being asked questions, but she got lost in her own grilling.

"What kinds of things do you like to do?" a girl of about sixteen, with dark straight brown hair braided in a crown around her head and golden-brown skin, asked her. "I am Athena, by the way."

"I don't know. I like to read," Krystal replied.

"No, no. We want to figure out how to dress you. Do you climb trees? Do you run? Do you like dresses or not?" Athena asked.

Krystal stared at Athena a little unnerved. Girls didn't climb trees and weren't encouraged to run. She couldn't remember ever not wearing a dress or a shirt and a skirt. Then, she remembered where she was. She could be anything she wanted here. Within reason, she could do anything she wanted here. Krystal, no, Kay, she thought. She focused her attention back on Athena, who seemed to be grinning at her. "I don't know," she said slowly. "I want to be Kay. I've never climbed a tree or been encouraged to run, but I think I would like to try."

"Good, that's a start," Athena said quickly. "Listen up, everyone, this is Kay, do you hear?"

"Kay," a chorus of children repeated.

"Ze's a small; find Kay some leggings and a shirt," Athena commanded. "Is there a bright color that you like, Kay, and how do you want your hair?"

"Oh, Athena, let me do ze's hair. You know how I love long hair," said a dark-skinned boy in a form fitting pants and shirt set, accented with a bright yellow fabric flower at his throat. "I'm Pansy, and the pronoun I favor is he. May I?" he asked, his hand poised near zirs head.

"Sure," Kay answered hesitantly. And then ze felt his fingers undo zirs braids and run his fingers through zirs hair gently. He started brushing zirs hair and yet there was something different about the way he brushed. Kay realized he was taking the measure of zirs hair, the feel of it, the weight of it. He walked around zir, playing with the ways zirs hair could frame zirs face.

"Color?" demanded Athena, pulling Kay out of zirs thoughts.

"Purple," ze answered absently as a small olive-skinned girl stepped forward with a tray of what had to be make-up.

"I'm Camille, and I am a she. I love to do make-up. Would you let me do yours?" she asked softly.

"Okay, I guess," Kay answered timidly. Ze had never really worn make-up before and was a little daunted by the quantity of color on Camille's face. Her eyes were a yellowy-green, and her lids were painted a bright green that brought out their color with kohl eyeliner accenting her eyes. Her lips were painted a pale sharp pink, and a dusty rose colored her cheeks. "Over the top like me?" Camille asked preening. "Or just a test?"

Kay laughed at the pose, and answered, "Just a test, I think, today."

Camille gave a fake pout, but then set to her task, "Close your eyes." Kay felt Camille apply a line of paint across zirs lids. "Good, now open and look up at the sky," and Kay felt a line of paint applied just under zirs eyes. All the while Pansy was positioning zirs hair. "What about zirs lips, Pansy? I mean look at the coloring, such fair skin, with the dark hair and the blue eyes."

"Too dark, Camille. Ze just wants a test; there will lots of other days—when ze's ready," the boy answered. Kay felt a sense of relief at the words. "What do you think of Kay's hair?" And Kay felt the end of a braid being tied off with string, and Pansy was done.

"Lovely," answered Camille. "Hold still, Kay; just a minute longer. Part your lips just a bit." Kay complied and felt a thin layer of creamy paint applied to zir lips.

Pansy and Camille stepped back to look at Kay, and then what seemed to be a boy in a form fitting dress stepped forward, "I am Suzette, and I am a she." She held up a shirt and a pair of leggings in a dusty blue, "What do you think?"

"Wait, wait," called a young girl with curly, short, blond hair and a shock of painted butterflies adorning her face, "I am Melissa Blue; I am a she, and I just love butterflies, don't you?" and she held a tray of brightly colored fabric butterflies on one side and brightly colored fabric flowers on the other. "See anything you like?"

Kay felt drawn to a beautiful purple bearded-iris, so ze chose that. "Think about where you would like to wear it while you change. We could put it in your hair, or around your neck in a choker, or at your waist in a belt."

"Or at your wrist in a corsage," Pansy added. "Go to that cabin there and change. Think about whether you want to keep your old clothes. If you don't, they'll be added to the communal store."

Kay did as ze was told, but it felt odd. Ze didn't know whose cabin it was, but it was neat and quiet. Ze stripped off zirs dress and petticoats and things. Putting on the simple clingy shirt and leggings felt strange. Ze was fully clothed and yet ze felt so exposed. Never had zirs true body shape been on such display. It had always been covered by the layers and layers of clothes. Kay felt zir hair; it was braided around zirs head, ze guessed somewhat like Athena's. Then Kay realized that ze had been so busy with zir own transformation that ze didn't know what had happened to Kyle or to Jamie. Ze grabbed zirs old things and rushed out the door.

The crowd of children was back. It made way and gently urged zir into the center where Kay found zirself looking at two children she knew and yet didn't. Before ze could speak, Athena's voice rang out. "Attention, everyone. I would like to present our guests. They are trying some identities out, and they are new at this, so those identities might change as they try to find out what represents their true selves. First, this is Jamie, and he's trying out being a gay boy."

Pansy stepped forward and took the clothes Jamie handed him and passed them off to someone else. Then Pansy took the pale pink fabric rose that Jamie held in his hand, "Where would you like it?"

"Around my neck," Jamie answered softly. A young girl handed Pansy a length of ribbon, and Pansy fastened the flower to the ribbon and then fastened the choker around Jamie's neck.

Jamie laughed nervously, but pirouetted around. He was wearing heavy make-up like Camille and form fitting clothing much like Kay had on.

"Welcome, Jamie," the children responded, and there was clapping and whistling to emphasize the welcoming words.

"Next," Athena continued, "is Kyla who is trying out being a girl," and Kay found zirself staring at zir brother, zir sister, ze corrected in zirs head. Kyla looked like a girl, her hair had been styled differently, her make-up was much softer than Jamie's, but she wore more than Kay, and she wore a form fitting dress much like Suzette. She was pretty, this Kyla, in her own way, Kay realized with a smile (different than the prettiness Kyle had

had) but pretty all the same.

Again, Pansy stepped forward to take the clothes Kyla handed him. Next, he took the bright yellow butterfly that Kyla held in her hand. "Where would you like it?" he asked.

"In my hair," Kyla answered quietly. The same young girl handed a small bobby pin to Pansy who attached it to the butterfly and pinned it neatly in Kyla's hair behind her ear.

Kyla looked nervously at Kay. Ze felt a mixed set of emotions at the weight zirs approval or disapproval held over zirs twin. Ze returned Kyla's nervous look with a blazing smile, and Kay felt zirs eyes well with tears just as Kyla's did as she smiled to the crowd and spun around to the words, "Welcome, Kyla," and the clapping and whistling.

"Last, but not least, this is Kay who is trying on being non-binary."

One last time, Pansy stepped forward and took Kay's clothes. Then, he took the purple flower from zirs hand and asked where ze wanted it.

"In my hair, like my sister," Kay answered. Pansy accepted another bobby pin and placed the flower in the center of the mass of Kay's encircling braids.

Thus adorned, Kay stepped forward and spun around to, "Welcome, Kay," and more clapping and whistling.

"Alright, alright, introductions are through. There's still daylight yet and some chores to do. Off with you now, until it's supper time," and with that, Athena dismissed the crowd.

Kay, Kyla, and Jamie weren't sure what to do, but Peter appeared. "Let me show you around, and then tomorrow at breakfast you can pick something you'd like to do or be assigned to a task." Peter walked them around to the various gardens, through the orchards, to the chicken pens and yards, to the meadows with the goats and the sheep, to the various food makers and craftspeople, to Mother Wendy's infirmary, to the small lake and to the nearest beach. It took them several hours, and the children were beginning to feel very weary indeed when

Peter left them to themselves in a small orchard not far from dining area.

"How do you feel?" Jamie asked the twins bluntly.

"Good," Kay said slowly, "different...even a little outrageous. I didn't know I could present myself to others this way. I am not even sure that I am not presenting myself to myself in a whole new way. I don't know whether that makes sense. Does it?"

"Yes," answered Kyla, taking ze's hand and squeezing it gently. "I feel like I am acting out a part of myself that I have never been able to make public before. And the presentation is as much for myself as it is for others. It does feel almost out of control because I never felt I was allowed to do this before."

"I know," said Jamie excitedly, "and we can keep trying other identities out. I like this one, but I know I also want to try being a girl and then a non-binary. Is that weird?" Jamie asked suddenly self-conscious.

"No, it's not weird, not here anyway, and here's where we are. Three cheers for Beyondland and P who brought us here," exclaimed Kay.

"Hip, hip, hooray! Hip, hip, hooray! Hip, hip hooray!" they cried.

And just like that, Kay and Kyla, and Jamie settled into life in Beyondland and rarely ever gave their old lives second thoughts.

The Huntsman and the Beast

THE HUNTSMAN WAS disgusted with himself. The evil queen had ordered him to kill Snow White, and he had actually meant to obey the command. He had taken the girl out into the woods, in his trance-like state. The girl plainly knew she was in danger. She begged him to keep her safe, to spare her life. He got her into the deep woods and had drawn his knife. She saw and turned a ghostly white and had actually kneeled to accept a death-blow. He had lost his nerve at that point or recovered his sense, or a bit of both. She was completely innocent and helpless. Everything he knew about good and evil pushed itself into his mind. This was fundamentally wrong, he told himself. He could not harm her or he would lose his soul. The queen had clearly traded hers for her strange powers, but the huntsman would not damn his own or hurt such an innocent.

"Run, Snow White," he told the wide-eyed princess who clearly thought she was about to be slaughtered.

She didn't wait for clarification. She ran, and the huntsman ran in another direction away from the queen's palace. He would be hunted now too, the same as the girl. He prayed to God for luck for both of them. He crashed through the woods, trying to get as much distance as he could from the scene of his nearly sinful act and the queen's palace. Murderer, murderer of an innocent, a helpless young woman. He didn't even think Snow White was eighteen. He fell to his knees, weeping. How had he even considered this? Then he sat back and thought. When the evil queen had commanded him to kill the princess, he had felt helpless to disobey her will. But there in the woods, away from her influence and power, he was able to assert his own morality and reject the death-sentence. He continued to run—to free himself from guilt and influence. He ran and ran and finally found a sheltered spot to spend the night. He covered himself in pine-needles and fell asleep.

In the morning, he continued to run and move deeper into the woods, deeper than he had ever gone before. Suddenly, he saw the print and froze, and there were others, similarly strange and unnatural. He had seen all sorts of bear prints, wolf prints, cat prints, but he had never seen anything like this before. It seemed vaguely human and yet animal. His whole being cried out that this creature was dangerous. He was scared. What he wanted was to return to those woods he knew, but he had effectively banished himself by disobeying the queen and letting Snow White go.

With his bow, he brought down a duck and had a tasty lunch. He kept pushing on. By night fall, he had killed a rabbit and found a cave that offered good shelter. He had met no one on his travels. During the night, he was awoken by the snarls and shrieks of a cougar being killed. He couldn't imagine what was killing the animal. The bears around were small brown bear; the cougar would be a bigger threat to a bear than the other way around. Wolves could bring down a cougar, but there was no howling or barking or wolf snarling. Suddenly he thought of the strange prints he had seen. In some of the prints, the animal had stood on two feet but had claws; in others, it had seemed four legged. What was that thing that had made the prints and was it responsible for killing the cougar somewhere near where he was hidden? He felt a wave of fear that the animal might find him, but why would it look with an ample supply of food nearby. The noise of the struggle ceased, and the huntsman was too far away to hear the victorious animal feeding. He was thankful for that and slowly sank back into an uneasy sleep.

He woke the next day later than would have liked. He saw the ravens circling what he assumed was the corpse of the cougar. He went to take a look at the body. The throat had been eaten away, and the animal had concentrated its feeding on the chest cavity, eating the heart and other vital organs. The sides of the cougar had been slashed by powerful claws, and the left foreleg had been torn or gnawed off. The cougar had never had a chance. Perhaps, there was some giant grizzly bear that had somehow found its way here. But the strange prints pushed themselves back into the huntsman's mind. Not one to waste what was offered, the huntsman cut off a back leg and roasted that for his breakfast before setting out further. He heard riders at one point and hid. Hiding and waiting, until he couldn't hear the riders anymore, made him wonder after Snow White. Was she safe? Had she eluded capture too? Had she found help somewhere?

By dusk, he had brought down another duck, but he had found no shelter. He had made himself a quick dinner of roast duck, and then picked a tree with a particularly large tangle of forking branches so that he was able to wedge himself among them without much risk of falling out of the tree during the night. He fell asleep easily, tired from the night before. Again, late during the night, he was awoken by the panic of birds nearby. There was a strange, deep, loud howl of some kind. The sound of it made the hairs on the back of the huntsman's neck stand up. It was both sorrowful and full of rage. A huge animal was running close by. The huntsman could hear it crashing through the trees, and then it was going in another direction, away from him. He felt relief sweep over him, and he let himself fall back into sleep.

The next morning the sun and the birds had him up at dawn. He found a large stream and stripped his clothes off to wash himself properly. He speared some fish easily and had them roasted to break his fast. He pushed on. He didn't know how far he'd had to go, but he knew he hadn't gone far enough. He was relieved to hear no riders as he traveled. He shot two squirrels during the afternoon and roasted them. He reached the top of a hill at dusk and couldn't believe his eyes. In the lands below lay a beautiful castle with sprawling grounds. Though it had an abandoned or neglected look, there were rooms alight in what would have been some of the first main rooms. He made his way to the castle, hoping for sanctuary there.

The main door opened at his approach, though he saw no servant to open it. Lighted torches and candelabra guided him to a small dining room where a succulent dinner had been laid out for one person. The room sported a welcoming hearth fire. The huntsman warmed himself and waited to meet the host, the person the meal was presumably set for. No one came. He called out for the servants, but still no one came. The meal laid out was amazing—quail in red currant sauce, roasted potatoes smothered in butter, French green beans also smothered in butter and topped with roasted almonds, bread, hot and yeasty, and wine of a rich deep color that promised to be decadent. He waited an hour, and no one showed. Finally, he couldn't control himself and sat down and consumed the meal. It was even better than he thought it would be. Candles flared after he finished his meal, and he followed them. They led him to a door that was labeled, Anthony's Room. He stared at the sign. How could anyone here know his name? And yet someone obviously did.

Inside the room, the bed was so inviting after days in the woods that he stripped off his clothes, washed hastily in the wash basin, and fell asleep in a nest of soft fabric and quilts. In the morning, to his surprise, there were fine clean clothes in his size hanging on the armoire. He opened the armoire to put the hanger back in it and found more clothes—all looking like they would fit him. He resumed his search for the host but could find no one. A wonderful breakfast was set out for him in the same small dining room. He ate some strawberries and then helped himself to a croissant, soft cheese, and a slice of cured ham. He poured himself hot coffee and sat looking around the room, trying to figure out where to find the inhabitants and what he should do if he failed to find someone.

As he wandered, he noticed how beautifully the castle was

decorated. Paintings and tapestries adorned the walls. Magnificent candelabra were everywhere. Though he searched and searched, he could find no one. Even in the kitchens, he could find no trace of a person or a means of the production of his breakfast. The only soul he did find was a magnificent stallion in the stable in a stall that was labeled Merlin. The huntsman laughed himself silly at the sight. He gasped when he finally began to gain control of himself, and he peered at the chestnut colored stallion. "An enchanted castle, of course, and you're the wizard, are you?" he asked.

He let himself into the stall and patted the powerful neck. Merlin whinnied in greeting and nuzzled his nose under the huntsman's arm. "You're a very handsome beast, Merlin," he said softly. "Let me look around a bit more, and then I'll come back and we'll go for a ride." He left the stable, but failed to find anyone else.

A lunch of venison stew, bread, and ale had been set out for him. He ate contentedly and then walked back to the stable to find Merlin bridled and saddled—ready to go. The huntsman, seeing the outfitted horse, searched the stable thoroughly and finding no one, he regarded the horse, "Nice trick," he said wryly. "Can you tell me how you did it?" At that point, he almost expected the horse to answer him, but Merlin just whinnied and stamped his hooves impatiently. The huntsman took the reins and mounted. Merlin was a pleasure to ride. They walked at first, but then the huntsman brought him to a trot, then a cantor, and then a gallop. Merlin was familiar with the grounds, so the huntsman often let the horse direct their paths.

The last place they went was a small apple orchard. Merlin ate happily the less rotted fruit on the ground, and the huntsman, noticing a saddle bag, filled it with ripe apples picked from the trees. They made their way back to the stable. Though the huntsman expected the magic of the castle could take care of Merlin, he did the work himself, both because he wanted something to do and because he liked horses. He took off the bridle and saddle and hung them up. He took down brushes and brushed Merlin thoroughly. He put some fresh straw in the stall and saw the beast was watered and fed. Then he bade Merlin good night, taking the saddle bag with him. He left the bag in the smallest kitchen.

He retired to his room and washed before dinner. He had seen a beautiful library in his earlier explorations of the castle and went there to select a book to read. *The Song of Roland* looked promising. With the book in hand, the huntsman went to the small dining room and was startled to find a large figure standing in front of the hearth fire wearing a long splendid tail-coat that obscured the figure's body. The huntsman froze, all the hairs on the back of his neck going rigid in panic and alarm. The figure before him was not quite human. The huntsman struggled to control himself.

"Huntsman, do you know what I am?" a deep growling voice asked quietly.

"I...I...can guess, my Lord," the huntsman said carefully. Enchantment. Magic. The evil queen had used black magic to gain and keep her throne. Had she done this too? Of course, there were different kinds of magic and enchantment. Something else might have done this, but what or who?

As if answering his thoughts, the figure spoke again, "I did this to myself. I was a vain and spoilt prince. I insulted a fairy queen, and she turned me into this," he waved theatrically at himself, "for my penance," he was silent for a moment. "Are you afraid?"

"Yes," the huntsman answered honestly. He watched in horrified fascination as the figure slowly turned from the fire to face him. He was enormous (nearly eight feet tall) and covered in dark brown fur. His face was something between a bear's and wolf's, but there was something human about it too. His eyes, perhaps, a golden-yellow-brown, the shape, the size in proportion to his face—but not animal eyes. He had massive, muscular shoulders and chest muscles. He wore breeches to cover his genitals and legs. He had large, dangerous talon-like claws on his hands and significant claws on his feet. This was the creature that had killed in the woods—powerful and dangerous, his thoughts told him. But some other part of him found that kind of raw power exciting.

The huntsman knew he had gone very pale, but he thought that was all his features betrayed. Why was he here? What did this poor enchanted prince want with him? "Why? What...do you want with me?" he asked.

"I...I...require a companion," the deep voice answered.

"A companion?" the huntsman echoed. "A companion to do what?" he asked, his face flushing with a sudden heat that he fought to control.

The creature had turned away. "I have been alone a very long time," the voice said, and the huntsman heard all the pain and humiliation that the speaker had to hold in place to make the admission, and he felt genuinely sorry for the creature in front of him. The voice continued, "It would be nice to have someone to talk to or to read to me," he said gesturing at the book in the huntsman's hand, pain and longing palpable in the voice. "Someone to eat with," he said motioning to the table, set, this time, for two.

The huntsman, moved by the desolation of the figure in front of him, smiled a little weakly and gestured toward the table. "It looks like dinner is served. Shall we?" he asked a little flippantly.

The figure in front of him went rigid with shock or tension or something else. Its eyes searched the huntsman's face. The pain and suspicion in the eyes made it clear it was looking for deception or ridicule or revulsion, and he felt again a wave of empathy for the poor tormented creature in front of him. He moved to the table, set down the book, pulled out the chair he had been sitting in for the last few meals, and said, "I am hungry. Shouldn't we eat?" He felt somehow reckless. The idea of eating with an enchanted prince in an enchanted castle made him think that anything was possible.

The figure nodded awkwardly, moved to the table, and pulled out the second chair. They sat down together. Boneless chicken breasts were stuffed with breading and apples and raisins, baked potatoes were amply buttered and topped with cheese, green beans were served in browned butter, and chilled white wine accompanied the meal. The creature's food had been cut up into strips. The huntsman noticed that while he had cutlery, the creature did not, which must have explained why his food was cut up.

Seeking to break the awkward silence that had descended, the huntsman took up his glass, "To companionship," he said.

The creature before him seemed to blanch at the words, but then resigned himself. His glass was different which made it easier for him to pick up in his clawed fist. He raised it and nodded in agreement, "To companionship."

"What is your name, my Lord?" the huntsman asked.

"Don't call me that!" the voice flared harshly. "I am a beast now, and Lord of no man or woman." He paused, trying to gain control of his emotions. "When I was human, I was Christopher, but that was long ago. You can call me Beast for that is what I am now."

"I know beasts, Christopher," Anthony said quietly, "and you are very different from any beast I know. You feel pain and regret as only a human can. I cannot, not, acknowledge that aspect of you. You are Christopher to me," he said and smiled slightly.

Christopher stared at him in open disbelief. Then he seemed to recover himself. "Okay, Anthony," he said. But a jolt of excitement rushed through him. The fairy queen had said that if someone could love him, he could change back. Surely, someone seeing him as human despite his hideous appearance could have that potential. Anthony seemed to be offering that potential. Love could be any kind of love, platonic, parental, familial, and amorous. It couldn't be parental or familial for them, but it could be platonic or romantic. He felt his penis throb at the thought before he really realized what he was thinking. He blushed furiously at his thoughts and his physical reaction to those thoughts. For the first time, he was glad he was a beast because otherwise Anthony might notice and guess at his thoughts. His thoughts were interrupted when he realized Anthony was speaking to him.

"How do you know my name?" he asked patiently, apparently asking the question for a second time.

"There is more than one magic mirror in the world," Christopher answered casually.

"You have seen me?" Anthony asked suspiciously. "You have watched me?" and his voice grew sharper, accusation and condemnation ringing in the tones of it.

Christopher stiffened. It wasn't like that. He wasn't stalking Anthony—that would be creepy and perhaps criminal—an invasion of personal privacy. How did he explain? "It is part of the enchantment, I think," he said softly. He had never actually articulated his suspicions about the mirror to anyone. There had been no one to tell. There was an immense sense of relief or gratitude in being able to speak of it. "I can see that others are happy and surrounded by people who love them while I am not," he continued. "It is a reminder of all I have lost."

Anthony had stopped eating and was staring at Christopher. His expression had changed from indignation to a genuine sympathy that wrenched at Christopher's heart. His beastly form was bad enough but the mirror—that was worse—it verged on torture. Self-torture, of course, that is why Christopher hardly ever looked at it. He didn't want to see others being happy, but the castle had lighted his way to the mirror with quiet insistence the day that Anthony had led Snow White into the woods and let her go.

Anthony seemed to be following Christopher's train of thought, because he suddenly asked, "Snow White, is...is... she...alright?" his voice fraught with concern.

Christopher felt his heart sink at what he perceived had

motivated Anthony's concern for the young woman. Of course, he must have feelings for her. Christopher forced himself to smile. "She is safe. She found a small cottage where a young woman named Aurora lives with three bumbling fairies. They seem content enough," he answered. "She is very pretty," he added.

"Pretty?" Anthony repeated, clearly surprised at the notion. "She is an innocent, and I nearly killed her," his tone was harsh and full of self-disgust. He shook his head trying to dismiss his thoughts.

Christopher stared at Anthony. So, it wasn't like that, Christopher thought, excitement coursing through him in a burst that made him blush again. He looked away and then glanced again at Anthony who was now blushing furiously as he seemed to read Christopher's thoughts despite the fur and animal features. They both looked away then and renewed assaults on their food. After an awkward silence, they talked about hunting and the castle—keeping clear, by mutual silent agreement, of anything vaguely suggesting romance. When they finished eating, they retired to the two armchairs on either side of the fire, and Anthony did in fact read from the book for an hour before they both retired to their chambers.

Having actually eaten in the castle, Christopher did not need to hunt, but he was much too excited to sleep either. Anthony was there. Someone was with him at long last. He could have a friend—and perhaps he could have more. There had been that moment when Christopher had thought of the possibility of a romantic relationship between them, and Anthony had realized it and hadn't looked repulsed or offended but had blushed in the same fashion. What did that mean?

He ran the grounds—running so hard that he could think of nothing else except drawing enough oxygen into his lungs and keeping his feet moving. He could hear the animals taking flight at the racket he was making thundering over the grounds. He could smell their fear at his scent, and he didn't care. He wasn't repulsed with himself by their fear for once. There was something else now.

He struggled, realizing that Anthony gave him hope. Hope, where there hadn't been hope, in so long. His pace slowed, and he came to a halt. His breathing steadied, and then it wasn't steady at all. He was sobbing, crying at the possibility that his life could be different. He sank to his knees and let himself weep. When the tears had spent themselves, he found himself drained, and he made his weary way back to the castle. He sank gratefully into his bed and was asleep nearly instantly.

Anthony alone in his room couldn't sleep either. He felt a confused excitement. He tossed and turned. He kept playing dinner over in his mind. Did he really see what he thought he saw? Was Christopher attracted to young men like he was? Christopher had assumed some kind of romantic attachment or attraction between Anthony and Snow White and had felt what were clearly relief and excitement at the prospect of Anthony not being attracted to her or to young women in general. That last part in particular had been the flash point. Not just that Anthony wasn't heterosexually attracted to Snow White but that he wasn't heterosexuality attracted at all. The thought had made both of them blush. But maybe that wasn't right. Maybe Christopher hadn't been blushing. Maybe it was just he who had blushed at that train of thought. Over and over images, questions, and doubts flashed through his mind. Sometime in the early morning, he fell into an exhausted sleep.

In the morning, Anthony found Christopher nervously pacing in the small dining room. Christopher stopped when Anthony came into the room appraising him quietly. "I didn't sleep well," Anthony said defensively.

"I am sorry," Christopher said softly. They sat down at the table together. Christopher reached awkwardly for the coffee pot.

"Let me do it, please," Anthony said impatiently, and he took the coffee pot from Christopher pushing the other young man's paws away. Christopher blushed at the contact but let Anthony pour coffee for them both.

"Why did you sleep badly?" Christopher asked. "Is there

something wrong with your room or the bed?" his voice anxious. He fell silent for a moment, and then he added, "Does it make you uncomfortable to be here?"

Anthony flushed; he couldn't tell him. "I had nightmares," he lied badly, but Christopher didn't seem to notice.

Christopher looked uncomfortable. "What did you have nightmares about?" he asked nervously.

The anxiety in Christopher's voice suddenly snapped Anthony out of his own. Christopher was drawing the wrong conclusions, he realized. "No, Christopher, I am fine here," he said, blushing. "Truly, I am fine." He was silent a moment and added in a barely audible voice, "You don't scare me."

Christopher looked at Anthony sharply, searching his face. Christopher flushed too, and the two young men distracted themselves by eating and drinking coffee. After breakfast, they played several matches of chess. They ate a small lunch of roast turkey sandwiches and greens and cider. It was a beautiful afternoon, and Christopher and Anthony took a walk through the grounds after their meal. Christopher showed Anthony the various formal gardens. Anthony particularly enjoyed the kitchen garden with the herbs and essential vegetables. Christopher found it amusing that Anthony wanted to pick the ripe vegetables, but the castle apparently didn't and conveniently produced a suitable basket just as Anthony couldn't carry anything more in his arms. They walked the basket back to the small kitchen and set off again. At dinner time, they made their way back. Poached salmon in a pesto-cream sauce was waiting for them along with pasta, bread, and chilled champagne. Anthony read to them until it was time to retire.

Anthony, tired from the night before, fell easily into sleep. Christopher felt a contented elation. They were getting along— they were also covertly flirting. Christopher happily let the best moments of the last two days—was it only two days?—yes, the last two days—linger in his mind. Part of him longed to rush forward with his relationship with Anthony, but it was all so new. Though he had been attracted to other boys before, he had never actually had a relationship. He wondered whether Anthony had. Anthony was slightly older than he was, but not by much, nineteen or twenty perhaps. Another part of him knew that he wanted to take things slowly. He wanted this relationship to be special. Intimacy could deepen naturally. Both he and Anthony needed time to know each other, and they had nothing but time. Thinking that way, he drifted off into a contented sleep.

Their days fell into an easy rhythm. They ate together and usually spent the mornings playing chess or cards. Christopher's paws and claws could usually push chess pieces where he wanted them to go. Where maneuvering was tricky, he could tell Anthony where he wanted a particular piece to go. Cards were trickier. He could hold the cards in his paws, but he couldn't manipulate them—at least not without dropping them half the time. At first, Christopher was angry and embarrassed, but Anthony calmed him and patiently held Christopher's hand of cards for him and manipulated the cards as Christopher instructed. The pleasure they both got from playing overcame the awkwardness of Christopher having to rely on Anthony.

After lunch, they strode the grounds and sometimes entered the woods so Anthony could hunt. The one absolute thing that Christopher would not let Anthony do was to see him hunt. Anthony tried to assure his friend that it wouldn't matter, but Christopher was equally firm that it would.

"You know in your mind that I am an animal, yet you choose to see me as a human. You can't imagine how special that is for me." He paused and continued, "I know that you saw and heard things in the woods when I was hunting, but you did not truly see me hunt as an animal. If you did, I don't think you could see me as human anymore, and I couldn't bear that."

Christopher's pain and distress were so apparent that Anthony gave his word to keep away, and Christopher always gave him clear markers not to cross, so Anthony never saw.

They experimented with Merlin—trying to get the stallion accustomed to Christopher's scent without going into full-fledged panic. That was a work in progress.

They grew closer as the days passed. They told each other the intimate details of their lives before they had met and of their dreams for the future. They held hands or close enough—Anthony would take Christopher's paw, and they twined their fingers/claws together. They had even kissed cautiously. Christopher was horribly self-conscious about his teeth, snout, and fur, but Anthony didn't care or at least made Christopher feel like it didn't matter.

It had been a few weeks, and they had settled into the armchairs for after dinner reading when the castle candelabra changed. Some dimmed while others flared. Christopher explained that it was the mirror. The candelabra had done the same thing the afternoon that the mirror had shown him Anthony with Snow White in the woods. They followed the lit path to a door by Christopher's room. It was a small room furnished with a bench facing a spectacular oval silver-gilt mirror. The frame was decorated with foliage and runes interspersed around the frame. The mirror itself was just a mirror when they walked in.

"It's beautiful," Anthony whispered. "What do the symbols mean?"

"I don't know," Christopher answered quietly.

As they sat on the bench, the mirror changed. It misted over, and the mist began to swirl, and then it parted, revealing a tiny cottage.

Anthony felt Christopher stiffen beside him at the sight. Before Anthony could ask, two young women, one blond-haired and the other black-haired, came skipping into view, holding hands, with the blond-haired woman holding a basket of fruit over her free arm.

Anthony, looking at the black-haired girl, gasped, "Snow White," he whispered. "Why?" he asked looking to Christopher for an explanation.

"I don't know," he answered back.

The mist returned, clouding the mirror. Then it swirled and parted again, revealing a tall cloaked figure traveling through the woods. The figure was accompanied by three wolves—the eyes of which glowed a sickening, unnatural red color. Anthony shuddered at the sight, and Christopher growled deep in his throat.

"They are not natural," Anthony said unnecessarily.

"Who?" Christopher asked looking at the hooded figure, but the hood of the cloaked figure snagged on a branch and fell back. Anthony had suspected, but he gasped at the sight of the woman.

"The evil queen," he whispered.

Christopher was studying the mirror carefully, so carefully that Anthony noticed. "What are you looking at?"

"She is three days from Snow White and her friend, and we are two—if we hurry and if she doesn't use magic," Christopher answered.

Anthony felt a jolt of panic. He had never wanted to be in the presence of the evil queen again. He didn't trust her. He didn't trust himself to be strong enough to resist her influence. Yet he felt a horrible obligation toward Snow White because the queen had used her influence over him to nearly kill her. Now the further complication was that he did not want to endanger Christopher. He did not know what kind of dark magic traveled with the queen, but he knew it was unnatural and therefore unnaturally dangerous. Two days' travel, but Christopher could travel much more quickly than he could. The thought of being separated from Christopher or of Christopher facing the queen alone made him go pale.

"I can't keep up with you," he said in alarm.

Christopher smiled ruefully, "Perhaps it is time to see just how well Merlin tolerates my presence. Last time wasn't so bad." The last time, Anthony had been riding Merlin; they were following Christopher, and it had been okay until the wind shifted, and Merlin must have gotten a full blast of Christopher's scent because he reared suddenly and then went down on all fours and bucked. Luckily, Christopher had sensed the stallion's fear and had run to the horse and rider in time to catch Anthony as he was thrown from the horse.

"What are those things?" Christopher asked to distract them from thinking about riding with Merlin.

"I don't know," Anthony said slowly. "The queen performs black magic. She is no white lady or white witch. She is concerned with power, death, and destruction. Whatever they are can't be good."

They looked at each other then. They were both scared, but they both seemed equally determined not to let the evil queen harm the young women.

"We don't have to go," Anthony said in a voice that lacked conviction.

"Don't we?" Christopher asked rhetorically. "The mirror summoned us to view these images. We must be meant to do something about them. Could you ever forgive yourself or find true happiness here with me if you knew the price of it was their blood?"

"No, but the mirror showed you me," Anthony said. He didn't know what he hoped to accomplish with this last comment, but the response took his breath away.

"I think it did it to give me hope." Christopher paused for moment. "I was very close to desolation before you came here, and you have given me hope and joy, Anthony," he said softly.

"And you me, Christopher," Anthony answered back, tears glistening in his eyes.

In a voice choked with emotion, Christopher said, "We...need to get...to bed. We should leave by dawn." They embraced then and kissed tenderly and made their way to their chambers hand in paw.

They woke before dawn—their pillows and quilts nudging and flapping at them to get them awake. They dressed and met in the small kitchen where provisioned saddle bags awaited them.

They walked to the stable. Christopher waited outside while Anthony walked in to find the bridled and saddled Merlin ready to go. He attached the saddle bags and talked to the stallion. He explained in an urgent voice their mission, to save two young women, to possibly battle a queen using black magic, and their urgent need to work with Christopher. Anthony felt distinctly ridiculous explaining all this until the horse butted him firmly in the chest in what seemed like a reprimand and shook its head.

"Are you talking to me after all, wizard?" he asked, amused. But when the horse nodded his head up and down in response, the smile slipped from his lips. He mounted then and rode out of the stable. Merlin's nostrils flared furiously at Christopher's scent, but when Christopher started to run, the stallion followed. They ran and rode hard. They ate only when they stopped to water the horse and relieve themselves. That first night they stopped at dusk. They were up again at dawn. Again, they ran and rode hard—only stopping to water Merlin. They reached the cottage by late afternoon. The young women and their fairy protectors were barricaded in the cottage by the time they arrived in a thunder of hoof beats, foot falls, and dust. Christopher and Anthony, consumed by their desire to shield the young women from the evil queen, had given no thought to their sudden appearance and how it could be seen as threatening. They tried to explain again and again, but the only responses they got were to be shot with fairy dust, which turned their clothes by turns from pink to blue and back again.

Exasperated, Anthony dismounted and stood in front of the door, "Snow White, look at me! I am the huntsman. Do you not remember me? The queen, do you hear me, the queen, is coming! We can get you way, but you must stop this nonsense and let us help you!"

The door opened a crack, and Anthony could see Snow White's face even paler than usual, if that was even possible, he thought absently; just behind her stood the blond-haired young woman holding Snow White's hand, and above them floated the three fairies who glowered at him.

"What is all this?" demanded the tallest fairy. "And what is that beast in the yard?"

Anthony explained it all. How the evil queen had held him in her power so that he nearly killed Snow White, letting Snow White go, finding the castle, how Christopher was an enchanted prince/beast, coming to know Christopher and his kindness, the warning from the mirror, Anthony and Christopher's mad journey to reach them, and the necessity to leave.

The tall fairy cocked an eye at Anthony, "I think you and your friend underestimate the power of fairies, and I would have thought your friend would have learned that lesson quite some time ago. We may not be fairy queens, but we are fairies and in the holy number of three. There is much that we can accomplish when properly motivated," she said tersely.

Christopher has been listening intently to the conversation. "Ladies," he said, bowing with a flourish, "is there power in an unholy number of three?"

"Indeed, there is. Why?" the tall fairy asked.

"The queen travels with three wolves with glowing red eyes," he answered solemnly.

The tall fairy bristled at that, and the other two gasped. The door flew open. Introductions were made. Aurora was a princess in hiding too and just as much in danger from the evil queen as Snow White. Almost instantly, the fairies had the young women ready for travel. They turned a squirrel into a lovely grey mare they dubbed Molly, and outfitted her with bridle and saddle. The young women mounted the mare with obvious horse-sense, much to Anthony's relief. They ran and rode hard, stopping at dusk and making camp. They ate quietly and talked for a while, getting to know each other. Christopher proposed to take a first watch, but the fairies insisted on keeping watch and bade him sleep with the others. The young women slept together, their arms curled around each other, both of the young men noted. They woke at dawn to a fabulous breakfast conjured by the fairies, yeasty bread with butter and honey, crisp bacon, candied apples, and hot cider. After eating quickly, they took to the woods again. At dusk, the fairies provided another excellent meal and sent them off to sleep.

The fairies woke them just before dawn, and the young people instantly knew why. The air itself seemed to shimmer with tension. The queen had reached the cottage and found it abandoned, and her rage was radiating out, feeling for her lost prey. The fairies insisted that the children eat. They forced down a few bites and sips to break their fasts, but they were too tense to do much more. They ran and rode to a broad clearing in the woods where they turned and waited for what would come.

After what seemed like hours, the queen stepped out of the woods first, followed by her pets. Christopher had taken off his coat, and he and Anthony stood in front of the young women at the far side of the clearing; the fairies floated behind Snow White and Aurora, and the horses stood in the shadows of the trees. The queen's eyes glinted in pleasure as she saw Anthony. Her eyes flickered slightly at the sight of Christopher but that was replaced quickly with a look of dismissal. She uttered something in a foreign tongue, and the wolves moved forward, transforming as they turned into wolf-men. They were not so tall or as big as Christopher, but their red eyes were unnerving, and there were three of them.

Anthony shot at them as they came. Arrow after arrow found its mark, but the wolf-men came on unphased by their wounds. Christopher groaned beside Anthony and then launched himself at the wolf-men. Anthony screamed in protest, shooting furiously until all his arrows were spent. Christopher slashed at the wolf-men with his huge claws, but though their flesh was slashed, they did not bleed, and they did not fall. They slashed at Christopher with their own claws, and they all heard him cry out in pain. Anthony was dropping his bow and preparing to run to Christopher's aid, when to his surprise, Aurora and Snow White ran past him, each holding a flaming sword which they used to cut through the wolf-men. Literally, Aurora and Snow White cut the wolf-men limb from limb. Whatever dark magic the queen had used to animate her creatures was extinguished in the flames. The queen shrieked with rage at the destruction of her pets.

Anthony had reached Christopher and held him cradled in his arms. The queen began to say something in the same strange tongue, and Anthony heard Merlin whinny in surprise, and then there was a great whoosh of air moving, and the ground shook as a great copper and brown and gold dragon exploded into being. He bellowed his arrival—with a note of triumph and satisfaction. Then he stretched himself, unfurled his wings, and poised his head. The queen tried to finish her incantation, but the dragon shot his flames at her in the next heartbeat, and she ignited in the flames, her cloak and clothes, her hair, her flesh. The dragon kept his flow of fire on her until there was nothing left. Then he closed his mouth briefly and roared in victory with a fury that shook the earth around them.

Anthony had ripped his shirt into pieces to bind Christopher's wounds; the worst of the bleeding was staunched, but Christopher was badly wounded. He struggled to sit up a little as the young women approached them, but it caused him pain, and he groaned heavily. He looked at Anthony. The fear and panic in Anthony's eyes confirmed his own assessment of his condition. He lifted his paw to caress Anthony's face.

"I love you," he whispered hoarsely.

"No! Don't you dare!" Anthony answered harshly. "I love you too, and you will not leave me!" he said hotly. Anthony felt Aurora and Snow White exchange glances at their words, but he did not care for anything except Christopher in his arms.

Christopher snorted and groaned, and then they all heard a pop. The air shimmered in haze of sparkling white light. A dazzling fairy clothed in silver and white stood in front of Christopher and Anthony. A wide smile graced her lips and lit up her face. She bowed toward Christopher, and he smiled a sad smile at the sight of her. She shook her head at him and stepped forward.

"Christopher, have you no faith?" she asked in a voice that sounded like running water. "You have done well, very well," and she bent and kissed him on the forehead. Christopher gasped and closed his eyes as his whole body felt like it was melting from his forehead to his toes—not burning—but melting and condensing. He felt his wounds mend, his body shrink, his fur fall away, his claws disappear, his teeth change, and his face transform. Anthony gasped still holding him. The young women also gasped behind him. Christopher opened his eyes and looked up at Anthony, and he could see tiny versions of himself reflected in Anthony's pupils. He was human again. He sighed and lifted his arm to see the brown skin and the human hand. He touched Anthony's face in a brief caress and sat upright. His breeches, suddenly much too big for his human frame, threatened to fall down and expose him, but they suddenly tightened to fit him. The three fairies snickered at his side, and Christopher shot them an appreciative grin. Anthony helped Christopher to his feet, and they all stood and bowed before the fairy queen.

She waved at them impatiently. "You have all done well," and she glanced at all of them in turn. "The future is what you will make of it," and she stood in front of each of the other young people and kissed them on the forehead. Next, she turned to the dragon who shook his head and spoke to the great surprise of the children.

"I like this form, my queen. May I not stay as I am and watch over the prince and his friend?" he asked in a rasping, smoky voice.

The fairy queen smiled and nodded in assent, "The choice is yours, Merlin," and she floated up to kiss his forehead. When she floated down again, the young people saw the mark on the dragon's forehead and felt their own foreheads, realizing that even if they could not see or feel it on each other that they were marked too by the fairy queen. The fairy queen then focused her gaze on Molly who nodded eagerly, accepting the kiss and transforming back into a squirrel. She stretched herself and shook her tail in pleasure and then scampered off into the woods. The fairy queen nodded to her sister fairies in approval and in acknowledgment. She bowed again. "I take my leave of you. Make the world a better place, and love and stand by each other," she commanded, and they all bowed their heads accepting the charges she made of them. The air shimmered again, and the fairy queen disappeared in a shower of glittering sparkles.

Left to themselves and free of the threat of the evil queen, Aurora and Snow White and the fairies decided to return to the cottage, but they promised to visit Christopher's castle every now and again. So, the young people parted. Merlin sprawled himself on the ground so that Christopher and Anthony could climb on his back. They flew back to the castle, which now bustled with activity, but no one seemed to notice them until they slid from Merlin's back.

"They can't see me," Merlin whispered somewhat unnecessarily, "that is part of the fairy queen's gift," he explained. "Come find me in the woods when you want me," he said, and with that, he launched himself back into the air and was gone.

Shouts of acknowledgment and greeting met the appearance of the prince. Anthony felt momentarily self-conscious and then felt Christopher grab his hand and lead him through the castle. Christopher's room was now labeled Christopher's and Anthony's Room, they noticed with some satisfaction, and it had expanded slightly to accommodate a couple rather than a single occupant. Splendid clothes had been laid out for them. They washed hastily and dressed themselves.

They strode holding hands to the Great Room. Outside Anthony hesitated, losing his nerve, but he glanced at Christopher who was looking at him tenderly. "You're with me now," he whispered, kissing Anthony's lips. Pulling away, he added, "Besides we have the fairy queen's blessing and Merlin's protection. Come, meet your new life with me." Christopher held out his hand, and Anthony took it, and they strode over the threshold of the room and into their future.

Snow White and Sleeping Beauty

SNOW WHITE HAD been increasingly uncomfortable. The queen radiated malice. Snow White did her best to keep out of the way, but she felt her panic growing. Young as she was, she was waiting for the queen to kill her. Every night she wondered if she would wake up in the morning. Snow White wanted to run away, but she wasn't allowed to the leave the castle. Her days were miserable. Some of the servants were nice to her, and they did their best to shield her from the queen and do small things for her. They provided her only happiness.

Snow White knew most of the servants, but such was the queen's power, that she could change them or control them somehow. Their personalities would change or get overridden or something. They became obedient and unexpressive. Snow White hated seeing them changed like that. She wondered what the queen made them do that required that state.

One day, Snow White tried to hide in the kitchen gardens. She had been sitting on a bench reading a book, when a figure loomed in front of her. She went rigid with panic until she looked up and saw it was Anthony, the huntsman. He had always been kind to her. She smiled at him, but he just stared at her, no recognition showing on his features. Her panic returned. He reached for her arm, and she flinched away from him. She backed away, but he grabbed her and pulled her against his body. He was huge, in comparison, and muscular. He was twenty and fully developed, and she was seventeen, nearly eighteen, and petite. She begged him to let her go, but he didn't or couldn't acknowledge her. He dragged her into the castle; she knew where he was taking her without being told. The queen was waiting for them impatiently.

"Take her to the woods and kill her!" she shrieked. The huntsman nodded obediently and dragged Snow White out of the room. "Bring me her heart!" the queen yelled after them.

The corridors were deserted as the huntsman forced Snow White before him—it was as if anyone who cared about her couldn't bear to see her walk to her death, and yet all she wanted was to see one sympathetic face, someone who cared about her and would miss her. Without anyone, not even the huntsman, acknowledging her, she felt utterly insignificant, as if her life had never and would never have any meaning. She wept, but he drove her forward. They entered the woods. Snow White started talking again, reminding him about her parents, telling him about her childhood, describing all her memories of him. It was as if as long as she talked, he would keep walking, driving them forward. She begged once more for her life or for him to let her go. Finally, she had run out of things to tell him, and he stopped. He loosened his knife and grabbed her wrist, but instead of fighting him, she knelt on the ground before him, resigned to her fate. He stared at her and blinked. He shook his head in disbelief and stepped away from her. "Snow White," he whispered, his face becoming ashen. He sheathed the knife.

"Run, Snow White," he said, and she scrambled to her feet and ran away from him. She heard him take off in a different direction. Clearly, he was not returning to the castle or the queen. She thought for a moment of going with him, but she realized that the queen would hunt both of them now, and two paths would divert the guards the queen sent after them. He was providing them with a distraction, and she hurried on gratefully.

It was frightening in the woods alone, but this was what she had wanted for so long. She found trees to sleep in so as not be exposed to predators at night while she slept. She found wild berries and dandelion leaves and flowers to eat and fresh water easily enough, but she was very hungry. Still she pushed on into the woods. She didn't know what she was looking for, but she kept going.

After about a week, she saw a small plume of smoke and followed it to a small cottage. She knocked on the cottage door, unsure of what she would find. A beautiful blond-haired young woman about her own age, opened the door with a look of surprise on her face. Snow White knew that she looked a mess, her clothes were dirty and tattered from getting caught on branches.

"I am sorry," she said haltingly. "I have nowhere else to go. I…I…was hoping to find shelter here. If…if…you…don't mind?" she finished lamely.

The young woman looked her over, and her surprise changed to concern. She held out her hand to help Snow White into the cottage and called over her shoulder, "Aunts, we have company." Snow White felt herself go weak in the knees, and she leaned on the young woman gratefully. The young woman steered her to the nearest chair. Seeing Snow White safely seated, the young woman turned and got her a glass of cool water. Handing her the water, the young woman introduced herself. "I am Aurora," she said softly. Snow White closed her eyes, savoring the cool water, and when she opened them, she nearly choked in surprise, floating on one side of Aurora were three small fairies. They couldn't be anything else. "These are the aunts, Nancy, Pansy, and Lavender," Aurora said by way of explanation.

"Who are you and what are you doing here?" the tallest fairy, Nancy, asked kindly. Aurora left the room and came back with a plate of bread, a small bowl of butter, and a knife. She put these on a small table which she placed in front of Snow White.

"I am Snow White," she answered. "The queen tried to have the huntsman kill me in the woods, but he let me go. I can't go back." She started crying then. When she had been struggling in the woods, her survival had been all she had allowed herself to think about, but here, in a place of shelter, her near miss with death overwhelmed her.

"Aunt Nancy, look what you have done to the poor thing," Aurora said reproachfully. "She is more than half starved and scared out of her mind. Let her be until she has eaten something." Then Aurora pulled up a chair and put her arms around Snow White, patting her hair and stroking her back. It felt so good to be held tenderly that Snow White cried a little harder for a moment, and then started to try and calm herself. Snow White sat up and dried her tears on her sleeve. Aurora broke of a piece of bread, buttered it, and handed it to her. Snow White ate gratefully, and Pansy, the short fairy, had a mug of hot cider float its way across the room to her. Snow White ate two more big pieces of bread and drank all of the cider. It felt wonderful to have the filling bread and the hot liquid in her belly.

Snow White then told them everything about what her life had been like before her parents had died and the queen had arrived and taken the throne. She tried to describe the dark magic the queen used. Her descriptions made the aunts cast nervous looks at each other. When she had told them everything, Aurora told her their story. They too were hiding from the evil queen. It was decided that Snow White would live with them. Aurora was lonely anyway. The aunts were company, but they weren't human, and they weren't Aurora's age.

The young women did everything together. They searched for mushrooms, fished and set nets and snares to catch fish, rabbits and small game in the woods. They explored the woods together. They told each other everything, did the wash together, bathed together. They were such contrasts. Aurora was tall and slender with her long, curling blond hair and bright, crystal blue eyes. Snow White was smaller and fuller with long jet-black hair, red full lips, and dark blue eyes.

They explored each other too—touching, kissing, embracing, touching more, kissing more, gently biting, licking, sucking, nibbling. The combination of nipple and clitoral stimulation brought them to sexual nirvana, and that they could do it again and again was a marvel to them. So, the aunts had each other, and Snow White and Sleeping Beauty had each other. Aurora's nick name was Sleeping Beauty from when she was a child and the aunts watched her nap and sleep, fascinated that someone could require so much sleep.

As the young women became more attached, Aurora grew slightly troubled in her heart. She knew her parents expected her to return in about a year, and expected her to marry the young man she had been betrothed to since infancy. But she loved Snow White and couldn't imagine being separated from her.

Then, one day, they all felt oddly jumpy. The last few days had held a funny sense of foreboding, something the fairies and the young women refused to acknowledge or put into words, lest it come true.

They heard someone coming through the woods. Panicked, they barricaded themselves in the cottage. A male voice called out to them, saying something, but it was obscured by the aunts bickering with each other, arguing on what spells to use, yelling when the spells went wrong, and blaming each other for being so out of practice with offensive and defensive spells.

Finally, the voice called out again, and they all froze when it addressed Snow White directly.

"Snow White, look at me! I am the huntsman. Do you not remember me? The queen, do you hear me, the queen, is coming! We can get you away, but you must stop this nonsense and let us help you!"

It was the huntsman; Snow White could see him. It was Anthony. She opened the door with Aurora holding her hand tightly in support, the fairies hovering around them.

Nancy demanded an explanation for his presence and the beast he traveled with, and Anthony explained it all. How the evil queen had held him in her power so that he nearly killed Snow White, letting Snow White go, finding the castle, who and what Christopher was, coming to know Christopher and his kindness, the warning from the mirror, the queen and the three red-eyed wolves, their hasty journey to reach them, and the necessity to leave.

The fairies had everything sorted in minutes. Pansy brought a squirming squirrel forward, and Nancy turned it into a pretty gray mare. Pansy named it Molly and outfitted the beast with a bridle and saddle. Then they had the young women mount Molly, and they all set off with the fairies flying protectively around Snow White and Aurora.

Anthony and the young women rode, Anthony on a fine chestnut stallion, and Christopher ran. At dusk, they made camp. The beast, or Christopher, as Anthony called him, tried to take the first watch, but the fairies sent him off to bed with the rest of them. Snow White curled up with Aurora like they always did without thinking about it, and fell asleep. Sometime in the night, Snow White woke to a flash of lights. At first, she was alarmed, but she heard the fairy voices and realized they were practicing—not wanting to repeat their misadventures with Anthony and Christopher when faced with the much more menacing threat of the evil queen. She snuggled against Aurora and fell back to sleep.

The young people woke the next day to find that the fairies, apparently pleased with themselves, had conjured a magnificent breakfast. They ate quickly and were moving again. They traveled all the next day until dusk again, stopping only to water the horses. The fairies conjured them a tasty dinner and then sent them to bed.

The girls were woken by the fairies before dawn, and Snow White could feel the queen's malice radiating around them. They all could, she realized from their tense expressions. The queen had found the abandoned cottage and sought them. Snow White trembled, and Aurora tried to assure her—but Aurora was scared too.

Anthony and the young women mounted the horses, and they were off again. When they came to a large clearing, Christopher and Anthony had them stop. At the far-side of the clearing, Anthony led the horses into the shade of the trees and bade them stay, but he did not tether them. He had Snow White and Aurora stand by the trees with the fairies hovering protectively. If it went badly, the young women were to flee on the horses. Christopher and Anthony stood together in front of the young women, and they all waited.

Finally, the queen walked out of the trees opposite them. Three red-eyed wolves followed her, and they all gasped. Snow White watched as the queen leered at Anthony, and she felt a defensive surge for this young man who was risking his life for her, for them. The queen's gaze shifted to Christopher, and Snow White saw the dismissive way she looked at him—which she questioned, re-assessing Christopher again herself.

The queen said something in that language of dark magic, and the wolves stepped forward, transforming as they did into wolf-men. Snow White and Aurora and the fairies all gasped, and Christopher and Anthony stiffened. Anthony raised his bow and shot at them. Every arrow, Snow White was impressed to see, hit one of the wolf-men, but the arrows did not halt their advance. Snow White felt her skin break out in goose bumps. What were those things, she thought? What had the queen done? Snow White heard Christopher growl and then saw him launch himself forward to attack the wolf-men. Anthony screamed in protest and shot the last of his arrows. Heedless of six to nine arrows protruding from them, the wolf-men met Christopher. He slashed at them with his massive claws, and Snow White watched in horror as the flesh of the wolf-men was ripped open in gashes—with no effect. There was no blood, and the wolf-men did not fall as a result of these new wounds.

Snow White was suddenly aware of the three fairies holding hands and casting twin spells. The air reverberated suddenly in front of her and Aurora and two flaming swords appeared in front of the startled young women.

"Take the swords, girls," the fairies said firmly. "Their flames will cut down the wolf-men. Go quickly! Before it is too late," urging them forward.

Snow White and Aurora then heard Christopher's cries of pain, and seizing the blazing swords, they ran forward, their skirts, under fairy influence, conveniently shortening to ease their movement. Snow White was afraid that the sword would be heavy and clumsy in her hands, but it felt remarkably light— almost like an extension of her hand. She moved it easily, testing it, and she saw out of the corner of her eye, Aurora doing the same. Christopher cried again, and suddenly the young women were there. Snow White brought her sword down without thinking. It sliced off the arm of one of the wolf-men. Aurora was engaged with another of the creatures, Snow White was vaguely aware. Snow White stabbed at the one still attacking Christopher, but then had to hack at her one-armed assailant, taking off his other arm and his head. Unbelievably it still stood, armless and headless, staggering around. Snow White saw that Aurora had cut hers to pieces—just as the fairies had said, she thought stupidly—legs as well as arms and head. Aurora had moved on to the one harassing Christopher. Snow White helped Aurora cut the wolf-man to pieces before returning to her original assailant and cutting off his legs. She heard the queen shriek in rage. She saw Anthony reach Christopher and rip his shirt off to tend to Christopher's wounds.

The queen began to speak again, and Snow White saw the fairies holding hands again in front of Anthony's horse, casting a spell, and quickly breaking apart. The air was reverberating again. The horse made a shocked kind of sound, and then it was growing, writhing, twisting, changing, and shooting up to an enormous size. Snow White stepped back in shock, with Aurora beside her, equally shocked. Horse no longer, the dragon stretched, spreading his wings and cocking his head, Fire shot out of his mouth, engulfing the queen in flames before she could finish her incantation. Snow White watched in mingled fascination and horror as the queen was consumed in the flames. The dragon roared in triumph.

As Snow White's shock began to fade, she felt her adrenaline level crash, and she felt suddenly weak-kneed and sick to her stomach. Aurora touched her hand, and both young women looked at the gore splattered on themselves from the unnatural flesh. The swords were burned clean, and somehow Snow White wished she could be burned clean of the carnage she had committed, too. The fairies took the swords from them, and Snow White threw up. As her retching eased, Snow White realized that Aurora was sick beside her. The fairies hovered near them. Lavender produced cups of cool water scented with mint. "Wash out your mouths, girls, and spit it out. Then drink some of the water slowly," she admonished them.

The water cleaned the sickness out of Snow White's mouth. She took only a few sips of it before the cup disappeared. Snow White looked up to find Nancy looking over the young women, with an expression of deepest sympathy.

"It is a horrible thing to kill another of one's own kind, even ones such as those," she said waving in the direction of the corpses. "Killing damages the soul. We cannot lighten that burden for you; it would not be right to do so. You must make your peace with it, but you had little other choice. You had to kill them or be killed, and let others die at their hands, or paws, in this case." She smiled a weak smile. "We should see if we can help the boys," Nancy said to the other fairies, and they all turned to join Anthony and Christopher.

Snow White went pale looking at Christopher. He was struggling to sit up. He was badly wounded, and she wondered if he would die. She felt Aurora take her hand, and Snow White gently squeezed the other young woman's hand. Snow White watched wide-eyed as Christopher caressed Anthony's face in what was clearly a tender gesture. Christopher told Anthony how much he loved him, and Anthony was angry at first, but then admitted he loved Christopher too. Snow White looked at Aurora, both exchanging glances of surprise and relief. Then the air changed, followed by a popping sound.

A beautiful, dazzling fairy appeared in a burst of white light.

She was dressed in silver and pearl and pale flashing opal, and seemed bigger than the other fairies. Snow White glanced at Aurora, but it was clear that Aurora had never seen this fairy, from the look on her face. The fairies, however, had bowed their heads toward what Snow White realized belatedly must be a fairy queen. Aurora came to the same conclusion, and both quickly bowed their heads.

Christopher and the fairy queen seemed to know each other. She bowed to him, and he shook his head with a sad smile. Snow White realized that Christopher thought he was going to die and was preparing himself. She felt tears sting in her eyes, but the fairy queen was chastising Christopher's lack of faith. She bent and kissed his forehead—and Christopher began to change. He shrank in size, his wounds disappeared, his fur fell away—revealing smooth, brown skin—his claws disappeared, his face transformed to a strikingly handsome young man's face. She gasped in surprise and heard the others gasp around her. Of course, Snow White realized, Anthony had said that Christopher had been under an enchantment, and the love between Anthony and Christopher had somehow broken it. How romantic, she thought. Aurora squeezed her hand again, apparently thinking so too. Christopher sat up, and just as his breeches threatened to fall down, they suddenly tightened to fit the young man's new shape, and Snow White heard the fairies snicker quietly. Anthony helped Christopher to his feet.

The fairy queen stepped back and surveyed them all. "You have all done well," she said. "The future is what you will make of it," she added. Then, she stood before each of the other young people and kissed each one. She turned to the dragon, who shook his head and spoke, much to Snow White's surprise. He told the queen he wanted to remain a dragon, and asked to be permitted to watch over Christopher and Anthony. The fairy queen called him Merlin—and Snow White wondered briefly at just how many forms Merlin might have had, but she was distracted from these thoughts by the mark the kiss of the fairy queen had left on the dragon's forehead. Her hand instantly went to her own forehead, and she saw the other young people reaching for their own. They must all be marked—even if they couldn't see or feel it. The fairy queen then turned to the gray mare who was nodding her head eagerly. With a pang of regret, Snow White watched as the fairy queen kissed the horse and transformed her back into a squirrel, who scampered happily back into the woods. Lastly, she turned and acknowledged her sister fairies.

The fairy queen faced them all and bowed again. "I take my leave of you. Make the world a better place, love and stand by each other," she commanded them. Snow White bowed her head to accept the command and acknowledge it, and she realized that the others were doing the same. In a burst of sparkling air, the fairy queen was gone, and they were alone in the clearing.

Anthony, holding Christopher's hand and radiating pure joy and relief, turned to Snow White, Aurora, and the fairies. "Thank you," he said, his voice charged with emotion. "Thank you for saving Christopher."

Snow White was caught off guard, so apparently was Aurora. The two young women shook their heads in befuddlement. "We…didn't…we…there wasn't any other choice," Snow White said, falling back on the words Nancy had said to them.

"And it wasn't just for Christopher," Aurora added.

"And it wasn't the girls or us who healed Christopher's wounds," Nancy said in a firm voice.

Christopher smiled at them, "We are grateful, nevertheless," he said, bursting with the same kindred joy and happiness as his boyfriend.

"What happens now?" Aurora asked.

"I don't know," Christopher said slowly. "If the enchantment is truly broken, life at the castle has been restored. You, ladies, would be most welcome guests," he said bowing his head in invitation.

The fairies fluttered at that, but Snow White realized they were deliberately not saying anything—allowing the young women to decide what they wanted to do. Aurora and Snow White looked at each other consideringly. No, they wanted time alone still. They wanted time to figure out how to present themselves to Aurora's parents—especially now that Anthony and Christopher had shown them an example of a same-sexed couple, for clearly having faced death, the two young men would not be parted from each other by mere conventional dictates of heterosexual coupling. If it could work for the young men, surely it could work for the young women. Snow White smiled a sly smile, watching a similar train of thought play itself across Aurora's face.

"No," Snow White said slowly. "Thank you for the invitation, but I think we want to return to the cottage." Aurora smiled and nodded in agreement, and the fairies relaxed their anxious fluttering.

"Should we accompany you?" Anthony asked, and the young men looked at Snow White and Aurora questioningly.

"No, I think we will be fine," Aurora said, and then without thinking, she added, "I think we can take care of ourselves."

"Obviously," the young men said at the same time. Both the young women blushed a little awkwardly, and they all laughed.

Recovering himself, Christopher said, "You'll come visit, though, wouldn't you? The fairy queen said that we needed to stick together. We can only do that if we see you now and again."

"Yes, of course," Snow White answered.

Aurora added, "We might even enlist your aid with my parents." She took Snow White's hand. "They still expect me to marry my betrothed," she said, blushing faintly.

Christopher and Anthony glanced at each other, blushing slightly too. "I am not sure that we don't have some challenges in that regard ourselves," Christopher said, "but anything we can do, we would do happily."

"And you can visit us, too," Snow White added.

"Yes, we know the way," Anthony added.

The young people embraced affectionately. The young women said goodbye to Merlin, and the young men said their goodbyes to the fairies, and they parted ways until they would meet again.

It took the young women and the fairies three days to reach the cottage, but with the death of the evil queen, they felt a sense of security that none of them had felt for a very long time.

Once back at the cottage, life settled into its normal routine, and Snow White and Sleeping Beauty were very happy together.

The Troll Council and the Intersex Savior

Oh, Trollie Woellie Stones,
the Halfling-Child will come,
It/She/He will break the spell
and set you free,
so, like in the Ancient Past,
you can look after Us and Me.

THAT IS THE rhyme the women of my family whispered to us at night. It seemed like complete nonsense. What were "Trollie Woellie Stones" and what was a child that could be a "Halfling" and described as "it/she/he"? And it contrasted so strongly with the grim prayer that the Church Fathers made us all memorize:

Now I lay me down to sleep,
I pray the Lord my soul to keep.
If I should die before I wake,
I pray to God my soul to take.

Even as a child, the tones of the two rhymes seemed so different. The odd Trolls were paternal and nurturing while the Lord God was judgmental and punishing—demanding a child to beg for acceptance lest he or she be damned to hell. The juxtaposition was not lost on me. The two "prayers" seemed to represent two very different world-views or relationship-pictures of humans to their gods. And there was another contradiction, the Trolls of most stories we were told as children were brutish and grotesque, large and clumsy, violent and mean. But that was not how they were pictured in the "Trollie Woellie" rhyme; in that rhyme, they were benevolent and the guardians of human beings, and they had been cursed and turned into stones.

Granny Grace and Nanna Nancy were grooming me to be a midwife. I am Helen, and I love what I am learning, but I am often so confused. The Church Fathers are so judgmental and unforgiving. Humans sin; then they need to confess it and be punished and humiliated for their sinning. The God of the Church Fathers is an angry God, determined to hold humans to a standard that they can't, by their very natures, meet. Yet Granny and Nanna never treated people like that. They try very hard not to judge anything they see or witness. And traveling with them, my eyes were opened: pregnant too-young girls, boys and men with anal fissures, children with bruises that they shouldn't have had, and more. Sex is sinful for the Church Fathers, especially for girls and women. Sex within marriage is necessary for creating children, they said, but it shouldn't be enjoyed or engaged in too often. Sex is for procreation, not pleasure. Desire and attraction were linked to lust, one of the Seven Deadly Sins. Somehow, the soul which could control mind and bodily functions should be able to control the passions of the flesh or lusts and sexual attraction, and sexual attraction and sexual action on that attraction were wrong and sinful. It seemed a central contradiction of being a Christian: humans were sexual from birth to death, and yet sex and sexuality were sinful or associated with sin and shame. The God of the Church Fathers was a sadist, or so it seemed.

But in visiting real people, I saw that sex was a driving force in their lives. Though procreation was the aim of all sexual encounters in the views of the Church Fathers, it was clear from what I saw that sexual attraction actually drove a lot of relationships. And relations that drove them, for one reason or another (according to Granny and Nanna and scandalously to me at first) were not always between men and women of relatively the same age and sometimes not between a man and a woman at all.

Actually, Granny and Nanna, I realized, weren't two women related to each other or thrust together by circumstances; they are committed partners—in every sense of the word. They were in a relationship found evil by the Church Fathers, but I knew there was nothing evil about them; they were the most generous, giving, and charitable women I knew. They were Trollie Woellie women and worshippers of whatever gods, actually goddesses, that meant. I knew the Trollie Woellies worshiped the Great Goddess and her manifestations in the Maiden, the Mother, and the Crone—a Holy Trinity of women and their consorts (six in all)—all revering the parent/child bond as the model of god/goddess and human relations—loving, nurturing, and forgiving—such a different view from the Church Fathers and their angry sky God who judged and punished and didn't have a partner.

Granny and Nanna had been taking me with them for some time, so I could treat a child (or adult for that matter) with worms; I could help with fevers. I knew my uses of herbs, poultices, teas, salves, and even simple songs and lullabies. I had gone on birth vigils followed by the actual birth. I had set bones and stitched wounds.

We had been called to a birth in the late afternoon of the night before the full moon. Nanna was strangely elated. "Gran, Gran, I feel the Goddess! Can you?" she exclaimed.

Granny paused, seeming to read the air, if that is possible, "Yes, Nan, I feel it too. This birth—there is something...I don't know...it is different...it is special."

The family was distraught; the sisters and their girls were all there, even Sarah's wizened mother, Mother Henley. They were anxious. Sarah Bourke had been pregnant three times and miscarried each time. The worried father, Ben Bourke, was being distracted at a neighbor's house. One of the Church Fathers, Father Lucius, waited down stairs with most of the girls and Mother Henley; he sat praying in his somber robes. We were greeted warmly by Mother Henley, but Father Lucius eyed us warily, and I could feel Granny and Nanna tense and radiate a subtle outrage.

"Oh, Grace and Nancy, thank heavens you've come," the old woman said, rushing forward and hugging Granny and Nanna. "You'll see our Sarah through. Please help her."

"We'll do our best, Lizzy. We'll do our best," Nanna assured her, disengaging from the hug and looking about.

"What do you need? We have water boiling, and there are clean linens upstairs," Mother Henley said.

"Helen is helping us, now. Let her set some smaller pots to boil, so that she can make a raspberry leaf tea, and some herb infused water for soaking rags," Granny said quickly, and I was dispatched into the kitchen with a small gang of girls offering to help. "Come up with the tea and rags as soon as you can, Helen."

Granny and Nanna went up to the room. Karen, a young woman of about my own age, carried the pot of tea and a few cups while I carried a bowl with the steaming fragrant rags. I could feel the tension as soon as we were inside the room. Father Lucius had sent his sister, Marion, to attend the birth, and Granny and Nanna didn't like the woman in the room one bit. Sarah's labor was progressing, and her sisters, Camille and Sharon, sat on either side of her bed holding her hands and whispering encouragement. Marion stood awkwardly near the door.

"There, on the table, ladies," Nanna motioned to me and Karen. Karen didn't know Granny and Nanna, but she fled the room as soon as she could. "Bring a larger pot of boiling water, as soon as you can," Nanna called to the young woman's back.

"Come look, Helen," Granny called. Between Sarah's spread legs and the labia of her vagina, I could see a tiny patch of bloody woolly something, of scalp, I realized.

"Is…that…its head with hair on it?" I asked.

"That's just what it is," Granny said proudly. "Sarah, you hear that. The baby is in good position. Camille, Sharon, get her up and have her walk around the room a bit."

"Do you think that wise?" Marion said awkwardly.

Granny and Nanna both visibly bristled at this comment.

"Gravity works in our favor, Marion. The baby needs to come out, down through the birth canal. Standing and walking add pressure naturally," Nanna said tersely. "Of course, there is not a lot of room, so feel free to wait downstairs."

As if to emphasize this point, Camille knocked into Marion as she and Sharon walked about with Sarah. "Oh, excuse me; I am so sorry," she said, the lack of sincerity clear in her voice.

"Oh, no, Lucius wants me to stay," the woman said, flattening herself against the wall.

"Why?" Granny asked, a little too pointedly.

"He just does," she answered evasively.

"The Church Fathers don't trust women, so this one's sent his spy into a birthing room," Sharon spat.

"I am not a spy," Marion said indignantly.

"Then, why are you here?" Camille asked.

"To observe," she answered.

"To observe us," Nanna said softly to Granny and me. "To see that we follow the teachings of the Church Fathers in a birthing situation—in terms of the mother and the child and their sin or lack of sin."

"You, witch! How dare you try to judge me or my child!" Sarah exploded at the woman. "Open the door, Camille!" Camille obeyed her sister, moving away from her and opening the door. "Get out, Marion! Mother, get this woman out of here!" Sarah screamed into the hall way. Mortified, Marion fled the room.

"Camille, perhaps you or Sharon should go down and explain to your mother. Helen can help with Sarah in your absence," Gran suggested.

"I'll go," Sharon said, letting me take her place. She shut the door behind her, and we easily ignored the angry voices that spoke from below as Sarah worked through a contraction. A little later, Sharon returned with the large pot of very hot water. Nanna put the knives and other instruments into the water to sterilize them. Sharon recounted the scenes she witnessed of her outraged mother screaming at Father Lucius for daring to insult the best mid-wives around and for putting her daughter and the unborn child in danger and distress. She did a great impression of the blustering Father Lucius trying to explain how he was protecting their souls from pagan influences.

"You know he'll succeed, in the end?" Nanna said gravelly. "Men will eventually control birth with horrible consequences for women and their children until women are able to take it back again."

"But why do they want to encroach on things that women have always tended themselves?" Camille asked both bewildered and suspicious.

"Power and control," Granny answered grimly. "They can't bear that women retain power in this realm—it smacks of the 'pagan' influence of the Great Goddess and her priestesses. Midwives, to the Church Fathers, are linked to those ancient priestesses by their extensive knowledge of myth and medical lore."

"Oh, Trollie, Woellie Stones," Sharon sang out mockingly.

"Laugh if you want, but the Church Fathers have begun punishing people for knowing the song and teaching it to children and any of the related stories," Nanna countered.

Sarah screamed, and Nanna and Granny had Camille and Sharon lay her down again. Much more of the baby's head was visible now. The contractions quickened and became more regular. The birth progressed with the head, then the shoulders, and then the baby was out. Granny had gotten a sterilized knife out from the water and severed the umbilical cord. The baby started crying, and Nanna worked at cleaning it off and wrapping it.

"What is it?" Sarah asked weakly.

"Life, Sarah, is a great mystery. You understand that, don't you?" Nanna said softly with an intense excitement quivering in her voice. I looked at her, trying to understand what she meant. Sarah nodded obediently. "Let's all take a look," Nanna said, laying the little infant on Sarah's lap. Sarah was sitting propped up on pillows, but she unwrapped the baby and stared. Sharon gasped and crossed herself.

"Don't do that, Sharon," said Granny with a quiet authority. "The God of the Church Fathers has no place for such a child. Only the Great Goddess, in her mercy and love, sees this is an opportunity—a crossing or a merging."

As I stared at the infant who seemed to have both a scrotum and a vagina, the words from the song flew into my head: "Oh, Trollie Woellie Stones/the Halfling-Child will come/It, She, He will break the spell/and set you free," I recited under my breath. In the dead silence that filled the room, they all heard me, and I blushed. Granny and Nanna looked oddly satisfied and even slightly triumphant.

"But, what do we do?" Sarah asked, panic climbing into her voice.

"We pick a name and raise the child as best we can," Camille answered.

"We wanted Tom for a boy, and Rose for a girl. But what do we do now?"

As if in answer, the strangest thing happened. A small kaleidoscope of butterflies flew in the window. Odder still, almost all of them landed themselves on the bed around Sarah and the baby. They were Eclipse butterflies, the males yellow (like the sun) with streaks of black (eclipse) and the females (the eclipsed sun) black-ish in that iridescent way many insects could show color, six in total, three yellow and three black. Once they were settled, we all looked up to see the final butterfly settle on the open blanket of the sleeping infant. It was neither yellow nor black; it was both—one wing, yellow flecked with black, and the other, black flecked with yellow.

"What does it mean?" I blurted out, astonished at this display.

"It is a sign, Helen. Explain it to them," Granny prompted me.

I felt them all looking at me and blushed. "Butterflies are a symbol of the Great Goddess," I struggled to explain. "Their transformations from caterpillar to chrysalis to butterfly are powerful symbols of regeneration and rebirth. Three females are accompanied by three males like the Maid, the Maiden, and the Crone and their consorts. Really, really rare is the single butterfly; it is both male and female. I have never seen one before. These are signs from the Great Goddess, and not just ordinary signs, the single butterfly mirrors the child."

As soon as the words were out of my mouth, the butterflies took flight. They circled the room and then flew out the window, leaving us all in an awed and confused silence.

"Do you believe that?" Sharon asked, staring from me to Granny and Nanna.

"Yes," Nanna answered firmly. "But the child is in great danger. If Father Lucius was to find out, he would want the child killed."

"Killed?" Sarah whispered, wrapping up the child in its blankets and hugging the baby to her.

"How do we protect it?" Camille answered, laying her hand on Sarah's shoulder.

"Name it a girl's name," Granny suggested.

"Why a girl's name?" Sharon asked.

"To keep the father at a distance," I said, as the logic of it settled on me.

"But later, what if that is wrong?" Sarah asked. "What if the girl grows up and is more like a boy?"

"We can cross that bridge when we get to it," Nanna answered. "You could always move and start over somewhere else with a son instead of a daughter. If you were careful, who would have to know?"

"This is dangerous," Sharon said ominously.

"Yes, absolutely; this is dangerous. We are the only ones who know, me, Helen, Nanna, Sarah, Camille, and you, Sharon," Granny said quietly. "Sarah, what is the child's name?"

"Rose," Sarah answered and kissed the baby's head, "my sweet Rose," she murmured.

"Swear by the Great Goddess and on Sarah's life that you will protect Rose now and always," Granny commanded, and she had each of us swear the oath. That finished, we busied ourselves cleaning up the birthing things. Camille and Sharon and I took pots and things back down to the kitchen, and Mother Henley was allowed up to see her daughter and new grand-daughter. When the time came, we left and returned to our cottage. We came to check on Rose every once in a while. Sarah and her sisters kept the secret well. Mother Henley came to know and so did Ben, Sarah's husband. But Rose was such a happy and sweet child that they loved her more than life and kept Rose's special qualities a careful secret.

As Rose grew though, other special qualities became apparent. Rose loved the woods. She loved to wander in them and to listen to them—to all the wondrous noises that animals and creatures made in the woods. However, this was not standard girl behavior. But before the Church Fathers could condemn Rose's wanderings, Camille had her son, Danny, and Sharon had her daughter, Lena, accompany their cousin on her wanderings. So, the three children would venture into the woods, and when they were comfortably away from the eyes of others, Danny and Lena would hang back and let Rose lose herself in the magic she seemed to find in the woods.

"I don't know how to explain it, Mother," Lena had tried to explain to Sharon. "The woods are a part of her. She reads the woods, its creatures. She can make things happen."

"Make things happen?" Sharon said skeptically.

"She had some of the fawns come over to us the other day," Lena said breathlessly. "They were so beautiful and sweet. Delicate. They let us touch them and pet them, and then Rose released them and they bounded away. It was like magic."

"Hush, Lena. You can't talk like that. You know how the Church Fathers are," Sharon said crossly.

"Yes, I know. They are frightened little men who have more power than is good for them. They are narrow-minded and would only feel threatened by Rose's gifts, but Rose is special. I don't know how to explain," Lena added.

"She is special. More special than you know. Protect her,

Lena, for me and for your Aunt Sarah."

"Of course, Mother." After a slight pause, Lena said, "You know she makes me think of that lullaby, 'Oh Trollie, Woellie Stones.'"

"Yes, she does, but let's keep that between ourselves," Sharon warned.

Granny, Nanna, and I kept Rose on our minds. We checked in with Sharon and Camille and Sarah. From Camille and Sharon, we heard things about Rose's gifts. We were all nine years older, and Granny and Nanna sent me to assess Rose. I found her in the woods, Lena and Danny hovering just in case any assistance was needed. As I neared, Rose turned and smiled at me.

"Good Day, Helen. I hope you are well," she said sweetly.

"I am well, Rose. How are you?" I asked companionably.

"I am fine, Helen," she answered, a smile playing on her lips. "You want to see what I can do?" The smile changed to a smirk, and mischief sparkled in her eyes. "Let's look for truffles, shall we?"

I didn't understand; it was a challenge, that much I knew. I watched as Danny and Lena seemed to tense, and then to my astonishment and horror, a wild boar stepped through the undergrowth. I gasped.

"Don't be alarmed, sweet Helen; she will help us," said Rose. And miraculously the wild boar didn't charge us or act threateningly. It grunted encouragingly and started sniffing determinedly. It rooted through the forest and brought us to a particular stand of old trees, where it started digging and then stopped and backed off. Rose bent down and ran her hands through the disturbed soil, pulling up a few truffles. Danny and Lena stepped up and began collecting them with pleasure. Rose handed me one, and I smiled as I smelled at the earthy, heady scent. The Grands, Granny and Nanna, would be pleased. Before I realized it, the boar was gone. Danny saw me looking around for the boar and smiled.

"I am not really sure how she does it. She calls them somehow, and they just come, and when she releases them, they leave," he explained, shrugging at the vague explanation.

"Do you forage often?" I asked, pointing to the basket he held teaming with truffles.

"Often, but not always. Sometimes its mushrooms…"

"The chanterelles are my favorites," Lena interrupted, joining us.

"But other times its herbs or berries, and sometimes it's nothing at all," he continued.

"And she likes the stones," Lena added softly.

"The Standing Stones?" I asked, an unanticipated excitement surprising me.

Danny and Lena nodded mutely. The Church Fathers said the Standing Stones were pagan and used in devil worship. Few people really believed that. The old ways had nothing to do with devil worship. The Great Goddess and the Standing Stones were harvest and fertility centered. The people of the valley mostly tolerated the Church Fathers and their talk, but most believed in something more and found comfort in the old tales and the "Trollie Woellie" rhyme, so though they hid their knowledge of the old ways from the Church Fathers, most were not committed converts to Church ways. Danny and Lena were being careful, for their own sakes and for Rose's.

"The Stones are special," Rose said, suddenly right beside us. Her face was serious and contemplative at the same time. "They're sad and yet powerful. They call to me. There's something I have to figure out, but I am not sure what it is," and there was a heart-breaking regret in her voice. "Perhaps we can go tomorrow. Would you like to go, Helen?" she asked, turning to look at me.

"Yes, Rose. I would like that," I answered with genuine enthusiasm.

"You'll need gifts. Look for things tomorrow, a pretty leaf or flower, a bright stone, a bird's feather, a bit of string or ribbon. You know, a token," she tried to explain.

I nodded, and Rose seemed content with that, and we walked back to the village. Danny and Lena talked idly, engaging me now and then in conversation, but Rose said no more, lost in her own thoughts or listening to the woods. At Camille's, Danny divvied up the truffles, the children insisting that I get an even fourth to take home to the Grands.

At home in our cottage, the Grands asked me all sorts of questions about the day. I did the best I could to describe the odd aura that seemed to surround Rose and her intense listening to the world around her, but what interested them the most was the Standing Stones.

"Gifts? What kind of gifts are you to bring?" Granny asked.

As I explained what Rose had said, Nanna smiled, "Tokens...this is old magic, Grace, ways of the Great Goddess," her voice charged with excitement.

Granny looked at Nanna in surprise, "She's nine, right? Helen, Rose is nine?"

"Yes, nine," I answered, sensing the excitement radiating from them, but not understanding. "What is it?"

"It's months away, Grace," Nanna said soothingly.

"Yes, but the child is struggling to figure out her role. We can help. She has to be the one!" Granny said in a rush.

"I don't understand," I said.

"The rhyme, the Standing Stones, Samhain, Rose—the Halfling-child, nine years old (three times three)—the time to break the spell is coming," Nanna said softly.

"The spell?" I repeated stupidly. The words of the rhyme rushed through my head ("Oh, Trollie Woellie Stones/ the Halfling-Child will come,/ It, She, He will break the spell/ and set you free,/ so like in the Ancient Past,/ you can look after Us and Me"). "Rose?" I asked. "This is real? You think this can actually happen? The stones come back to life. The stones as Trolls?"

I looked between them frantically.

"Helen, it is okay. It is old magic. Magic that hasn't been

seen or felt in a long time, but the time is coming," Granny said trying to re-assure me. I wasn't convinced, but we let the matter drop. We ate a lovely meal of scrambled eggs with fresh truffle shavings. I went to bed confused and excited, but all the activity of the day weighed on me, and I fell into a deep sleep.

I woke at dawn and went to do my chores around the cottage farm. I gathered eggs and fed the chickens. I fed and milked the goats and brought a pitcher of the milk into the kitchen. I picked some squash and herbs and left those in the kitchen too. Along the way, I found two Cardinal feathers, two pieces of clear quartz, and some pretty bluebells. Granny and Nanna had a breakfast of portage and goats' milk waiting for me. We ate together. As I prepared to go to meet Rose, Danny, and Lena, I was surprised to find Granny and Nanna getting ready to leave too.

"Are you coming with me?" I asked.

"No, we are going straight to the stones. We'll talk to Rose there," Nanna answered, and I remembered their excited bits of conversation from the night before about helping and Samhain or Halloween. It was June; there were literally four months until October.

"Why Halloween?" I asked.

"The Feast of the Dead has magic and power. If Rose can tap into that, and channel her own power, that could do it!" Granny answered happily.

"Much remains to be seen, Grace. Let's not get ahead of ourselves," Nanna said quietly.

I had the distinct feeling that this was only the beginning, so I went on my way with my gifts wrapped in a piece of yellow cloth. The children were waiting for me outside Sarah's cottage. As we walked, we picked up more gifts, some dandelion flowers and some wild roses. Danny found a few reddish rocks. Lena and Danny talked politely, allowing me to join their conversation as I wished. Rose seemed lost in her own thoughts. The stones were at the top of Gaia's Mound. It wasn't terribly steep, but conversation died as we labored up the slope. At the summit, we paused to take in the majesty of the circle of towering stones. Then, Danny, Lena, and I hung back, as Rose wandered among the stones. She was murmuring to them or chanting.

"What does she say to them?" I asked.

"We don't know," Lena answered. "She doesn't answer many questions about what she does or feels. We accompany her, but we don't pry. Rose is just special."

I nodded, and I felt a great surge of affection toward Danny and Lena. I wasn't sure if they knew what I knew about Rose's physical anatomy. But it was more than just that. Rose was different—she saw and interacted with the world differently. In some places and with some people, that would cause untold pain and humiliation for someone like Rose—bullied, picked on, made fun of, even beaten up. But Danny and Lena just loved their cousin. Though Rose was different and did things they didn't understand, they just offered her their love and support. It was beautiful. I thanked the Great Goddess, not for the first time, that we had managed to get the awful woman, Marion, out of the birthing room before Rose was born. What the Church Fathers would do with someone like Rose I shuddered to think.

Rose had wandered around the ring of stones, but now she had turned to us and was calling. "Do you have your gifts?" she asked.

I had more flowers in my hand, but I reached for the bundle of fabric and stepped forward. Rose looked over our offerings and regrouped them into twelve relatively equal piles.

"Take one each, and place it at the base of a stone. While you place it, sing the 'Trollie Woellie' rhyme," she instructed.

There were the four of us, so we each placed three. There was something particularly moving about placing the offerings and saying the prayer. I found myself watching Rose in particular as she set down her offerings. She touched the stones—one hand extended at her full height and then letting that hand trail down the stone as she knelt to place the offering with the other hand. It seemed intimate or personal in a way that I couldn't explain.

Though I knew the Grands intended to be there, it surprised me when they stepped into the circle of stones when we were done. Danny and Lena were also surprised. If Rose was surprised, it didn't show. On the contrary, she knelt before the Grands, tears streaming down her cheeks.

"You can help me, Granny Grace and Nanna Nancy? You can help them? Please," she cried in a pleading set of questions.

Alarmed, Danny and Lena both cried their cousin's name, "Rose!" and moved toward her.

Nanna held out one arm in protest. "Children, do not be alarmed," she said to Danny and Lena.

Granny had walked to Rose and pulled her to her feet, "Yes, my darling Rose, we can help. Don't cry, my child; they will be free soon," Granny told her. "Tell us what you feel or hear from the stones," she demanded.

Rose reflected for a moment and then said, "They are trapped in the stones. They feel sorrow and loss. They need us; they need to protect us, to watch over us. The sorcerers betrayed them and separated us. I feel their pain, their sorrow, and I ache for the connection that they long for as well," she answered, her voice quivering with emotion.

Danny turned to me, "You mean this is real—all of it—the Trolls in the stones—Rose as the Halfling—magic?" his voice spiking at different points.

Lena and Danny looked at me. I struggled to answer them. I fell back on words the Grands had used, "Life is mysterious, and we can't know the design or the why. There are obvious divisions, but mergers too, that confuse us. There is no absolute reading of the world as just black and white—there are many blacks and many whites and all the greys in between—and that is just a black and white palette—imagine how complicated it gets in the multifaceted rainbow—five different yellows or a thousand—and then for every color in the rainbow. We think of gender as binary (male/female)—but maybe it isn't—maybe there are a lot of in-betweens like Rose."

"But Rose is the only one we know who is…different," Lena said.

"Have you even paid attention? Have you looked beyond what you expect?" I cried, surprised at my own emotion on the subject.

Danny and Lena looked alarmed at first, but they seemed to pause and think on the demands.

"Sam and Harry," Danny said quietly.

"Melissa and Meredith," said Lena, "and Granny Grace and Nanna Nancy," she whispered.

I nodded. "You won't tell?" I asked.

"Of course not," they said in unison. "You've never told about Rose."

So, it was agreed, Rose and her companions would come to us at least once week after lunch for instruction in the folklore of the old ways. They knew sketches of it from their mothers, but Granny and Nanna knew the stories in detail. Since one could work with his or her hands and listen at the same time, we were all set to indoor work at these sessions. The tasks varied from preparing herbs and poultices and such, to carding wool, spinning, knitting, or weaving. While we worked, the Grands told us stories about the Great Goddess and the old ways where the Maiden, the Mother, and the Crone represented the Great Goddess in their rituals. Being mortal women, they were accompanied by their male consorts, the Lad, the Father, and the Sage. In the traditions of the Great Goddess, all life was a sacred, interconnected web with the Great Goddess at the center—the great spider spinning and connecting all the strands of the sacred web. She was both the giver of live and the bestower of death—mighty and terrible, beautiful and revolting, warmth and coldness, harbor and tempest, harvest and famine. The ways of the Great Goddess were mysterious—and that was not frightening nor bad. Thus, many rituals involved darkness (dusk/dawn/caves)—places were the rituals' magic and mystery could be enhanced and celebrated. Faith in the Great Goddess, in her human manifestations, in the community, and in the great web of life were more important than "knowing" or "seeing" in an absolute way. Dark was not evil, nor was the light. Both were tools of the Great Goddess. The dynamism of the Great Goddess centered on her powers over life. And creating life, at least for mortal, living things, involved sexual expression from flowers and the birds and the bees, to the fish in the seas and the animals of the land to human beings. For humans, sexual expression was both absolutely common and mundane and yet could also be profoundly sacred and holy. For humans, sexual expression was about pleasure whether self-pleasuring to partnered-pleasuring, and humans were sexual from birth to death. Puberty was the marker of fertility—the possibility of being capable of procreation.

As I listened, I thought about how it was such a different way of thinking about human relationships than what the Church Fathers claimed (with sexuality and sexual pleasure as sinful). I also thought about our real-life travels as healers and mid-wives and how sexuality (repressed under the teachings of the Church Fathers or not) seemed to too often drive human actions and human abuses of other humans. What the Grands were telling us made sense to me on a fundamental level, and yet Father Lucius and his brethren held influence and would never reconcile themselves to the sinless sexuality of the Great Goddess. But maybe the time of Church Fathers was coming to an end—if the stones really woke or were brought back to life.

"The Church Fathers would be outraged by such notions," Danny said, struggling to take in what the Grands were telling us and finding it just as at odds with the Church Fathers' teachings as I was finding it.

"Absolutely, they are outraged," Nanna said, agreeing. "That's why they suppress the stories and have started punishing people for saying the 'Trollie Woellie' rhyme. But our people, the people of the Lower Valley, they ache for the old ways. They hide our stories and now the rhyme from the Church Fathers, but they aren't ardent followers of the Church."

"How do you know?" I asked, for it seemed to me that we were about to engage in direct conflict with the Church Fathers. If the stones really turned into Trolls, the two religions, that of the Great Goddess with her Troll guardians of human beings and that of the Church Fathers with their angry, punitive God, would oppose each other.

Granny smiled at me in that knowing way. "Very good, Helen. You see the danger. The matriarchs have been sending us messages. The Church Fathers seek to subjugate women, and to some men, that is very attractive. But the people of the Lower Valley are an old people and they are proud of their strong and fierce women. The matriarchs know Samhain is coming; they know what is at stake, and they stand with us."

"What will happen on Samhain?" Lena asked.

"We will attempt an old ceremony of rebirth and see what happens," Nanna said very softly.

"And the stones?" Danny asked.

"They will return to us," Rose said, with a conviction that surprised us and closed the conversation. Granny and Nanna continued telling some of the stories until it was close to dinner time, and then Rose, Danny, and Lena left us until the next week.

The days flew by. The seasons began to change. The heat of summer was mixed with brisk mornings and chill breezes. The squirrels were struck with their seasonal insanity, frantically gathering nuts and burying them. The flocks of geese and ducks started to take to the air, heading south. And suddenly it was Samhain, a clear, crisp day. People were excited. They were busy cooking up specialties. Children had tied up kindling into bundles for the bonfire that night. The Grands were excited. As the sun began to set, Mother Henley and her children and grandchildren arrived at the cottage. Some people dressed up in fanciful costumes for Samhain. As a feast of the dead, it was a time of crossings. Mother Henley was dressed as priestess of sorts—in a white sheet tied with bold blue cording across and around her body. Rose wore a simple white tunic, but her hair had been cut. It was in a style that was neither traditionally feminine nor masculine. It came down past her ears and was blunt-cut at her jawline. The effect was disorienting, and then I remembered who Rose was—"the halfling-child" who was both male and female or something in between—not one sex but intersex. The look suited her perfectly, once I thought about it.

Almost everyone carried a covered basket or pot with specialties or a bundle of kindling. As we walked, families joined us. Most of the families of the Lower Valley joined us, so we became quite a grouping, a number that could be considered an army. We walked to the cemetery first, where people placed food offerings on the graves of their ancestors and deceased love ones. As darkness settled, people lit torches, and we walked on to the Standing Stones. As we neared the end of the climb of Gaia's Mound, the Grands began the "Trollie Woellie" rhyme, which everyone picked up and chanted.

When we reached the summit, Nanna directed people into stations around the stones. Six fires were set outside the stones, and one was set in the center of the stones. When they were lit, Granny had most of the people ring the stones, while she, Nanna, and Rose moved to the center.

"Call to them, Rose," Nanna commanded.

"I am not Rose any longer; I am Ray—like a sunbeam ray or a moonbeam ray."

There was a murmuring in the crowd, and then they were chanting the "Trollie Woellie" rhyme again, but with a passion that had not been there before.

"Trolls," cried Ray, "come back to us!"

The Grands were doing things I didn't quite understand. They had mixed milk, honey, and blood, and were pouring it on the ground and spattering it as they danced around the stones to the chanting.

"Trolls come back to us! Please come back to us!" Ray's voice screamed.

And in the crystal-clear night, lightening streaked through

the sky and lit it up, and then it went dark. The fires still burned, but there was a rumbling. Nanna and Granny kept up the chanting, and then the earth moved. We were disoriented as the ground moved and then the stones moved and took shape and stood up. The Grands fell silent and knelt on the ground. We, in the outer circle, did the same. Only Ray stood with her arms outstretched in supplication. The Trolls were different than I could have imagined, though it was hard to see very clearly in the light by the bonfire in the center of the circle. They were graceful beings, tall and lanky. They stood about seven feet high. Their skin colors varied just like ours, some dark-skinned (brown, nearly black), others still dark but not as dark (a bronzy ruddy color), others a golden yellowish, and the remaining a pale pinkish white. Most were dark-haired, but they wore it in a range of different styles. Their eyes were all the same, however, a shocking moss green that filled their entire eyes and cat-like pupils. They were dressed in drapes of green and brown, tied with cords of the same hues, but their dress was not gendered but unisex. The females and the males wore the same thing. The two closest to Ray also seemed to be the most senior, judging from the grey that streaked their hair.

"I am Sabeline, and this is Olisagh, my consort," the female said pointing to the male near her. Her voice was soft yet commanding and with a quality that seemed like running water, somehow. It was hypnotic and calming at the same time. "Are you the Halfling?" she asked of Ray.

Ray nodded, and then sank to zirs knees.

"Do not kneel before us, child," Olisagh said in a deep voice that again was commanding but not threatening, compelling and somehow like water. Then he turned from Ray and looked at the Grands and us outside the circle of Trolls, and motioned us to rise with his arms.

"Come to us, child, and tell us the how and why we all gathered here," Sabeline said.

Ray rose and walked to Sabeline and Olisagh. Each of them

held out a hand to Ray, palms face up, and Ray put zirs hands face down over theirs. They then moved their hands, slightly, so that their hands were just below Ray's forearms, and they grasped zirs arms; Ray returned to the gesture, and the two Trolls closed their eyes and seemed to read Ray's thoughts and memories. After a few minutes, they opened their eyes, and released Ray's arms.

"Children of the Great Goddess, please link," Sabeline said softly, and the other Trolls obeyed, so that the circle of Trolls all held hands in that same way that they held Ray's arms and hands. The circle of Trolls all closed their eyes in concentration. After a few minutes, they released each other.

"Are your people prepared?" Sabeline asked, moving her gaze from Ray to Granny and Nanna. "The Church Fathers are probably on their way. A choice will need to be made."

Nanna stepped forward, "I believe that the people of the Lower Valley choose you and the Great Goddess, Greatmother Sabeline," she said, "but we should confirm that now."

Sabeline nodded. "People of the Lower Valley," she said turning to face some of us and encouraging us with a gesture to break our outer circle and converge in single group facing her and Olisagh, Ray, and the Grands. "I am Sabeline, and this is Olisagh," she repeated to us. "We are the Greatmother and Greatfather of the Troll Council. This is Ganna and Aphra," and two female Trolls stepped out of their positions in the circle and stood behind Sabeline and Olisagh. "This is Maev and Jenico, the Grandmother and Grandfather," and a female and male Troll stepped out of their positions in the circle and joined Ganna and Aphra. "This is Mureil and Foylan," and again a female and male Troll stepped away from the circle to join the others. "This is Hanlon and Thoran," she continued, as two male Trolls stepped away from the circle and joined the others. "And this is Brighid and Iolo, the Mother and Father," she concluded, and the last female and male Troll left the circle and joined the others. "Will you stand with us, and allow us to fulfill our traditional roles as protectors of your kind as charged to us by the Great Goddess? In pledging to us, you pledge to follow the old ways of the Great Goddess, so do not make your pledge idly."

People looked to me to help lead our response. I wasn't sure what to say so I just began repeating the rhyme: "Oh, Trollie Woellie Stones,/ the Halfling-Child will come,/ It, She, He will break the spell/ and set you free,/ so like in the Ancient Past,/ you can look after Us and Me." People were quick to pick up the rhyme, and it echoed through the night. The Trolls all smiled listening to us, and then they bowed to us and to Ray and the Grands.

"It is our honor, to serve once more," Olisagh said in his deep voice.

Just then, we saw twenty or so people on horseback with torches ascending Gaia's Mound. We were not surprised to see the Church Fathers and some of their followers as they reached the summit, Father Lucius joined by Fathers Boniface and Alexander. Even in the darkness, you could see their faces contorted with rage and revulsion. The Trolls stepped in front of us; behind them stood Ray and the Grands and then the rest of us.

"What have you done?" screamed Father Lucius. "What are these demons you have conjured with your devil worship?"

One of the Trolls, perhaps Maev, opened her mouth and made a call, the strangest call I have ever heard, something like an eagle's peal and a cougar's growl. Then, Jenico also made a call, a neighing sound that also sounded like "brothers and sisters."

"Gentlemen," Sabeline began.

But Father Boniface cut her off, "Silence, Demon. You will not work your dark magic on us," and he welded a staff menacingly.

Nanna stepped forward, "Father Boniface, these are not demons but the stones brought back to us—the Trollie Woelli Stones—a miracle."

Father Lucius circled back to Nanna. "I always knew you and Grace were witches," he spat. "They should all be burned at the stake!" He too brandished a staff.

But before the Church Fathers could muster their group to attack, the sky erupted in noise as twelve magnificent griffins menaced one side of the mounted riders while twelve winged centaurs menaced the other side. The horses snorted and reared, clearly threatened by the new arrivals.

"This is black magic!" screamed Father Alexander. "These new creatures are worse than the Trolls; they are unnatural aberrations. Repent, people of the Lower Valley or be damned to the flames of hell and eternal suffering!" he yelled.

Granny stepped forward next to Nanna. "Get yourselves gone, Church Fathers. You are not welcome here! And take your followers with you!"

The combination of the twelve Trolls, the larger number of the hovering and menacing Halfling beasts, the defiant Nanna and Granny and the rest of us were too much for the superstitious, bigoted, fearful, fanatical Church Fathers. "Devil worshippers, damn you all!" they screamed at us, and turned and rode off into the night.

We watched them descend, and as they trailed out of sight, the griffins and the winged centaurs landed. The griffins were as big as the centaurs—their massive eagle heads, wings, and legs melding into their substantial lion haunches and back legs. The Trolls could communicate with them, and they pointed out Talon and Claw, Tawny and Silver. Some of the male centaurs introduced themselves, Chromis, Bromus, Pholus, and Medon. The female centaurs were more withdrawn, and only Hylonome and Melanippe introduced themselves.

Once the introductions, such as they were, were made, Sabeline spoke to us. "The Great Goddess makes all life possible and all things sacred. The tragedy of the religion of the Church Fathers is that they see things in binaries: good and bad, heaven and hell, light and dark, male and female, eagle and lion or man and horse. But the Great Goddess is about more than such limited associations. Life is as varied as we can imagine. There is rarely just one way to view a creature or a situation—

but multiple. We celebrate those that are different and embrace a range of ways to be. The griffins and the centaurs help us as we are prepared to help them. But we all keep the ways of the Great Goddess." Then she turned and nodded first to the cohort of griffins and then to the cohort of centaurs. They cried a salute of sorts and then took to the air in a storm of wings.

Olisagh now spoke to us. "The Church Fathers will be back, and back with reinforcements. To truly protect you and us, there is a magic that we can perform, but it means sealing off the Lower Valley from non-believers. Consider this carefully."

Nanna and Granny spoke to Ray, and then they fanned out among the families to speak to the matriarchs. Granny came to me.

"Helen, you too, speak with the matriarchs," she commanded.

So, I went and was relieved that nearly everyone wanted the Church Fathers and their followers barred from the Lower Valley. The few that didn't, lit torches and left us. It was a sad parting, but then the Trolls had us all move into the center of the summit, and they positioned themselves around us in a circle. They chanted words we didn't understand, and they had us say the words too—as best we could. As we chanted, the air charged, and something changed. I couldn't really explain it, but I knew we were sealed away. I knew we were safe.

With all of that over, we built up the bonfires and shared the food that we still had left and curled up under the stars, Trolls and humans, and fell asleep. The new day would bring a new beginning, and we all seemed pleased and content with that opportunity.

Snow White's Father and the Transgender Queen

SNOW WHITE WAS the apple of her parents' eyes. Queen Anna had wished for a child with skin as white as snow, lips as red as blood, and hair as black as coal, and Snow White was an exceptionally pale girl with shockingly large blue eyes, a small nose, full, red lips, and beautifully thick, raven's wing black hair, and she was a beauty, inside and out. Though she was the princess, she delighted in helping old Sasha in the kitchens. Sasha was a baker who let Snow White help with her baking breads and sweets for the castle, and Sasha told the most wonderful stories of lands far away and peoples who practiced all sorts of strange customs.

Though both Snow White's parents loved her unconditionally, they did not love each other. They had been betrothed as infants, and Queen Anna always felt that in marrying King David, she had married down, so she treated him with a cold distain that ate away at their marriage. Thus, though the queen was very beautiful, when she became sick and then died when Snow White was a young woman, the king was sad, but far from heart broken. The following spring, kings and knights across the kingdoms were called to join a great army and fight their enemies. Though King David was loathed to be separated from his daughter, he was also eager to travel and see if he could find a new queen.

King David appointed his sister, Lady Jessica, as Queen Regent to rule Avonvale in his absence and tend to Snow White's education. With many of the kingdom's knights and soldiers, King David left. Lady Jessica preferred her regular title to Queen Regent Jessica but would use the more formal title when she had to. She was a kind and beautiful woman. She had Snow White attend her in court sessions, so that Snow White could learn the ways of the court and see and learn the ways the people were ruled. Lady Jessica believed that rulers should be like parents to their people: they should provide opportunities to their people to better and improve themselves and the kingdom; they should minimize conflict; when necessary, they should provide just punishment for transgressors of the public peace and harmony; they should provide protection and shelter to their people; etc. There had to be responsibility on both sides: the ruler for the ruled and the ruled for the ruler. Lady Jessica and King David had been taught this style of leadership by their own parents, Queen Beth and King Michael, but Queen Anna had had a harsher view of rulership, and the people of Avonvale responded gratefully to the return of the old ways under Lady Jessica's care.

Snow White bloomed into a sweet, lovely, and kind young woman. Her quiet work in the kitchens with Sasha kept her humble and down to earth. Her studies with Lady Jessica and her tutors introduced her to different languages, the literature and history of her kingdom, the literature and histories of neighboring kingdoms, music and art, and the duties of rulers. As Snow White reached her eighteenth birthday, Prince Christos, a prince of Lakeland, a neighboring kingdom and her mother's former home, became a frequent guest. Prince Christos was very handsome. He had golden skin, golden curly locks, and deep green eyes. He was twenty and tall and strong and arrogant. Snow White found him very attractive, but she had strong reservations about him. He was rude or dismissive toward Sasha. He found Lady Jessica's style of rulership, "womanly" and "soft." Lady Jessica did not like the match either and put off Prince Christos and his parents—Queen Sara and King Edgar—because King David was away.

King Edgar called for the return of King David so the matter might be settled, and some months after the call, King David sent word that he, his men, and some guests would be returning to Avonvale. The kingdom buzzed with tension, anticipating the return of the king and his men and his guests. Food stores and live foul and livestock where sent to the castle in preparation for days of feasting. Additionally, temporary pens were built to hold the overflow. Snow White was desperately excited to be reunited with her father.

At last, the great day came, and a great swarm of men, some on horseback and some on foot, filed up the hills of Avonvale toward the castle, kicking up clouds of dust in their wake. The king's standard in white and light blue and silver marked the swarm. As they traveled through the villages, many of the men on foot and a few of the men on horseback, left the main swarm, returning to their families and loved ones after three years away. The main group of the king's men continued to the castle. King David was warmly received at the castle, both by his noblemen and noblewomen and by the staff of the castle, but his warmest welcomes were from his daughter and sister.

"Poppa," cried Snow White, running to her father after he dismounted and throwing her arms around his neck.

"Snow White," he said, emotion straining his voice, "I hardly recognize you, child," catching her up in his arms, showering her with kisses, hugging her, and then setting her down on her feet again. "There, there, child; don't cry. I am home, and I have someone I would like you to meet," he said, though his emotion threatened to break through his cool manner.

"David," Lady Jessica said, embracing him, "We have missed you so," a few tears escaping her eyes as well.

"Jessica, not you too," King David replied, working to steady his voice and hold back the tears swelling in his own eyes. He hugged his sister and kissed her on the forehead. "Come," he said, steadying himself and beckoning them toward the carriage at the rear of the first train of his men.

Opening the carriage, King David reached his hand in, and it was grasped by a dark-skinned hand that King David gently pulled forward. Emerging from the carriage was a beautiful dark-skinned woman wearing a beautiful light blue gown and a sumptuous robe of white and silver, the king's colors, both Snow White and Lady Jessica noted. Her bearing was elegant and regal. Her skin was like dark walnut but smooth and glossy, almost satiny. She had full wine-dark lips, high cheek bones, full black lashes and lush, large dark brown eyes. Her hair was black like Snow White's but different, coarser somehow, and braided in many braids and tied up, or perhaps braided, into a crown coiling around her head. She was like no woman either Snow White or Lady Jessica had ever seen, but they both curtseyed before her as soon as she stepped from the carriage. "This, my lovely ladies, is Princess Eriana and her lovely children, Prince Hakim and Princess Tanya." Then the prince and princess followed their mother out of the carriage and stood on either side of her. The children clearly resembled their mother; they had her striking good looks, dark satiny skin, and dark coarse hair. Princess Tanya's hair was done in a simpler version of her mother's, and she seemed to be about Snow White's own age, whereas Prince Hakim whose hair was cropped close to his head seemed to be a few years older, perhaps twenty. They all, the princesses and prince, greeted Snow White and Lady Jessica warmly, which Snow White and Lady Jessica returned in kind.

Apartments in the castle had been prepared for the guests, and Princess Eriana was shown to the grandest by the king himself, Snow White showed Tanya to hers, and Lady Jessica showed the prince to his. Their rooms were clustered together in the south wing. Their baggage was brought up by the servants, and they were left to refresh themselves before a feast would begin in four hours' time.

The king had Jessica and Snow White conference with him in his apartments in the north wing of the castle. They talked for hours, catching up on their separate adventures. Jessica and

Snow White explained about the events in the kingdom, Snow White's studies, and Prince Christos' advances. David told them about their campaigns, both the successes and the defeats. He told them about meeting Princess Eriana and her children. He tried to explain how and why she was so special to him. Snow White saw that her father felt deeply for this woman—more deeply than he had felt for her own mother, she realized sadly. But she also remembered how her mother had been so condescending toward her husband, and another part of her was happy for his happiness. And yet, there was something, something her father was not telling her—like a secret. She couldn't say why she felt that way, but she did.

Jessica talked to her brother about matters of state in more sophistication, and when Snow White fidgeted restlessly, they dismissed her to prepare for the feast. Not being sleepy and having over an hour to kill, she wandered back to the south wing and knocked on Tanya's door. Tanya seemed genuinely delighted to see her and ushered Snow White into the apartments. Hakim was there too, and he also seemed glad for her company. All of them seemed happy, even relieved, for their parents' overt happiness, and they were anxious that it be maintained. Snow White tried to warn them about the nasty children at court, the spoilt ones who she didn't trust, who would stab you in the back and smile the whole time. They told her about themselves, and Snow White was so thoroughly enjoying their company that she regretted the need to leave them to dress for the feast.

Tanya hugged her as she left, and Snow White found herself hugging the princess back with equal enthusiasm. They could be sisters, she realized—if the king and the princess married—and she realized that she wanted more than she knew, a sister. Hakim took her hand and kissed it, and she flushed. He could be her brother, and yet he was not, and he seemed so much kinder and more sensitive than Prince Christos that she didn't want to think of him as her brother. Her flush darkened, and his brow furrowed in confusion, and then, though it was hard to tell with his dark skin, Hakim's cheeks seemed to darken as well as if he suddenly understood her thoughts.

She excused herself hastily and walked back to her apartments feeling intensely confused. Tasked with a bath and dressing for the ball, she pushed her confused thoughts from her mind. Her maid was giddy with her accomplishment as she made Snow White look at herself in the mirror: her hair was pinned elegantly so that tendrils fell seductively around her shoulders and down her back. Her dress was a beautiful deep blue that brought out her eyes. A garnet choker highlighted the red of her lips and was echoed in the trim of the dress. She looked beautiful and more grown up than she had ever felt. She was thrilled that her father would see her this way. And she was thrilled that Hakim would see her this way too—for completely different reasons.

Dressed, she went to her father's apartments, and they walked together to the grand ballroom. They took their place on the dais and were joined by Jessica and Eriana and her children. Tanya kissed Snow White on the cheeks in welcome, and so Eriana and Hakim followed suit, both Snow White and Hakim blushing slightly at the kisses between them.

The feast and the dance were wonderful. Snow White talked easily with Tanya and Eriana, and they with her. Her talk with Hakim was shier and more forced, and Snow White noticed that this gave both Tanya and Eriana and even her father a kind of pleasure. She danced with her father and with nobles of the kingdom. When she danced with Christos, it felt odious to her. All he wanted was domination over her—she could feel it in the way he led. She was stiff and formal in his arms. She knew he sensed it because she felt his irritation at her resistance. He wanted her swooning over him, captive to his looks and his charms, but he repulsed her more than anything.

At the end of their dance, Hakim cut in, and she relaxed immediately in his arms, and their faces both flushed at the realization. Snow White raised such confusing emotions in him. He had never felt anything like it before. She was shockingly beautiful in a way he hadn't seen previously, so he was attracted to her physically. But if their parents married, they would be like siblings. Tanya was drawn to her like a sister. He could feel his sister's affection for Snow White. Tanya had watched Snow White and Christos dancing with growing alarm and anxiety. Finally, she had begged him to cut in, to save Snow White from having to dance with him again, and he had seen how uncomfortable Snow White was in the other young man's arms. He wanted to protect her, to take her away from the man who threatened her. And then they were blushing, and she was in his arms, her body melting against his. Hakim spun her away before Christos could see the way she changed in his arms, or the blush on her face.

"My lady," Hakim began, but she interrupted him.

"Please, get me away from him," she pleaded softly, and a shudder ran through her body at the thought of being reclaimed by Christos.

Hakim felt it and pulled her closer. He led her further into the dancing crowd. She was light and graceful. They danced well together, matching each other's movements with the give and take of attentive partners. When the dance ended, she didn't leave his arms, so they danced the next dance too. When they started to walk back to the dais together, a young man stopped them and claimed Snow White for the next dance. She consented, but her eyes lingered on Hakim as they parted, or did he imagine it? Back on the dais, his mother, Tanya, and even the king engaged him in conversation, and he talked happily with them, but he was distracted every now and then, searching the crowd of dancers for Snow White and finding a strange relief when he could see her.

King Edgar, Queen Sara, and Prince Christos joined them on the dais for a while. The king and queen of Lakeland pushed for the betrothal of their son and Snow White. Hakim listened with dismay. He knew that Snow White did not like this young man, felt threatened by him even. He saw that Lady Jessica was tense over this conversation. She obviously did not like this match for her niece. King David was also tense, so he knew of Lady Jessica and Snow White's objections. Tanya and even his mother were tense beside him, reading the emotions around them. Hakim studied the Lakeland royalty. They were handsome and polite, but not in a wholly genuine way. Beauty and civility were means to acquire or take or subdue what they wanted, whether objects or other beings. They were dangerous because once they had what they wanted, they would do whatever they wanted with their acquisitions. They thought of themselves as superior, above their people, above even other royalty. If you were a good reader of people, you could feel the contempt they felt for Lady Jessica and King David and Snow White. They weren't looking for a princess who would become a queen of Lakeland. They were looking for a servant who would become the plaything of their son. Hakim flushed with rage. Snow White deserved so much better than that. He felt bound to protect her from Christos. He searched the crowd for her. He could not see her at first. His anxiety spiked, and then he caught a glimpse of her pressed against a pillar trying not to be seen and watching the dais warily.

King David, to Hakim's relief, put off King Edgar and Queen Sara's requests by pointing out that he had only just returned and needed time to reacquaint himself with his daughter and the feelings of her heart. They acquiesced reluctantly and withdrew. Once they were gone, Lady Jessica vented the objections she had to the match, all of which Hakim agreed with. He was relieved to see the king agreed with his sister. Lady Jessica then surprised them by appealing to Princess Eriana to assess the Lakelanders and weigh in herself on what was in the best interest of Snow White. Hakim felt his mother blush and tense. Though almost everyone guessed that King David would marry his mother shortly, she was not the queen, and yet, Lady Jessica, by seeking her opinion in this matter, was treating her as such. It was an honor and a compliment. It was also a brilliant strategic move. King David would be grateful for his sister's compliment to his new queen, and he would support her assessment of the unsuitability of Prince Christos for Snow White. The Lakelanders were foolish for thinking Lady Jessica soft. More could be won by generosity than threat or might.

"Of course, I only have the most fleeting sense of these people, Lady Jessica, but my gut reaction is against them," Eriana offered softly.

Snow White joined them suddenly on the dais. She looked frightened, and Hakim's heart ached at the sight of her fear. They all felt it radiating off her body.

"Snow White?" King David said, and there was pain in his voice as he read her distress.

"Please, father, I can't stand him," Snow White said quietly. She looked so meek and miserable. Hakim wanted to comfort her badly. Tanya reached out and took Snow White's hand, pulling Snow White down next to her on the bench between her and her mother, and providing her comfort. Eriana took Snow White's other hand and stroked it reassuringly.

King David nodded, his face etched with sorrow and concern. "I would never force you to marry someone, my child. I have my own wounds on that score. It hurts me to find you so worried about that." Then his face changed and softened with traces of adoration and amusement, and he waved his hand around the dais, "Besides your own objections, you have the support of the royal household against such a match. Who am I to go against such opposition?" And a wry smile formed on his lips. "Relax and enjoy this evening. We will come up with some excuse to put off the Lakelanders." They all relaxed at his words. Hakim watched as Snow White visibly relaxed, and Tanya wrapped her arms around Snow White and hugged her. Lady Jessica looked a little smug for a moment, but that look disappeared in an instant, and relief and then contentment were the only emotions on her face.

Jolting them from their shared relief, Prince Christos appeared, looking arrogant and cocky. He asked Snow White to dance. She tried to decline, but he was insistent. They all realized that he must have been watching Snow White's return to the dais and had interpreted the scene in completely the wrong way. He thought that Tanya's hug was one of congratulations for a betrothal rather than one of congratulations for escaping one. Snow White went with him unwillingly, the tension and stiffness in her body was obvious to Hakim and the others. How could Christos not read it? Perhaps he didn't care or was so wrapped up in his own feelings that he didn't notice. Hakim watched them, and he did not need his sister's urging this time to get up and cut in on Christos at the end of the dance.

This time, however, he was not as adroit at shielding Snow White from Christos. She flushed and smiled at Hakim with such obvious relief and pleasure as she moved into his arms that Christos saw. Fury distorted his features as he looked between them, and his dark cruelty showed through the veneer of his good looks. Snow White tried to master her face, but it was too late. She trembled at the realization, and Hakim pulled her closer to him to comfort her, but this only enraged Christos further. Hakim spun them into the crowd away from him.

"Snow White? Are you all right?" he whispered in her ear.

"Yes, no," she answered. "In your arms, yes, but he frightens me."

Hakim was so confused. He had only just met her. They would be step-siblings, and yet he was fiercely attracted to her, to her beauty and her vulnerability. He wanted to protect her like he wanted to protect his mother and his sister, but differently too. They weren't blood relatives. He didn't want her to be with Christos not only because Christos was horrid but because Hakim was jealous, thinking of Snow White with another young man. She seemed just as taken with him as he was for her, and suddenly he had to know. "I seem to care for you, Snow White, in an almost irrational manner. I will do what I can to protect you," he said softly, pulling away from her only slightly to plant a soft, swift kiss on her forehead. He heard her breath catch, but she did not pull away. Her face flushed, and a smile played at the corners of her mouth.

She looked up at him, her deep blue eyes searching his with an intensity that took his breath away. Her smile quirked mischievously for a moment. "I don't know how well I could protect you," and the smirk suddenly disappeared, replaced by a sweet vulnerability, "but I also feel oddly irrational about you," her voice turning so quiet that he barely caught the words. He exhaled and pulled her against him more tightly, and he felt her meet his embrace with a joy he had never felt before.

When the dance was over, they avoided Christos and made their way through the crowd hand-in-hand. As they neared the dais, she unlaced her fingers from his, and with regret, he let their hands fall apart. Neither one, later, felt that this precaution had been effective. Everyone on the dais seemed to have seen their closeness on the dance floor. Tanya was bubbling with enthusiasm. King David and Princess Eriana seemed surprised, but bemused. Lady Jessica was surprised and reserved, keeping her feelings to herself until she knew them more fully. Snow White blushed and tensed slightly.

"Father," she began. "I...I don't want to encounter Christos again. May I retire?" she asked, with her eyes and her expression all begging him to grant her request.

He studied her face for a moment and smiled at her indulgently, "Yes, child, go." He stood, and she came forward to kiss his cheeks good night.

Tanya leapt to her feet, grabbing Hakim's hand and propelling him forward with her, "May we go as well, Mother? My king?" Her enthusiasm made the king chuckle and shake his head.

Tanya certainly could accompany Snow White, as a young woman and as a soon-to-be-step-sibling, but it was unseemly, now that the possibility loomed for Hakim and Snow White to be something more than step-siblings, for him to be alone with her. Tanya's enthusiasm for the match did not present a seemingly strong enough deterrent for distance between the couple. The king hesitated. Lady Jessica stood, "David, I will attend them," she said softly, an amused smile playing at edges of her mouth. With that she kissed her brother's cheeks, while Tanya and Hakim kissed their mother, and then Lady Jessica embraced the princess too and took her leave. Tanya nearly skipped across the floor to catch up with Snow White, dragging her brother with her.

Snow White led them to small library where they passed the rest of the evening quietly, sometimes talking as a group and sometimes in pairs. Tanya probed both Snow White and Hakim about their feelings separately. She was amazingly good at listening and extracting even the most sensitive information out of a person, Snow White thought, as she found herself confiding her confused attraction to Hakim. Lady Jessica, in a more reserved fashion, questioned Hakim about himself and his intentions. He flushed when she questioned him about Snow White. Despite the suddenness of whatever was happening between them, Lady Jessica was convinced that Hakim cared for her niece, was a sensitive and sincere young man, and was surprised at his own feelings for Snow White.

Lady Jessica did not try to speak to Snow White while in the library. She would wait to speak with her niece when they were alone. Tanya brought her brother over to Snow White in a rather transparent gesture and left the two alone, moving to speak with Lady Jessica who indulged Tanya's orchestrations. Lady Jessica found Tanya to be a loving and protective sister but was pleasantly surprised by the sincere depth of affection that the young woman had for Snow White.

Hakim sat down on the sofa next to Snow White, watching her blush as his sister scampered away. Hakim reached over and put his hand on Snow White's, and she turned her hand over and laced her fingers through his. Once their fingers were entwined, he squeezed her hand gently. "What happens now?" he asked her quietly.

"I don't know," she said back, "but I would like to get to know you better."

"Yes, Snow," he began, watching her eyes flash at his shorting of her name and then soften as if, after considering his liberty, she liked it. "I would like to know you better too. Perhaps we could ride tomorrow," he suggested.

"Yes, I would like that," she said. They chatted quietly for a while, but when it was quite late and Snow White yawned, Hakim stood and pulled her to her feet. "You're tired. Tanya and I should leave you to your rest." He squeezed her hand and then brought it to his lips and kissed it. She flushed as he did it. "Good night, Snow. Sleep well," he whispered. He released her hand and found his sister waiting for him. Tanya hugged Snow White and kissed her cheeks before leaving the library with her brother to return to their rooms in the south wing of the castle.

Snow White sat back down as her aunt sat next to her on the sofa, and they talked. Snow White tried to explain her confused feelings toward Hakim to Lady Jessica. She feared that she did not do them justice, but her aunt seemed increasingly sympathetic as she spoke. When Snow White yawned again sometime later, Lady Jessica sent her to bed.

The next morning, King David spent several hours with Snow White and Lady Jessica. They discussed everything in more detail. Both Snow White and Lady Jessica were happy that the king had found Princess Eriana. They hoped to know her better before the wedding, but they had no objections to the wedding which was then set to happen in two months' time. The king told his daughter and sister about the angry confrontation he had had with King Edgar over the apparent affection between Hakim and Snow White. King David had deflected the accusations, but he also felt that the current situation was significant in derailing Prince Christos' pursuit of Snow White. He then turned his attention to finding out just what was going on between the young people. Lady Jessica intervened and spoke on both Hakim's and Snow White's defenses, explaining that both were surprised by their emotions, but that both were kind and sweet individuals, and that though it was sudden, it seemed genuine.

The king left Lady Jessica and Snow White to study for an hour before lunch. They joined the king and Princess Eriana and her children for lunch. Princess Eriana made a significant effort to engage Snow White in conversation as the king did with Hakim. After lunch, the three young people were allowed to go riding alone. They rode and talked together, but Tanya also found occasions to lag behind, allowing Hakim and Snow White to talk together by themselves.

The days fell into a pattern, in the mornings Lady Jessica tutored not just Snow White, but Tanya and Hakim too. Then, with the king and soon-to-be-queen, they ate lunch together. When weather permitted, the young people spent time in the afternoons outside, riding, hawking, walking, exploring. On days when the weather was bad, they read together in the library or played a range of games. Tanya found ways for Hakim and Snow White to spend time alone, and the more time they spent together, the more their affections grew. Snow White introduced Hakim to Sasha in the kitchens and found satisfaction in the respectful way he interacted with the old woman and took criticism in the way he crimped the edges of fruit tarts or shaped his croissants. Sasha even knew some of the tales of Hakim's people, which she recited to them to both Snow White's and Hakim's amusement. Also, the more time Snow White and her aunt and father and Princess Eriana and her children spent as a family, the more Snow White, Hakim, Tanya, and Lady Jessica saw the obvious love between the king and soon-to-be-queen. After so many years of the king's unhappiness with Queen Anna, both Snow White and Lady Jessica were happy for him. Yet as much as Snow White longed for the union of her father and Princess Eriana because of their obvious affection and passion for each other, there was something that bothered her—something she found different about how her father and the princess interacted.

Tanya felt so close to Snow White that she often barged into Snow White's rooms unannounced just like she did to her brother and mother. On more than one occasion, Tanya, dragging Snow White with her, barged into Hakim's rooms. One evening just before dinner, the young women rushed through his rooms to find him in his bedroom in the process of changing his shirt. He stood in his bedroom, shirtless, his muscled torso completely exposed and his dark skin gleaming in the soft light. Snow White froze and gasped at the sight of him, blushing a deep shade of crimson. Startled by her gasp, Hakim looked up and flushed as well. He grabbed up the clean shirt and threw it on hastily. Tanya clucked at them both for being awkward, and when Snow White and Hakim recovered themselves, they walked down to dinner together.

Just before the wedding, one of the servants found Snow White and told her that Tanya had been desperately searching the castle for her. Snow White went to Tanya's rooms and didn't find her there. She checked Hakim's rooms as well. She could find neither of them. Becoming more and more anxious, she went to Princess Eriana's rooms, and in her frantic state, she burst into the rooms. She found Princess Eriana and Tanya in the rooms but was rendered speechless. Princess Eriana was in a state of undress, her chest exposed. Snow White stared, and they all gasped.

"Snow White?" the princess whispered stricken, except that she couldn't be a princess, not with the torso of a man.

"I…don't…understand," was all Snow White could manage to say. She felt her face flush. She had intruded. She had grossly invaded the princess' privacy, and there were secrets, obviously. She was horribly confused. "I am sorry. I shouldn't have. I was worried about Tanya, and I couldn't find her," she said in a rush. "I should go," and she turned to leave.

But suddenly Tanya was blocking her way through the door. "Snow White," she said softly but firmly. "We should have told you, but many people don't understand. Please sit and let us explain." Snow White felt numb. She didn't know what to think, but she let Tanya lead her to the bed. Slowly, together, Tanya and Princess Eriana explained that though Eriana was physically male, he had always felt like a female, even when he was just a boy. He learned to hide his feelings from his parents, from his siblings, and from his friends. Whenever he tried to express his desire to be a girl or feminine, he had been ridiculed and even beaten. Yet the feelings didn't change. He had been forced to marry a woman by his parents, and Tanya and Hakim were the children of that union. But more and more, he felt uncomfortable. Then a plague swept through the land, and his wife caught the fever. It took her life when the children were still quite young. He had been sad for her loss, as a fellow human being and as the mother of his children, but he felt a relief as well. He no longer felt the need to perform his maleness. In sorting through her things, it occurred to him that he could transform himself into Princess Eriana and leave with the children. They could resettle somewhere new where he would only be known as Princess Eriana; he had jewels enough to finance it, and so they left, and he became her more fully than the lie of being a man. They had been a family for so many years that Tanya and Hakim identified her as female, as their mother, the only mother they truly knew.

"Does my father know?" Snow White asked quietly.

"Yes, he knows, and he still loves me," the princess answered.

Snow White was silent. She thought about everything that Princess Eriana had said. She wished she had been told before this, but she understood that Eriana's choice to reject her physical nature and embrace her emotional nature was different—and at first, people resisted difference—Lady Jessica had shown her example after example of difference being persecuted in her lessons. And though she was annoyed that neither Tanya nor Hakim had told her, she also realized that the secret was not theirs to tell. The simple truth was that her father was happy, and Eriana was happy. She also thought about how unhappy her father had been in his "traditional" marriage. If this was what he wanted, who was she to judge it or get in the way of it. Certainly, she expected her father's willingness to allow her to love freely—to reject Prince Christos despite the considerable pressure for the match—and to accept Hakim as their affections grew.

"Snow White?" Tanya said softly, the tension and anxiety in her voice pliable and in the frantic look in her eyes.

Snow White patted Tanya's hand and smiled. She stood and walked to the princess. Princess Eriana regarded her curiously and warily. Snow White kissed the princess' cheeks and said softly, "I wish you and my father every happiness." Tears sprung up in the princess' eyes, and Tanya gave a small shriek of triumph. Snow White felt a wave of bitterness that her culture could make it so difficult for people to be happy, especially when they were different and, therefore, the most vulnerable.

"Help us," Tanya demanded, and the two young women attended the princess and helped her try on various dresses, veils, jewels, gloves, petticoats, and shoes for the wedding until they found the ones that the princess liked the best. The emergency, that had driven Tanya's desperation to find Snow White, had been to be able to look through Snow White's jewels and accessories for her mother. Snow White offered to go and bring them, but the princess was content with what Tanya had found. Tanya and Snow White helped the princess change back into her regular clothes, and then the two young women left the princess and went searching for Hakim. They found him in the small library reading poetry. To amuse them, he read aloud, glancing furtively at Snow White when reading a love poem. Before going down to dinner, Tanya had a brief whispered conversation with her brother. Snow White guessed that she was telling him that Snow White now knew about their mother, and he had the grace to look sheepish for having withheld the truth from her. Tanya skipped into the dining room as Hakim came to a stop and faced Snow White by the door. They were alone in the hallway.

"Snow," he said softly. "I should have...I wanted to tell you," he began.

She looked up at him, searching his face. He was clearly uncomfortable and worried that he had damaged their relationship. "Shh," she whispered and held a finger to his lips. "It wasn't your secret to tell. I understand that. I wish I had been told, but now I know."

He covered her hand with his and moved it from in front of his face. "And you don't care about my mother?" he asked, doubt clear in his voice.

"I want my father to be happy. If your mother makes him happy and he makes her happy, it is fine with me," she answered, and then added, "Just as I hope that my father would only care about my happiness in a match that I chose," her face reddening as she said the last words. His hand released hers, and she felt his hand stroke her cheek, and then he bent down and brushed his lips against hers, and they were kissing.

After a few minutes, they pulled apart, and he pressed his forehead against hers. "I love you, Snow. I loved you before, but that you could forgive me for not telling you and that you could accept my mother...You are such a special young woman. I love you so much." His words were breathless and rushed, but they thrilled her.

"I love you too, Hakim," and she pulled her head back and kissed him briefly, before pulling away, grabbing his hand, and walking into the dining room. They took their places at the table. King David looked at his daughter guiltily, and she knew that he knew that she knew and that he felt badly about not telling her himself.

The next few days flew past. King David and Snow White told Lady Jessica about Princess Eriana, and the older woman didn't seem particularly surprised, knowing her brother as intimately as she did, and also being slightly savvier at spotting slightly masculine features in the princess. The thing that mattered to Lady Jessica was the happiness of her brother and the princess, and she was just as accepting of the king and soon-to-be-queen and their union as Snow White was.

Snow White wondered about how her father and the princess were together alone. As two physical men, they could kiss and touch erotically. They wouldn't be able to have intercourse like a man and a woman could, but they could make each other come in a range of ways, and as long as it was pleasing to both of them. Whose business was it anyway? The bedroom was a private place—past the judgment of those outside it.

The wedding was splendid. Princess Eriana looked magnificent. King David looked dashing, and the two of them were bursting with joy and happiness. After the ceremony, the princess was presented as Queen Eriana. At the reception, the king and queen announced the engagement of Prince Hakim and Princess Snow White with the wedding taking place in three months' time. The announcement infuriated King Edgar and his family, but at such a public setting, there was little they could do, and with the whole realm hearing the announcement, Prince Christos' pursuit was dead.

As an engaged couple, Hakim and Snow White got to spend more time alone together, which they used to explore each other in ways they had not imagined. They found they liked being touched in some of the same ways and in ways that were different because of their different sexual parts. He was always gentle with her, and she was so grateful to be with Hakim and not Christos. Hakim loved arousing her. Her arousal never failed to further excite him. He made her come and was fascinated by her capacity to come again and again and again. He had never imagined how good it would feel to be inside her and to come like that. Neither one of them were, therefore, much surprised that she was about a month pregnant by the time of the wedding.

The queen and Tanya and Lady Jessica helped Snow White choose a beautiful dress and accessories, and the day of the wedding, they helped her dress, while King David distracted the anxious groom. The wedding was on a lesser scale than that of the king and queen's. Mercifully, the Lakelanders were absent from the event, which no one seemed to mind. Both Snow White and Hakim were infectiously happy. Everyone had a great time, and they all lived happily ever after.

Wendy and Polly Pan

THE LOVE FAMILY children were nestled in their beds in the nursery. Jack clung to his teddy, and Matt to his blankey while Wendy read to them. Their favorite stories were ones with magic whether with merpeople and fairies or gods and heroes and magic beasts or pirates and treasure or giants and elves and dwarves. Mother and Father Love were at a formal dinner, and Nanna Love was sitting contently in the parlor knitting and humming to herself after presiding over the children's getting-ready-for-bed-routine. When the children had their fill of stories, they drifted off to sleep, each to her or his own unique combination of dream characters and stories.

The following morning was Saturday, and the children rose early. The Love family was to spend the afternoon at Kew Gardens, and the children were looking forward to it immensely. Mother Love fussed over their clothes and had Wendy change into a much more elegant dress than Wendy thought was warranted for an afternoon of walking and looking at all manner of flora.

It was a stunningly beautiful day for London in early June—clear and bright. Wendy found the Orchid House spectacular and didn't want to leave. Matt and Jack liked the Cactus House best. Mother Love loved the Lily Pad and Pond House. Father Love said he didn't have a favorite, but he was looking forward to tea at Museum No. 1, which overlooked the Palm House.

When the family entered the formal dining room, it was so grand and sumptuous that the children fell silent and gaped at the room around them. The host dressed in formal attire led them to an ample table and held the chairs out for Wendy and Mother Love, tucking them both in and laying their napkins on their laps with a flourish. Once the ladies were seated, Father Love and the boys seated themselves. The table was dressed with a crisp white cotton cloth. White cotton napkins, the ones not on the ladies' laps, were elegantly folded between the cutlery. A small salt and pepper set was on the table along with a small vase of tiny roses in a variety of pinks.

Almost immediately a waiter appeared, placing a large tray on a stand beside the table and setting down a large tea pot and small plates of scones for each of the Loves and carefully placing pots of butter, clotted cream, and jam among them. Next came tea cups and saucers and a bowl of lemon slices, a small pitcher of cream, several sugar bowls with different kinds of sugar, and a small bowl of honey.

"The supplemental cart will pass shortly. How is this to start, Sir? Can I get you anything else?" the waiter asked solicitously.

"This looks wonderful," answered Father Love. Mother Love leaned forward to pour tea into the five cups. Then she passed around the lemons, cream, sugar, and honey, and the Loves started to fix their individual cups of tea. Wendy was contently sipping her tea and eating a scone when a family of four approached them. The Mother and Father were elegantly dressed, and two boys accompanied them. One, Wendy thought, was about her own age, and the other was a few years older than Wendy. Mother and Father Love got to their feet as the family approached, and the Love children followed their example.

This was the Hook family—Mother and Father Hook and James and Andrew Hook. James was the elder, and Wendy realized he was strikingly good looking, but the way he regarded her, arrogantly, hungrily, made her distinctly uncomfortable. She felt her face flush under his appraising gaze. She suddenly knew this was why her mother had fussed over her clothing. Her mother and father were interested in Wendy being courted by James Hook. The introductions were made. Andrew shook her hand and smiled at her warmly. He was less handsome than his brother, but she felt more comfortable with him and less ill at ease. James took her hand confidently. He didn't shake her hand but brought it to his lips and kissed it. "The pleasure is all mine," he murmured softly, somehow only for her. "Miss Love, how charming to make your acquaintance," he simpered. He smiled, and his eyes sparkled with excitement and malice.

Wendy felt the muscles in her stomach clench. He was dangerous, her gut told her. She felt her parents and his parents watching her. She blushed and lowered her eyes, "It is nice to meet you, Mr. Hook," she forced herself to say because she knew that was the response they all expected. How could any of them want this, she thought. How could they not see this young man's predatory nature? She was just a girl, seventeen years old. Yes, she had bloomed. Her blood flowed regularly, but she still slept in the nursery with her brothers. Next, they would be suggesting a room of her own.

After introductions and pleasantries were exchanged, the Hook family took its leave and was ushered to its own table across the room for tea. As much as Wendy tried to put thoughts of James Hook out of her mind and return to her former enjoyment of her tea and scones, she felt his gaze drift toward her and linger on her. It was unsettling, and she knew instinctively that he did it explicitly to unsettle her. When the supplemental cart came with its many delights, Wendy didn't care to get anything, and it was with profound relief that she left the grand dining room with her family.

When they got home, Mother Love helped Wendy change out of the fancy dress. "Well, what did you think of the Hook boys?" she asked.

Wendy plucked up her courage and answered softly, "I liked Andrew, but I don't know about James. I wish you had told me we were meeting them." Wendy watched her mother's face fall. Clearly, she wanted Wendy to be taken with James. But that was just the point Wendy thought. James had "taken" other girls—just how far, she was afraid to imagine—but she didn't want to be his latest conquest.

"But James is so handsome and charming, Wendy. Don't you think so?" Mother Love plead.

"No, I don't," Wendy answered boldly. "And I'm just a little girl. I am not ready for this."

"No, sweet girl, you are not a little girl. You haven't been one for some time. It is time you moved into your own room. The room next to ours will be painted and decorated next week, and we can move you in next weekend."

Wendy stared at her mother. It was all happening too fast—being courted by a young man who scared her, the prospect of marriage hinted at through courting, and being thrown out of the nursery. The tears came unbidden. Anger, fury, frustration, and hurt flashed over her face. Her mother gaped at Wendy—bewildered by her tears and her read of Wendy's emotions. Clearly Mother Love thought she was offering Wendy great things in being courted by James and her own room. But she knew nothing of Wendy's heart. Wendy had no interest in young men. She loved her girlfriends at school— who knew her and talked to her—who comforted her and scolded her—who hugged her and kissed her innocently. James Hook was something else entirely.

"NO!" Wendy screamed. "Why…why are you doing this to me? I don't want this!"

Mother Love was so surprised at the outburst that she struggled to regain her composure. "It is almost time for supper, Wendy. Let's drop this conversation for now, and we can talk about it tomorrow after you have had some time to think about it." She left Wendy then, and Wendy changed into a simpler dress. She wandered to the nursery's great window, which was also a door, and opened it and stood on the narrow balcony. The cool evening air felt refreshing on her face. She looked at the fading sun and glanced at the sky. It was still too early for the stars she was desperate to wish upon to save her. Before she knew what she was doing, she fell down on her knees crying, "Help me! My parents are forcing a hideous man on me, and I don't want to grow up. I don't want to leave my girlfriends and my childhood!" She wept softly, and then she heard Jack calling for her, asking for a story.

Wendy pulled herself together and got a book on Greek mythology and read to Jack and Matt about Hercules and his labors. The boys delighted in the stories, but the stories left Wendy decidedly unsettled. Why were the stories always predominantly about boys or men? Why did they have all the adventures? Why were women only valued as mothers or virgins? Why were women presented as petty and trivial or as sources of evil? Zeus had visited Alcmena disguised as her husband, Amphitryon. When it was established that the real Amphitryon had been away with his men at war and Alcmena had slept with a man she thought was her husband, it was her life that was threatened—not the impostor. Getting revenge of Zeus would have been impossible—but still—that Alcmena's life was on the line through no fault of her own was a problem for Wendy. And Hera was just a mean and vindictive portrayal of a female deity— with no real power of her own. She turned on the women her husband had already victimized—victimizing them again instead of helping them. Why did women gang up on other women? Shouldn't it be the other way around—women supporting other women and perhaps even ganging up on men? Then Deianira, fearful that Hercules would cast her aside for a younger woman, becomes the instrument of his death, spreading a robe with a sample of Nessus' blood which was contaminated with the Hydra's venom. Why couldn't she be the instrument of his salvation instead of his torment and death?

Her head full of confused thoughts, she struggled to fall asleep long after her brothers had drifted into easy dreams. She felt herself just begin to doze when the window onto the tiny balcony opened quietly and a figure stepped through into the room. Wendy was trying to incorporate this new development into her dream when the figure walked over to her bed and stood looking down at her. It wasn't a dream, and Wendy scrambled to a sitting position, clutching at her blankets. "What…what do you want?" she whispered. "Who are you?" she asked.

The figure seemed to radiate out a source of light at her words, so that Wendy could see her more clearly even in the dark nursery. She was unlike anyone that Wendy had seen before. She was about Wendy's height and build, but her skin was a chocolate brown color, her eyes seemed black in the soft light, her hair was long, dark, and braided in thin braids which were tied together with a leather cord and hung neatly down her back. She was wearing a fitted brown leather jacket almost like a riding jacket, and like a jockey, she was wearing matching brown leather pants that were quite close fitting. She seemed slightly older than Wendy, twenty or perhaps nineteen. There were knives sheathed on each hip, and she was smiling down at Wendy with excitement and possibility dancing in her eyes. Wendy realized that she wasn't afraid of this person.

"Who are you?" she asked again, relaxing slightly.

A smile crooked in the corner of her mouth. "I am Polly, Polly Pan," she said. "What's your name?" she asked in return.

"I am Wendy, Wendy Love. And why are you here?" Wendy asked.

"This evening you asked for help. You said that your parents were forcing a man on you and that you didn't want to grow up. I can help with that," Polly answered, matter-of-factly.

"What do you mean?" Wendy asked. Wendy didn't understand how Polly could have heard her that evening.

"I live in Everland where it stays the same. There we stay the same too. It's a haven of sorts. I find unhappy children and take them there, and we live happily there, our own big family, looking after each other and working together to get what needs to be done, done," Polly explained.

"I would have to leave my family?" Wendy questioned.

"I am afraid that is the price," Polly said, sympathy clear in her voice.

"Could I never return?" Wendy asked.

"I have returned children back to their families. I am not a pirate who spirits children away and holds them against their wills, after all. But it can be tricky to return. You won't have aged—that is part of Everland's magic—but your family members will have done."

"Magic? What kind of magic?" Wendy asked.

"Well, aside from not aging, there are magical beings in Everland, fairies and merpeople, magical beasts too, and fairies can do magic themselves," Polly said.

Wendy was excited, confused, and shocked at the same time. She wanted to go in a terrible way. She didn't want to grow up. She wanted nothing to do with James Hook, and she wanted to be in a place where there was magic. However, as much as wanted to go, she loved her brothers and her parents and her life at school. She couldn't imagine what her parents would think if they found her missing (worried, sad, betrayed, angry). And yet, how often did such an opportunity happen?

"Do you do this a lot?" Wendy found herself asking.

"Enough, Everland is quite inhabited. Look, I know this is a lot to take in," Polly said gently. "Why don't you think about it, and I can come back in a week to see what your answer is. How does that sound?" she asked.

"That's quite generous," Wendy answered. "Thank you."

"Wendy, it is a big step. There is hard work to do in Everland, planting and harvesting, weaving and sewing, cooking and cleaning up, but there are friends and no forced marriages and times to relax and enjoy oneself. Think about it. Anon," she said softly, and with that, she turned, exited the window, and was gone.

Wendy leapt to her feet and rushed to the window, realizing that both Polly's entrance and exit should have been impossible. She looked around wildly but could see no trace of the mysterious young woman. She closed the window and then pinched herself.

"Ouch," she muttered. Okay, so not dreaming but perhaps crazy or hallucinating. She got into bed thinking sleep would be impossible after such an encounter, but perhaps the shock itself was tiring because she found herself asleep before she realized it.

In the morning, Mother Love was all a flutter. She was bursting with it at breakfast, but contained herself until after they had all eaten. Once they were done, she said sweetly, "Wendy, dear, James Hook will be coming over today after tea to take you for a walk in the park across the square."

Wendy gasped while her brothers giggled. Wendy felt trapped and betrayed. How could her mother have done this after the things Wendy had said yesterday? "Why have you done this?" Wendy asked, her voice heavy with resentment and irritation.

"Watch your tone, dear," Mother Love said sharply. "His mother sent a note over this morning requesting it. The Hooks are very well connected, Wendy. It is a smart match," she added.

"Smart match? What have you done? I am only seventeen. I don't want to marry, and I do not find him remotely likeable," Wendy said indignantly.

"Wendy," her father said sternly, "we have accepted the invitation. Go for the walk with the young man, and we can talk afterward." His tone said that there would be no further discussion on the topic.

Wendy, who had opened her mouth to respond, closed it. She was on the brink of tears, so she excused herself and rushed from the table, running up the stairs to be alone in the nursery.

The day passed miserably. Matt and Jack tried to engage her in games and distractions. Though they had giggled at the breakfast table, they sensed her genuine dismay and distress over this outing and were full of sympathy.

Tea was more like a wake than anything. Straight afterward, Mother Love took Wendy upstairs to her parents' bedroom and helped her change into a dress that Wendy had never seen before. It was a pale blue woman's dress—the most adult thing she had ever worn. It revealed more cleavage than she realized she had. Her mother fussed putting up her hair in pins and commenting about how she picked it out to match the color of her eyes. White lace trimmed the sleeves and accented the bodice and skirt. She had to be laced into it. The constraint she felt wearing the dress was overwhelming. Polly in her form fitting leather flitted through her mind. The leather seemed fitted but not so tight as to limit her breathing, and Wendy couldn't imagine the freedom of movement that pants would give her. Why hadn't she said "yes" when Polly asked her?

Wendy heard the doorbell ring and begged her mother to tell James that she was ill and couldn't go with him. "You heard your father," her mother chided. Unwillingly, Wendy plastered a false smile on her face and went to face James Hook. He said all the right things to her father and mother. He was superficially sweet with his smile and words, but there was nothing but ridicule, derision, and contempt in his eyes. Why couldn't they see it?

"Miss Love, what a delight to see you," he said, coming to take her hand and kissing it. She wanted to yank her hand away from his, but she nodded at him mutely, suppressing her emotions and revulsion. Her mother gave her hat, gloves, and wrap, and James ushered the two of them out the door.

"You're very quiet, Miss Love. Are you not happy to see me?" he asked when they were on the street, but not having reached the park yet.

Wendy turned to stare at him. He was so arrogant that he expected her to fawn over him, but with Polly's offer to take her away from all this, she was emboldened and answered him truthfully. "No, actually, Mr. Hook. I would rather be anywhere than here with you."

Now it was his turn to stare. After a few moments of appraising her, he laughed. "You are a surprise, Miss Love. I believe that you can see beyond my striking good looks into my dark heart. How ironic, you are one of the few who can, but it won't help you. You will be mine," he hissed, the last word causing drops of sweat to run down the back of Wendy's neck.

"What on earth do you mean?" she asked startled. "I am only seventeen," she protested.

"But you will be eighteen in September, and we will be married by the end of that month," he said menacingly.

"What?" she hissed. He grabbed her elbow and marched them down the street to the park. Wendy was too stunned by this new information to do more than allow herself to be led mutely. He found a bench and motioned for her to sit. Once she was settled, he sat next to her.

"Why? How?" she whispered.

"I have noticed you for some time now, Miss Love. I am twenty and a marriageable young man. You are beautiful, and I want you, so you shall be mine. We are quite wealthy, and your parents are intoxicated at the prospect of the match. You will be mine," he repeated.

"You can't own a person," she said bitterly.

"Young women and wives have no legal standing. Once you are my wife, you will be mine," he said dismissively.

She realized with horror that he believed what he said. Though she knew it was true, the words made her heart sink. What kind of man entered a marriage assuming his wife was his possession like any other object he possessed?

"But I am not done with my schooling. I am not ready," she protested again.

"Schooling? What do you need schooling for? Once you are with child, you will have all you need to occupy your time. You bleed; you are ready for all you need to be," he said coldly.

With child, she thought wildly. Her bleeding. Her face burned with shame. These were intimate female matters, and he was discussing them in the most shockingly bold and direct manner. It just wasn't done, not between a young woman and a young man who were unrelated, not even between a young woman and a young man who were related. God, she hated him. How could her parents consider marrying her to this monster? "I would like to go home now," she said curtly.

"But we are not done our walk," he said threateningly. He pulled her to her feet, and grasping her elbow, he steered her around the park. He talked to her about his studies and travels and where he hoped they would live. In some ways, it could be considered courting, but as with everything with him, there was condescension, in the way he felt so superior to her, and menace, in that he would force himself on her, regardless of her wishes, desires, and dreams. She could picture her life with him as his servant in all things, and it made her skin crawl with revulsion. She wondered how far his domination and cruelty would go. He would delight in being emotionally abusive that was clear already, but would he be physically abusive as well? He would force her to have intimate relations with him which was revolting enough, but would he beat her as well?

She felt intense relief when the length of their walk seemed to satisfy him, and he steered her back to the street and toward her house. All she wanted to do was get away from him. Her parents, to her horror, invited him to stay for dinner, but he declined and bid them all a good evening. Wendy flew to the nursery. She stripped off the dress, throwing it on the floor, tears streamed down her face, and she changed into a regular dress—something more age appropriate. Her mother blustered into the room. "Wendy," but she stopped when she saw the dress on the floor and the tears on her daughter's face.

"He is horrid and foul. I hate him. I can't believe that you would think of marrying me to someone so awful. You haven't even talked to me about what I want," Wendy shouted at her bitterly. "Don't you care about me at all?"

Mother Love was utterly dumbfounded, "But he is perfectly charming, Wendy."

"Then you marry him," Wendy responded acidly.

Mother Love collected herself. "That dress is the most expensive thing you have. You should treat it better."

Wendy picked up the dress and handed it to her mother. "You take it, Mother, if you leave it with me, I will shred it into ribbons. You have betrayed me in the most grievous way that I can imagine. Please leave me. I do not want dinner. I want to cry and mourn what you and father are condemning me to." She turned from her mother and got into her bed and shut her eyes. Her mother tried to talk to her, but Wendy wouldn't acknowledge her presence.

James Hook imposed himself on Wendy two more times that week, and her parents, despite her protests, enabled his assaults on her person. He joined them for tea on Wednesday afternoon. She ignored him as much as she could despite the glares from both her parents. After he left, she was threatened and scolded by both her parents. Just has her mother had said, the bedroom next to her parents' room was re-wall papered and painted and new furnishings were provided. Mother Love asked Wendy constantly about what she thought of the decorations and the furnishings. Clearly, this was supposed to be a boon that she should appreciate and be grateful for. It was finished by Thursday. Wendy could not bear to leave the nursery and begged to able to stay through the weekend. Her parents agreed provided that she go out with James on Saturday afternoon for a carriage ride. Andrew would be joining them as chaperone. Wendy didn't like the terms, but she accepted them. At least, in front of other people he couldn't be verbally abusive—at least not easily.

It had been a beautiful day. They had gone to Covent Garden, and James had bought her strawberries to take home and have with her family after dinner. On the surface, it seemed like an idyllic outing: the young couple, a carriage ride, a beautiful day, the festive market, the strawberries. But because Andrew was discrete and hung back from James and Wendy, James had plenty of opportunities to say nasty and intimidating things to Wendy. She was shaking with fury by the time to she got through her front door. She pushed the strawberries into her mother's hands and didn't even say goodbye to James. She just ran up the stairs and closed herself in the nursery. She cried so piteously that Mother Love scolded her only mildly and then left her alone.

Mother Love made Wendy join the family for dinner. Wendy picked at her food and flatly refused to touch a strawberry. She longed for evening and Polly and escape from this nightmare.

She read to Jack and Matt about pirates and treasure maps and gold. As usual, the stories were filled with cabin boys and pirate boys and men, but a few women (who were not slaves, servants, or prostitutes) showed up as she read; Charlotte de Berry, Anne Bonny, and Mary Read had all been notable English pirates. It just must have been a difficult life around so many men in such a violent occupation, Wendy thought. Wendy pictured them in men's clothes like Polly, and she wondered with a slight thrill if she would be able to ditch her skirts and petticoats for pants in Everland. Wendy tried to imagine all the things that one could do in pants that one couldn't do in skirts or as a respectable young woman in a skirt: climb a tree, ride a bicycle, ride a horse the regular way instead of side-saddle, run as fast as you could, put your legs up, and she was sure that there were other possibilities that she couldn't even imagine.

And the letter. She had agonized over the letter. She loved her parents, and she hated them for driving her to run away:

> *Dear Mother and Father Love,*
>
> *You cannot know how much I love you, but I feel that you cannot possibly love me as I love you. I hate James Hook. He is a horrid, horrid man. He has promised to torment me and brutalize me once I am his wife. I have begged you to end this courtship, and you have not. I have taken the only other option that seems tolerable to me. I am leaving. Do not look for me. Please tell my brothers that I love them and that I regret I will never see them again.*
>
> *Your daughter,*
> *Wendy Love*

She couldn't imagine how they would take the information from the letter. Would they believe her? Would they look for her? Would they understand the wrong they had done to her? It wasn't her concern anymore.

Her brothers were asleep; Wendy could tell from their breathing. She went over silently and kissed each one gently on the cheek. Then, Wendy had packed a small bag of her favorite few dresses and clothes. She had several books for fairy tales (Hans Christian Andersen, Oscar Wilde, and the Brothers Grimm collections). She brought a few other odd things—a small photograph of her family together, a thimble (Polly said there would be sewing), some hair ribbons, and Libby, her doll. Everything was in the bag and under her bed in preparation for Polly. The later it got, the more anxious Wendy became. Finally, when Wendy was falling into utter despair and had nearly given up hope, the window opened, and Polly Pan was there, just as she had been the week before.

"Polly," Wendy gasped, "I...I...I thought you weren't coming," and Wendy was surprised at the desperation in her voice.

It apparently shocked Polly too, because she looked at Wendy sharply, her welcoming smile changing into a look concern and alarm. "What has happened to you?" she asked.

Wendy wasn't sure what to say. She had only just met James Hook the last time Polly and Wendy had spoken. Since then, there were the three awful encounters—the one in the park, the wretched tea, and the one in the carriage where he had revealed more of himself. What had changed was that her opinion of him had changed from just a gut feeling of dislike to a confirmed knowledge that he was a loathsome human being. "I've...I've had...to spend time with him...alone," she said softly.

Polly's expression softened slightly, "That bad, was it?" There was just enough trace of sympathy and humor and relief in Polly's voice, that even Wendy laughed. Yes, it was that bad, but it didn't matter now; she was leaving. She would be beyond his grasp. Her guilt, about what her disappearance would do to her parents, had evaporated the more and more they were deaf to her protests about James.

"Do you want to come with me?" Polly asked.

"Yes, I'd rather die than stay here," Wendy answered.

"Do you have the things you want to bring with you?" Polly inquired.

"Yes," said Wendy, and she reached under the bed and grabbed her bag. She pulled the blankets over her bed and took the letter to her parents from the bag and set it on her pillow.

"You're sure?" Polly asked. "This is a big step."

"I am so absolutely sure. This is the only option I can live with," Wendy answered with conviction.

"Okay," Polly said. Polly led her to the window. "Take my hand and let's go."

Wendy took Polly's hand and felt a zing go through her. It was like she could do anything or be anyone. Wendy looked at Polly as Polly led her to the window, and she saw Polly as a great leader and a great mother at the same time: a woman who would command of others the best of themselves and who trusted and believed that she would not be disappointed by the results. And Wendy wanted to be all of that—the best that she could be and connected to others for the greater good.

Polly reached in her jacket pocket with her other hand and then held her pinched fingers above Wendy's head. Polly sprinkled Wendy with what seemed like sparkling powder. "Fairy dust," Polly announced to answer Wendy's unspoken question, "to help you fly."

Fly! thought Wendy in horror, but before she could say anything or even do anything, Polly leapt through the window, pulling Wendy with her. Wendy was shocked to realize that she wasn't falling like a stone. She was actually sort of floating with Polly steering her along. How Polly could fly she wasn't sure.

"Are you okay?" Polly asked, the smile creeping across her face was playful and a little smug.

"You could have warned me," Wendy said reproachfully.

"I try to sometimes, but no one believes me. You just have to jump and see fairy dust in action to really believe."

Wendy hugged her bag to her chest with her free hand and stared out at London passing beneath them in a twinkle of lights. "Where is Everland?" she asked.

"It is beyond the known world. It is a between space; only through magic can one get there."

"But then how did you get there, Polly? You're a human woman like me, aren't you?" Wendy asked.

"Not exactly. I am a Polly Pandora: one of the many manifestations of Pandora since her first birth among the old gods and goddesses of Ancient Greece."

Wendy stared at her, trying to process this information and what she knew about Ancient Greek mythology. "Pandora was the gods' punishment to men for acquiring fire. Her and her box. Because of her curiosity, she released all manner of suffering into the world," Wendy said in a rush.

"That's one version. There is another version where Pandora was born a Titan just like Prometheus who gave men fire and was punished for it. So, she was immortal. Pandora's 'gift' was that she could not bear suffering, so she did what she could to ease the suffering of others including trying to ease Prometheus' when Zeus had him chained to the rocks and condemned him to suffer his liver being ripped out and eaten by an eagle evening after evening. Being immortal, the liver grew back, so Prometheus' torment was everlasting. Zeus punished Pandora for helping Prometheus by making her mortal, but being a Titan, even in her mortal form she had powers and abilities and has passed those down to her daughters ever since, Polly Pandoras all," Polly explained.

"But I have never heard that story," Wendy protested.

"Men, so far, have written most history and most literature and decided what was good or not good. They cast their stories to show themselves in the best possible lights, and they structure their stories and institutions to retain their power over women and children. Imagine what a different world it would be if women wrote history and literature and had control of what was read and what wasn't?" Polly challenged.

It was too much for Wendy at that moment, so she turned

her mind from a world transformed by female control to magic, Polly's magic. "So, your powers are that you can enter Everland and that you can fly?" she asked.

"Yes, there are other things that I can do too. I am a very skilled healer, for instance," and she smiled at Wendy.

"But the Greek gods are gone—why do you exist? I mean I don't mean to be rude, but I don't understand," Wendy tried to explain.

"Pandora was not immortal anymore; she was human of a sort, so she did not fade when the other gods faded," Polly answered.

Wendy's thoughts drifted as she tried to process all this information. She noticed that they were descending. Through the clouds, she saw a large island with smaller ones scattered about it at random. Polly told her about what could be found on the different islands, but their destination appeared to be the big island. Though it was dark, a beautiful bay came into view. Docks had been crafted along the eastern side, but it looked like there had been recent storm damage or something. Logs or planks floated in the water, and then one of the largest moved, and Wendy looked again, trying to make sense of what she saw.

"Avoid the bay," Polly said. "We have a congregation of alligators to deter unwanted guests."

Wendy gaped at Polly and then at the large alligator that had lifted its head and was staring fixedly at Polly. Polly smiled at the creature and saluted it. It opened its massive jaws in what almost looked like a smile, and through its open mouth, Wendy heard what sounded like a clock ticking even through the wind and the distance between herself and Polly and the beast.

"You...you...communicate with that...thing," Wendy asked in astonishment.

"Certainly," Polly answered crisply. "Alli-oop and I are old compatriots. He minds the congregation and keeps his fellows restricted to the bay. We haven't had company for a long time. The last pirate ship to try and 'take' the island got quite the surprise between us and the alligators. I stabbed the captain, and when he fell from his deck, Alli found him a tasty treat, hat, watch, boots, and all."

Wendy was too dumbstruck to respond. She stared at the large alligator until the darkness swallowed him up. Polly altered their course, and they flew over the island. Off to the left, there were points of light.

"Are you ready to enter your new home?" Polly asked, and she squeezed Wendy's hand for encouragement.

They landed in a small square with a series of fires burning to illuminate it. Two people awaited them, a boy of about fifteen and a girl a little younger, fourteen, Wendy guessed.

"Are you okay?" Polly asked as they landed, and Wendy touched ground and adjusted herself to being on firm ground again.

"Yes, thank you, Polly"; she kept her answer short, sensing that the two people waiting had things to say to Polly.

Nodding at Wendy, Polly turned and faced the two children. "Chad and Kira, is everything alright? Everyone has eaten and gone to bed?" Wendy noticed several things about Polly's voice—though she had complete confidence in these "captains" of hers, she was also genuinely worried about her "children," and her voice was amazingly persuasive. Hearing this, Wendy wanted nothing more than to earn the trust of Polly, to be in a position of authority, and to please this woman with how well she performed what was asked of her.

"Pandora, the boys and young men are fed and asleep," Chad answered respectfully. He was dark-skinned like Polly. In the dark, it was hard to see his features clearly.

"The girls and young women also," Kira answered. Kira was Asian with long jet- black hair and flashing black eyes.

"Thank you, Chad and Kira; this is Wendy. She will be joining our family."

Both of them nodded at her and smiled, "Welcome," they said in unison, and then they turned and separated, retreating to separate cabins.

Polly turned then to face Wendy. "Would you like to sleep in one of the girls' cabins or sleep in mine? Since you only know me, it is fine for you to sleep in my cabin," she added gently.

Wendy couldn't imagine sleeping with strangers. She had only ever slept with her brothers in the nursery. "May I sleep in yours? I don't know anyone here," she said quietly.

Polly led Wendy to a small cabin. The main room was small and dominated by a round table with seven chairs around it and a lit lantern. A fresh pitcher of water was on the table with two glasses. Along one wall was a washstand with another full pitcher and a washbasin. Toiletries were set on the side, a bar of soap, handmade brushes, combs, toothbrushes, and a pot of green paste that Wendy guessed was toothpaste. Off the main room, there seemed to be two small rooms. One had a large dark cloth drawn over it, obscuring it from view. The other had the cloth tied off to the side revealing a bed, a chest, a small table with a lantern on it, and a few bookshelves, some filled but others empty.

"Why don't you set your things in the spare room, and then I can take you to the privy before we turn in. Diana has gotten us fresh water and left the lantern burning for us," Polly said with a smile.

Wendy went into the small room with her mind whirling. Several things hit Wendy at once. They were beyond technology in Everland—no running water, no electricity or even gas lighting, no stoves. She had known this when Polly had described the hard work and chores, but the reality of needing to use a latrine instead of a water closet surprised her. They were also beyond the rules of English social convention. Polly's chosen companion was Diana—the object of the tender smile—the person she realized who was asleep behind the dark cloth and would share Polly's bed. She blushed at both realizations. At school, girls whispered about "very" close relationships between certain girls and young women, but she had always thought that this was the talk of girls trying to scandalize each other. Then she thought about James and his threats. She couldn't imagine his hands on her body or any young man's hands on her. Perhaps being with a girl or young woman was different than being with a boy or young man. She felt confused. Didn't every young girl dream about being married to a young man, and yet she was willing to give up everything to escape the fate of marrying James. She was snapped out of her thoughts by Polly who entered the room and lit her lantern.

"Ready?" Polly asked. Wendy blushed. She hadn't even emptied her bag. Polly seemed to realize she had caught Wendy off guard and said quietly, "I'll give you another minute," and left, untying the cloth so that Wendy was alone in the small room. Quickly, she rooted through her things, putting clothes in the chest and retrieving her toiletries. She stepped out of the room and walked to the washstand to place her things with the others. Polly took up the lantern and led Wendy to the privies; there was a line of ten of them. Polly used one while Wendy used another. It smelled, but not quite as badly as she had feared. Business finished, they walked back to the cabin. They washed their hands, and Polly led Wendy to the washstand to ready her teeth and hair for bed while she occupied herself by sitting at the table and drinking some water.

Wendy withdrew to her room afterward and changed into a nightgown and got into bed. She extinguished the lantern, realizing that she was desperately tired. She snuggled into the bed, wrapping the sheet and blankets about her and wondering what tomorrow would bring.

Though Wendy knew they were trying to be quiet, she heard Polly and Diana as they moved about the cabin the following morning. She dozed as they disappeared to the privies, but once she heard noise again, she got up and went out to join them.

Diana was sitting at the table alone with a mug of tea. She

was taller than Wendy and about the same age as Polly. She was dressed in a fitted blue shirt and a pair of fitted brown pants, both were made of cloth, a kind of linen. They weren't elegant, but they were completely functional. She was pretty with light brown skin and long curly dark brown hair, which she had tried to tame by braiding it in a single plait. She had big dark brown eyes framed with amazingly long dark lashes. She smiled at Wendy as she came in.

"Hi, Wendy, I am Diana. How did you sleep?" she asked.

"Fine, Diana. It is nice to meet you," Wendy answered politely.

"It's nice to meet you too. Why don't you hit the privies and then get dressed and groomed. When you are dressed, I will show you around, okay?"

Wendy nodded and excused herself to the privies. Diana was reading when she returned, so Wendy went to the washstand where she washed her hands and then her face and neck, brushed her hair, and tied it up. Then she retreated to her room where she dressed quickly.

They left the cabin together. There were about twenty-five cabins, Wendy guessed. Most were bigger than Polly's. A little past the cabins, there was a large area with tables and benches. On one side was a large brick oven, and on the other side were two large cook fires manned by a few children and young people handing out mugs of tea or bowls of porridge from pots hanging over the fires. Most of the children and young people seemed to have eaten but were sitting talking together at their tables. Diana got more tea and some porridge with Wendy. She motioned them to a table and introduced Wendy to the children at the table.

There were three girls and a boy at the table: Girija, Dong, Binta, and Jada. Girija was small, perhaps fourteen, Indian, with dark eyes and long silky black hair braided in a single plait. Dong was Chinese, young, about ten, with a mop of jet hair, dark eyes, a long scar across his left cheek, and a big goofy smile. Binta was dark-skinned, her coarse hair braided around her head like a crown. She looked about thirteen. She had dark eyes and what Wendy assumed were ceremonial scars on her face because the three slight scars on her right cheek were matched by three identical scars on her left cheek, so they couldn't be accidents. Jada was Middle Eastern, young, twelvish, with light brownish skin, glossy black hair, and dark eyes. They were all friendly and welcoming. They chatted politely while Diana and Wendy ate, but as soon as they were done eating, Wendy found herself grilled about how and why she had come.

Wendy told them about James Hook and her parents pushing her into a marriage with him. Jada nodded and explained that in Afghanistan she had been promised to a thirty-year-old man who terrified her. The others poured out their stories. Binta had feared female genital cutting. Wendy didn't understand what she meant at first until Binta explained that she would be held down and her female private parts would be cut off so that she could not feel sexual pleasure because, in her culture, if females enjoyed sex, they were considered depraved and wanton. Dong explained how his father beat him and sometimes worse. The last time, Dong thought that he might actually die. He had enough then and left. Girija did not offer her story, and Wendy realized that some stories might be too painful to tell and left the other girl to her silence.

Once they were done talking, they all cleared their bowls, cups, and spoons. A collection of girls and young women and boys and young men were gathered washing up the dishes or drying them and putting them away in cabinets underneath a lean-to near the fires and oven. Wendy observed from looking around the tables that there were significantly more girls and young women here than boys and young men and that though there were Caucasians like herself, there were more females and males of color. When she was alone with Diana, she asked about this.

"In most of the world, Wendy, girls and women have few or little rights. The men in their families own them (fathers, brothers, husbands, sons). They believe that girls and women are inferior. Worse things happen to girls than to boys in many instances, so there are more girls and young women who need rescuing than boys and young men—but that doesn't mean that some boys and young men don't need protection. You saw Dong today. His father slashed his face and beat him within an inch of his life the last time. Additionally, poor girls and women (i.e., girls and women in third world countries) are even less protected than girls and women in industrialized countries like England. Pandora is committed to alleviating suffering. She has this ability to sense pain and suffering, and she reaches out to those children and young people. Many will not leave despite their suffering, but those who do want to leave she brings here," Diana explained.

"What about you? What happened to you?" Wendy asked.

Diana's face changed, her eyes hardened and a grim determination lined her face, "My half-brother and his friends gang-raped me, and Pandora brought me here," she said so softly that Wendy had to strain her ears to hear her.

Wendy felt her face burn. She thought she understood what Diana meant, but she wasn't sure. Rape was a man forcing himself on a woman, knowing her in the most complete sexual way?

Diana read the confusion on Wendy's face, "Yes, they held me down and all had their wicked way with me. I wanted to die. It hurt so much, but more than that, I knew that I was ruined. No one would ever want me after that, but...Dora...Pandora made me feel otherwise," her voice choked, and Wendy was stunned to feel and understand the profound gratitude in Diana's voice. Polly, Pandora, Dora, saved Diana in a way that she could never forget or repay—and from her experiences, Diana could never be intimate with a young man ever again. They had robbed her of that, of ever trusting a male, even a brother, a family member. Wendy wondered if Pandora was scared as well. Men had demonized her as the source of evil and human suffering. Perhaps you never got over that kind of betrayal.

What if girls and young women realized that they could have meaningful emotionally and sexually fulfilling relationships with other females instead of boys and young men and rejected all the crap boys and men pushed on them? What would that look like? What if boys and men had to compete with much more female-positive relationships that girls and women had with other girls and women? What if boys and men had to respect girls and women in a manner that duplicated what boys and men demanded of girls and women? What would that look like? What if calling someone a boy or a man or a penis or a dick was the worst thing you could call a human being instead of the curses associated with being female and female genitalia? What if being stereotypically masculine or feminine was ridiculed because it stopped people from being fully human beings? Wendy pulled her thoughts back to the present. Victorian England couldn't handle these questions. Pandora and her actions raised them, but she was beyond, in a between place, and that was precisely why she could raise such questions, Wendy realized.

Over the next few weeks, Wendy envisioned seeing a variety of relationships—all beyond the social mores of Victorian England: girls and young women having relationships with other girls and young women, boys and young men having relationships with other boys and young men, girls and young women having relationships with boys and young men. She even envisioned the possibility of individuals having fluid identities and moving between being male and female. But the point in all these relationships in Everland was not the reproduction of the traditional family and the reproduction of the human species. The desired outcomes here were mutual companionship, respect, and pleasure. It didn't really matter who partnered with whom under those circumstances or even if one partnered with more than one person, if all partners understood that as a condition. Wendy thought of the Romantic rake, Lord Byron, and his group-sexual-partner escapades with both sexes and his pursuit of hedonistic pleasure. Girls whispered about his "supposed" sex life at school when they read his poetry. But perhaps that was the point—pleasure, pleasure in the company of another and even multiple others, sexual pleasure, emotional pleasure, physical pleasure. And the point here in Everland, just was it was for Byron, was the opposite of what it was in most of Victorian England with the threat of dominance and violence that James Hook had suggested to her and that her parents had not protected her from.

If only the freedom that could be achieved in Everland, could be achieved in the world beyond?

Baba Yaga, the Intersex Witch

I AM BABA Yaga, and no one knows what to do with me. I am a bundle of contradictions—associated with winter and spring, death and life, light and dark, male and female, the wild and the domestic, age and youth, human and animal, sky and earth. Mice, crows, and foxes are my pets. I am scavenger and hunter.R I am prey and predator.R I scurry, I fly, and I run.R I am meek and stealthy.R All this and more, my pets reflect. They call me a witch because they don't understand me. Their rigid and intolerant Christian blinders don't give them the imagination to appreciate me. They would burn me if they knew. When I was young, I was magnificent: the ultimate Janus god, not future and past, but both male and female—with breasts and scrotum.

I remember one Spring Equinox in particular. It is thousands of years now in the past. But the people had painted themselves in a variety of ways. Some of my followers had painted themselves for the grains and fruits and vegetables that they hoped with come with the harvest. Others had painted themselves for the game they hoped to catch or the kids and lambs they hoped the goats and sheep would birth. The children painted themselves or were painted as mice and crows and foxes. My priestesses, their consorts, and I would bless the grains and seeds that would be planted in the following days. As dark fell, the bonfires were lit. The people had been drinking wine and hard cider as they decorated themselves and prepared the bonfires. The feast would begin after the ceremony. The drums started beating. I was painted—my female breasts in a bright red color and my scrotum in bold blue. Snakes were painted coiling up my legs. Mice were painted on my arms, and I wore a black crow mask. The chanting began.

"Great One! Great One! Baba Yaga! Baba Yaga! Mysterious Baba Yaga Bring Us Spring and Harvest and Plenty! Great One! Great One!"

The priestesses fussed and escorted me naked from my house. People had thrown fresh leaves on the path all the way from my little house to the village center. The platform was there. The three consorts were kneeling, waiting for the priestesses. I took my position in the center. The Great Mother and her consort, the Great Father, approached me and gave me wine and honey and fresh water. Next, the Grand Mother and Grand Father came forward with dried fruits and vegetables and nuts. Lastly, the Mother and Father brought me an egg, a piece of deer liver, and the heart of a chicken. I consumed all these things in the ritual fashion with the important blessings. Then, I turned to the grains and seeds and blessed them and asked them to grow for me and for my grateful and respectful people. We sang and danced, and I left the platform to bless the goats and sheep and chickens and our most able hunters, foragers, and farmers—in short, all my people. The drums continued, and the priestesses and their consorts enacted rites of spring while people around them danced and sang to the drums beating. It was a beautiful night, and we were so happy. It was a simpler and more peaceful kind of life. Our gods were many—the spirits in the streams and rivers, in the trees, in the very mountains themselves. We were bound to the earth and our cousins—the creatures all around us. We killed creatures but always with respect and thanks. And then it all began to change.

The followers of Jesus of Nazareth said he was the One True God. His trinity was the Father, Son, and Holy Ghost (only males) instead of the Mother, the Crone, and the Maiden and their consorts. Whatever policies of love and forgiveness Jesus had taught, his followers insisted that they were only attainable through rigid intolerance of anything other.

As the last of my priestesses commented, with bitterness, "God, the Father, is a rigid sky God, placed in heaven, ruthless, vengeful, and unforgiving. His son becomes Christ through his gruesome death by crucifixion. Suffering and penance are the only offerings Christian followers can give to attain love and forgiveness, not on earth, but in heaven. So strange and unnatural. No feminine element or elements in Holy Trinity, no balance. Jesus' own mother must be a virgin—because sex has firmly been associated with sin and shame since Adam and Eve. So sad. Such a strange way to live. Women subjugated to men—inferior in the eyes of the Church and inferior in the Christian faith. Such a violent faith—how many killed in Christ's name? How many powerful men did violence to others cloaked under the (literal and figurative) veils of the Church?"

Ah, but doesn't it make sense now—that I fly through the air with both a womb and a phallus? Theoretically, I have both with my mortar and pestle. It is why I am associated with contradictory things—I am not one, but all.

My carriage, the mortar and pestle, left a mark behind. More specifically, the pestle left a trailing mark behind—as the phallus always leaves a trail or contamination and wreckage in its wake, at least in the patriarchal order. So, in addition, to the mortar and pestle, they associated me with a broom—for the Christians, the witches' means of transport, and with this broom, I swept away the marks of the pestle's passage.

My house is as contradictory as myself—a house on chicken legs. The house a symbol of a settled existence—usually a house in a village or community—and yet my house is not like others. It has legs and moves, and it is located in the woods, alone by itself. Where regular humans live in stationary houses in villages for mutual protection and security, my little house moves as it or I will and finds protection in isolation in the wilds of the woods—so un-Christian and suspicious in their self-righteous eyes.

Oh, how they have perverted my stories—Christianized

them beyond recognition, so their original meanings and lessons are lost. Take for example the story of the boy who comes to become a man where my priestesses showed him the passage to the underworld and told him how to position himself to make the crossing. He was too frightened and wouldn't take the position. But the story gets twisted, and the priestesses become my daughters doing my evil bidding, and the boy tricks them and cooks them in the oven and then, to my fury, escapes home a hero instead of a coward or villain.

But, consider how the story might be told alternately. Like so many of the essential elements, fire has the powers of both life and death. Benevolent fire cooks our food, warms us, and gives us light in the darkness. Fire, the destroyer, burns uncontrollably and lays waste to all that stands in its way. Fire is also a purifier in both forms, benevolent and destructive. Death by fire or by being burned to death is one of the most feared ways to die, and yet, people willingly and happily have fire in their homes. Russian homes, in particular, faced with the long and bitterly cold winters, had large, powerful ovens for both cooking and heating. My home has strange proportions depending on my needs, but there is a great oven. I am a guardian of the underworld—it is part of my symbolism of being associated with winter and death. The passage to the underworld must be guarded—and so it is by three priestesses and the oven itself—most people don't willingly venture into ovens, after all. So, this young fool comes brashly to my house. He brings none of the traditional gifts as respectful offerings— no wine or honey or fruit or meat. He asks to be a man, and I tell him to appease the priestesses. Again, the fool has not been properly prepared, and he doesn't understand the ritual sex that is part of his transition to manhood. The priestesses all overlook this slight and still try to help him by trying to explain how to position himself in the oven to make the passage to the underworld so that he will not be burned and can return from his journey—a return that will make him a man. But he fails to do this for all three of the priestesses, and finally runs away—as much a child and a fool as when he came.

The Christian priests hate the fact that people still tell my stories. Distorted as they are, one can, with the right lens, peel them back and see what is too scandalous for the poor Church Fathers to stomach. They plot my destruction. Silly fools. They do not know what I am. They do not know they cannot kill me. They see a strange old woman with too long arms (a man's arms), but they do not know my power. They can try to send me to the underworld—but that is my place as much as the upper world. I cross between worlds. They cannot contain me. But they will try.

Though I knew the priest was trying to get me, it was the Spring Equinox again. I went to the river and bathed. It was frightfully cold. But cleansing is part of the ritual. I had underestimated the old jackal. He had massed a group of angry villagers, and they came at me as I stepped out of the river.

"My God!" the priest exclaimed in shock. "W…what kind of demon are you?" The priest crossed himself and stepped back. "Beware," he bellowed, "it is an abomination," he announced to the crowd.

"No, I am not a demon. I am a merging of what can be— female and male, life and death, heaven and earth," I said, trying to defend myself.

"Speak not of heaven, witch. You are unnatural, and we cannot allow your contamination," spat the priest. "Bind her. And fire, ready a fire. The witch must burn!" he shrieked.

How fast they scurried to carry out his orders. Rough hands grabbed me, and my hands were tied behind my back. I couldn't believe that fat, old, lazy Tom could move so fast in his search for kindling, but he did, relieved that his own sins were being overshadowed by mine. People wouldn't look at me. I tried to speak, but then I was gagged. The pyre at the foot of a sapling Maple was assembled quicker than I thought possible. I was bound to the tree, and the priest brought the torch.

With demented glee, he took off the gag and said, "I condemn you to hell, witch," and lit the pyre. I could only imagine the sermons that would come out of this—scaring the faithful into blind obedience. Poor old women everywhere who could be accused of being witches—monsters, aberrations, freaks, like Baba Yaga. Only they are not Baba Yaga, but mortal women whose hair and flesh will burn—who will die in searing agony at the hands of small minded, intolerant men like this priest.

But I am Baba Yaga, and fire is one of my elements. The flames lapped up, and I simply crossed to the underworld. The poor priest and his followers—what would they do? Instead of their glorious execution—I just disappeared. No screams of unbearable agony, no smells of burning flesh. Just gone. I am sure they would run to my little house and try to torch that too. But my little house had already started walking away, into the sanctuary of the deep dark woods. It would find me when I crossed back. It always does.

Curiouser and Curiouser

MARGARET WAS READING that dreadful book with no illustrations. Everyone seemed to want me to grow up. No picture books, more lady-like clothing (so much more confining), more young lady training activities (needlework, painting, playing the piano, and the worst, dancing). I just wanted to play with my friends and my dolls. And yet, I knew I was changing. I was getting hair on my private parts and my breasts were budding. I didn't really like to think about it—it seemed scary and hideous—transforming into something else, someone else. I just wanted to be me, Alice, just plain Alice, the girl I used to be, the girl I understood myself to be.

I started to doze, and then I saw it—the white rabbit running by in a waistcoat, checking his pocket watch, and complaining about being late. I didn't think about it. I ran after the rabbit. I don't think Margaret even noticed. The rabbit ducked down a hole, and I followed and found myself falling. I screamed at first—but then I didn't hit the ground and just kept falling, so I glanced around at all the strange things that bordered the tunnel, bookshelves with books, pictures, toys, stuff of all sorts.

And then suddenly I was at the end, sitting on the ground looking down a large hall. There were big doors and little doors, I discovered. Some needed keys, but others did not. I opened a door and found myself at the start of a small wood. It smelled pleasantly of a funny kind of smoke, and I walked toward the smell. It seemed impossible, but sitting on the lower branches of a large gnarled tree was a giant caterpillar smoking a hookah. As I walked toward him, he watched me and blew out a huge puff of that funny, sweet-smelling smoke.

"Who are you?" he asked lazily.

I was taken aback. Animals didn't normally talk where I came from. But that couldn't be quite right, because the white rabbit had talked. Insects talking seemed even more impossible than a giant caterpillar smoking a hookah.

"Who are you?" he repeated with an edge to his voice.

"I'm Alice," I answered, finding my voice.

"And what is an Alice?" he asked.

"I am not exactly sure, now that you ask. I knew who I used to be, but now everyone seems to want me to grow up, and I don't think growing up seems very appealing."

"Why would that be? Everyone grows up," he answered.

"Yes, but growing up for a girl. Well, it's complicated, and I don't much care for some of changes involved in being a grown woman," I said. Being a grown woman meant getting married and having children. Male parts inside female parts and then baby parts inside female parts and then babies outside female parts and so much work—and it all seemed quite gross.

Strangely, the caterpillar seemed to understand. He sucked from the hookah again and blew an enormous cloud of smoke to the side of him, and through the smoky window he made, I saw birds and rabbits and foxes copulating through the trees. "I will change from this form into a chrysalis and then into a butterfly when I am grown. Life is transformation, Alice. But I fear, you do not know yourself."

"No, I don't know myself. That's just it. I feel so queer," I answered, truthfully.

The caterpillar laughed briefly, and then took another deep puff from the hookah and blew the smoke out in a different direction, and through that smoky window, I saw a small pool of water, with reeds sheltering it, making it like a private bath. "Take a bath, Alice. Find out who you are and what you like," he said in a very odd, almost leering, voice.

I turned from the pool to the caterpillar, but he was gone, another impossible thing. I stood frozen for a bit, but the pool looked so inviting that I went toward it. When I felt it, the water was pleasantly warm, so I took of my apron, my dress, my corset, my shift, my pantaloons, my stockings, and my shoes. I slid into the warm water and relaxed. I thought about what the caterpillar had said. "Who am I? Who is Alice? What does she want? What does she like? How will she transform? How will that change who she is and what she likes?"

The questions swam through my head. Male parts in female parts—but what if I don't like that? I had a feeling I knew what male parts wanted, but I had no idea what female parts wanted. Did they want different things? Did they do different things? Did they desire different things? Desire? What did Alice desire?

In the pool of warm water, I let my hands trace over my body. They caressed my budding breasts, and the wee nipples went hard or taut and the sensation was pleasurable. It made my private parts heat with desire, so with one hand toying with a nipple, I let the other one explore my private parts. Inside there was a button of flesh, and the more I toyed with it, the harder it seemed to get with a delightful pressure building and building, and then there was a little explosion of sensation radiating through me. It felt so good I realized I was moaning in pleasure.

So, there could be female pleasure in grown up life, and yet that seemed so at odds with everything that Margaret and my mother seemed to say about being a grown woman. Wives tolerated sexual relations with their husbands and then they had children to take care of. Naughty women, ruined women, women of the streets, harlots and prostitutes, they liked sex; they did sex work. The Madonna or the whore—there seemed to be no in-between in the world I knew. But here, in Wonderland, the rules were different. Perhaps there were other adventures to be had here, so I got out of the pool and dressed.

There was a path, and I followed it. Suddenly, there was a little house, and as I drew near, I saw the white rabbit. He was about to enter the little house.

"I say, hello there, Mr. Rabbit. Do you have a moment?"

"Who are you?" he asked.

"I am Alice. Who are you?"

"I am Blanc, and I would like to be at your service, Alice," he answered with a sly smile and a bow. "Won't you come in? I promise not to hurt you."

What a queer thing to say, I thought. "I should think not."

"Ah, but Alice, there are those who would hurt a trusting young woman. There are even those who would promise not to hurt but would," he explained, "but I am not like either of them."

I thought about it for a moment. I knew he was talking about rape and abuse. I knew that some men did that to some women. And yet there was something reassuring about Blanc, so as he opened the door to the little house and held it open for me, I walked in. He followed me in and shut the door. We were in a cozy little kitchen with a hearth fire burning low. On the stove, he put on a pot of apple cider, rum, and cinnamon. When it was warm, we sat by the hearth, drank the hot cider, ate apple tarts, and talked about all sorts of things. When we started to get sleepy, he took my hand and led me to his tiny room. Impossibly, he took off his waistcoat and laid it on a chair, and then he took off his rabbit suit to reveal himself as a naked young man. He smiled at me and got into bed, motioning me to do the same. So, I took of my clothes and joined him. We kissed and explored our bodies. He knew how to be gentle with me and how to give me pleasure. After I climaxed, he asked if he could. He was very gentle, guiding his hard part into my softness. It didn't take long for him to climax. The after sex was messier than I had imagined. He explained that while he had to wait a while before he could go again, that he could try to pleasure me again and again, if I wanted. It seemed amazing to me. He said that there were lots of different positions to try.

"Why would we try so many positions?" I asked.

He smiled lazily before answering. "While it is easiest to get you to climax by touching your clitoris, there is also another spot deeper inside that when rubbed just right by my cock will achieve a different kind of climax for you."

"A different kind?"

"So they say, but they also say, it can be difficult to find," he answered.

So, he pleasured me again, and when he was aroused again, he climaxed as well, and then we feel into a contented sleep entwined in each other's arms.

In the morning, Blanc asked if I wanted to stay. I was tempted, but I was not done with my adventures, so I said good-bye for the time being, but told him that I would be happy to come back some time. We kissed, and I left, following the path past his house.

I came to a larger brick house. With no one about, I knocked on the door. A cook let me in. She was bustling about, setting the table for two, a setting for me and a setting for a regal looking large woman, wearing elaborate clothes. "Who are you?" she asked.

"I am Alice. Who are you?"

The cook took a deep breath. "She's the duchess, of course!"

The duchess smiled. "The Duchess of Kent, or Lady Charlotte."

The cook set the fine meal before us, a Cornish hen each, some boiled potatoes, some sautéed carrots, some brown bread, and some red wine. Once we were served, the cook disappeared. The duchess was quite haughty at first, but as we ate and drank, she seemed kinder and sweeter. Finally, I realized I was tired. When I looked at the duchess with a dazed look, she smiled and stood, motioning me to follow her. She led me to her bedroom, and more impossible things happened. She took off her clothing and then she stepped out of her body, revealing a naked young woman about my own age. She climbed into bed and invited me to follow. I took off my clothes and joined her in the bed.

"Call me Char," the duchess said, and wrapped her arms around me, cuddling into my side.

We fell asleep in each other's arms. When we woke in the early evening, we got out of bed and brushed our teeth. Then we got back in bed and played and toyed with each other, I made her climax and then it was my turn, and back and forth again. It was lovely. I liked it. The cook knocked at the door to announce that supper was ready. We dressed, and entered the dining room to find another lovely meal, poached salmon in lemon sauce, Brussels sprouts with bacon, candied yams, and white wine. We ate and talked. Even though Char was wearing the large woman costume, she was kinder than she first appeared. That confused me.

"Char?" I began hesitantly.

"Yes, my dear Alice?"

"Why did you seem so so, I don't know, when we first met?" I finally asked.

"Oh, that. In the typical world, men boss around women. So, I find that if I am bossy first, I don't get bossed around. It is a terrible bore, I know. But being bossed around by most men is much worse."

"I met Blanc; he didn't seem so bad," I protested.

"Blanc is a darling—a very exceptional young man. You can't believe that most men treat women the way Blanc does. No, they're much more like the Hatter, who is as mad as they come. Mad crazy and mad angry—not a good combination—especially in a man. No, no, stay away from the Hatter, dear Alice."

After dinner, we retired to Char's bedroom for the night—indulging in the pleasures of the flesh until we were spent. I dreamed the most delicious dreams of petting and being petted all over and over. In the morning, Char asked me to stay, and I wanted to, but I also wanted to think about who Alice wanted to be. I said good-bye to the duchess and followed the path past her house.

Impossibly, it seemed I was back at the wood. I even smelled the funky, sweet smoke of the caterpillar's hookah. And then there he sat, just like that.

"Well, hello queer little Alice. Do you know who you are?" he asked sarcastically.

"No, not one hundred percent, but I do know that I am queer, and that is a place to start."

KATHLEEN MURPHEY IS an Associate Professor in the English Department at Community College of Philadelphia. She has a PhD in American Civilization from the University of Pennsylvania.

She has published poetry and short stories (mainly fairy tale retellings) through *The Voices Project, Writing in a Woman's Voice, Pennsylvania Literary Journal,* among other platforms. Her collection of fairy tale retellings, Other Tales, is available through Amazon. She turned her short story, *P Pan and Beyondland*, a retelling of the Peter Pan story with LGBTQ+ identifying characters, into a play which was performed as part of the 2018 Philadelphia Fringe Festival.

She is also a subversive knitting artist. Her piece, To Herself: Knitting, Poetry, Protest, was on display at Philadelphia's City Hall as part of its "Crafting Narratives" exhibition (9/30–12/31/2019). The knitted blanket was made up for 32 panels, each with the knitted title of a poem.

For more information, visit kathleenmurphey.com.

Made in the USA
Middletown, DE
26 November 2022

15719204R00121